SHINE
THE
Light

SHINE
THE
Light

April McGowan

WhiteFire
Publishing

This is a work of fiction. All characters and events portrayed in this novel are either fictitious or used fictitiously.

SHINE THE LIGHT

Cover design by Roseanna White Designs
Cover images from Shutterstock.com

WhiteFire Publishing
13607 Bedford Rd NE
Cumberland, MD 21502

ISBN: 978-1-946531-21-6 (digital)
          978-1-946531-20-9 (print)

For my loves,
~Ken, Madeline, and Seth~

And
My loving and supportive parents,
~Allan and Carol Solstad~
~Richard and Andrea Johnson~

And
My sister-scribes,
~Melody Roberts~
~Danika Cooley~

John 1:1-5

In the beginning was the Word, and the Word was with God, and the Word was God. He was in the beginning with God. All things were made through him, and without him was not any thing made that was made. In him was life, and the life was the light of men.

The light shines in the darkness, and the darkness has not overcome it. (ESV)

CHAPTER 1

A man reeking of body odor and urine shuffled by Shannon, an emptiness akin to a black hole shadowing his eyes. The soiled navy colored blanket slung over his shoulders enshrouded him like burial cloths that he clung to with nicotine-stained fingers.

Shannon focused her camera on those fingers and then on the man's eyes, capturing his despair. As she took his photograph, Shannon's heart wrenched in sympathy. She glanced up the sidewalk dotted with the lost and homeless. *Treat each as an individual and love them the best you can.* To do anything else would overwhelm Shannon. She tucked her Cannon Mark II away in her backpack and turned to those others who sat waiting. Only waiting. For a handout, for the weather to change, for time to pass.

She'd given that man a Ziploc packet with socks, protein bar, bottle of water, and a donated paperback of *Golden Apples in the Sun*. She might never see him again, or she'd see him next week. Homelessness overwhelmed her some days, but doing nothing was more abhorrent to her than doing something. She had to do *something*. She was thankful for all the books she'd collected from library cast off sales—and donations from friends who had more books than they knew what to do with.

Shannon handed off another packet to the life-worn homeless woman in front of her. The woman took it with grateful hands. They exchanged a smile before Shannon moved on down the block. Sometimes she felt like a bandage over a crack in the wall of a dam.

The air, heavy with an autumn musk, mixed with the late day heat radiating from the concrete office buildings that towered above them. Overhead, a sliver of blue sky and silky clouds funneled the day's last light down to them.

Queen Susie, one of the oldest women Shannon had met on the streets, moved toward her, holey boots scuffing the sidewalk as she pushed her rolling seat-walker ahead of her. Shannon greeted her and handed her a packet. Susie must have accumulated quite a library by this point if she'd had anywhere to store the books.

Queen Susie tucked the packet into the makeshift saddlebags that adorned her walker. She jangled the tattered Styrofoam change cup as a call for alms, but as a delivery truck raced by, honking angrily at a pedestrian, she lost her grip. Shannon caught the cup before it crashed to the sidewalk, spilling the old woman's gatherings for the day.

"Careful there, Queen Susie."

Queen Susie flashed Shannon a grateful grin and blinked at her from her one good eye. The other socket sagged open, the eye having been lost to infection many years ago. It was hard to look at, but she'd stopped trying to cover it when she found her deformity garnered larger donations.

"It's my rheumatism." Queen Susie took the cup in her stained, gnarled fingers and slid it into a holder she'd fashioned from duct tape on her chair.

"I know, sweetie. How are you and Magic Stan doing? You have a safe place to sleep tonight?"

Queen Susie locked on her with her good eye. "It's a secret." She nodded as if to draw Shannon into her conspiracy. "My Stan keeps us safe and sound."

"Speaking of, where is Magic Stan this evening?" Shannon was surprised he was out of earshot of Queen Susie. They usually traveled together.

"He's on his way." Queen Susie spoke of Stan like he was her personal attendant. And it often seemed that way to Shannon.

"You have a safe night, now. Okay?" She'd love to take Stan and Susie home, but she knew better than to put herself at risk. She had to opt for the next best thing—keeping an eye on them out here.

Despite it's being a hot fall, the nights were turning chilly in downtown Portland. The sunlight faded along with the busy traffic, blending into the buildings as streetlights flickered to life. Nearby restaurants opened their patios for dinner and somewhere in the distance someone started to play a piano. Dinner aromas of grilled onions wisped on the breeze. Shannon took out her Cannon and took a shot of the light, wanting to describe it to her best friend later. If only Amber could see the way it shone. But Amber's recent blindness kept her from experiencing that ever again.

The next best thing was to describe it to her and for Shannon to watch as Amber's interpretation formed on the canvasses she painted on. Often what Amber expressed caught the emotion of the moment even better than the camera. After losing her sight last year, she'd learned a new way to share her internal vision with the world around her—and the world connected with it. Orders for Amber's paintings had picked up significantly in the past few months, and she was running out of subject matter.

Shannon was too, truth be told. Many of her photographs weren't anything like Amber's work, but they helped pay the bills. Not everyone wanted photos of the homeless to adorn their living spaces. There was something there, though, that drew her to their plight. Often a wisdom of a shared humanity and how precious life was.

And maybe, if she was able to communicate that to another, they would see the homeless as hurting people, rather than just obstacles on the sidewalks.

In any case, she needed to plan a road trip for them—just the girls. They'd had little time together since Amber and Ethan had started seeing each other. Hope rose inside at the idea. It'd been a hard year. No matter how well things were going for Amber now, the last year had blurred into one of survival as Amber adjusted to her new sight loss and Shannon took on the role of comforter and encourager.

Shannon was ready to live again.

A tapping noise caught her attention, and she glanced up to see Magic Stan limping his way toward them down the street, his antique cane clicking on the sidewalk, top hat slanted just so over his mass of oily graying hair. At the same time, Shannon caught sight of Justin, her boyfriend, heading her way, a look of worry on his face. He didn't entirely trust Stan.

Shannon couldn't blame him. She knew very well the irrational unpredictability of those with mental illness—and Magic Stan suffered from multiple delusions. He was playwright and actor and magician. And the top orator of Burnside Boulevard.

"New books, Miss Shannon?" Magic Stan used an aloof tone that served to feed Queen Susie's idea of being lost royalty. They were quite a pair. With Magic around, Shannon knew she didn't have to worry over much about Queen Susie being mugged for her few earthy belongings. He'd dash the brains out of anyone who even looked askance at his queen and adopted street mother.

Justin came up and handed Magic Stan a Ziploc packet—this one held a copy of *Great Expectations* which Stan whipped out and caressed with deep affection.

"Kind, sir." Stan flipped open the pages and inhaled deeply. "Nothing like that aroma in the world." Stan gave Justin a cursory glance, eyes homing in on his neck. "Another tattoo, my boy? You'll never get a wife with all that ink. It isn't distinguished." Stan's gray, bushy eyebrows drew together in disapproval. Justin laughed it off, but Shannon came to his defense.

She cleared her throat and pointed out her own purple tipped hair, piercings and tattoos, particularly the tiny cross near her left eye—the one that covered the scar given to her by a fellow foster kid.

"But, you're not married, either." Magic Stan crossed his arms. "You look like one of those girls from the Korean punk band I saw down by the waterfront."

"Well, Stan, I'm not Korean, I'm part Thai. And as for marriage— there are worse things than being single." She sensed Justin stiffen next to her, but moved ahead. "Thanks, though, that you think I look like I could be in a band." She laughed at Stan's further scowl and gave him an extra protein bar. Then she and Justin moved down the street, offering several more packets and books.

She'd love more than anything to house every one of them on this street and make sure each one had a hot meal and warm bath. But there were too many. They multiplied every year. The camps by the mission and under the bridges swelled to capacity. In the city of Portland alone, camping along roadsides and in parks. Makeshift RV parks were cropping up along streets in otherwise residential neighborhoods, leaving garbage and waste. There simply wasn't enough room for them all. And winter was around the corner. Some would go south for warmer pastures, trading out the damp, incessant Oregon rain. Many, like Stan and Susie, were too infirm to move.

As they finished up for the day, she and Justin hoofed up the hill to his car. He'd been very quiet the past hour. Quiet even for Justin.

"We did good." Feeling the chill and dampness of an oncoming rain, Shannon untied her light jacket from around her waist and tugged it on. "Are you up for this again next week?"

He shrugged. His eyes carried the shadow of their earlier argument. "I've got a lot going on. I'll let you know." Justin smiled slightly, but it didn't look genuine. She could see the hurt in his eyes and her stomach clenched. If only he'd be willing to keep their relationship right where it was, she would have never had to break his heart.

"Everything okay?" She kept her voice light and encouraging—pretending all was well.

"Just got a lot on my mind." He leaned in and gave her a quick kiss. He looked deep into her eyes, and she saw a longing there she couldn't answer. Then he turned to get in his car.

They'd often finish up one of their days by grabbing dinner together, but he made no such offer this time. Something inside told her to stop him, to talk it over before he left—to try and make him understand. But she said nothing. Shannon wasn't going to change her mind. She wished he understood. He used to—or so she'd thought. Turns out he was just counting on wearing her down until she'd agree that marriage wasn't the bad idea she knew it to be. At least for *her*.

Justin rolled down his Fiat's windows and turned on the stereo. Rap music pounded through the car.

"I'll call you tomorrow." She waved.

Pursing his lips in thought, he nodded but didn't wave back. Her stomach sank three notches. As he pulled into traffic and headed away, she waited for the customary light tap of his car's horn.

It didn't come.

Shannon stood on the corner and watched him crest the next hill and disappear. She gulped for breath, drowning under the weight of her decision.

Her phone text sounded, and she pulled it out, hoping. It wasn't him. Instead she read Amber's text, inviting her for dinner.

Just us girls? Shannon tapped back. She could use some one-on-one with Amber.

Girls and boys. Ethan's here, Amber texted back.

A hard knot of emotion worked its way up into her throat.

Not tonight. Shannon couldn't bear to watch Ethan dote on Amber. Or worse that lovesick look in Amber's unseeing eyes.

You okay? Amber's Spidey sense was on full force, it seemed.

Yep. Gotta run. Say hi to Ethan. She put her phone on silent and tucked it into her pocket. She'd never lied to Amber before. Not bold-faced in type like that. But what could she say?

Things between Justin and her had been shaky at best the past few months. He wanted more. Shannon knew giving more really meant giving all—and she'd seen the damage of giving *all* too many times.

Shannon walked up 9th Street, past a stream of homeless heading south to the missions for the night. She tromped up the hill toward the food trucks, many of which were shuttering for the night, hoping Pho-Mazing wasn't closed yet. Getting there in time, she ordered soup and spring-wrapped tofu rolls and started the hike back to her studio apartment in China Town.

Walking never bothered her. She loved the feel of the city around her, its life of joys and sorrows ran through her blood. She never wanted to live anywhere else. She didn't want anything in her life to change.

She thought of Justin. Her wants mattered little, it seemed.

A bus whooshed by her, and she picked up her pace, passing the church where Amber attended her support group.

"Beautiful girl." The gravelly voice coming from a slumped man on the corner startled her. "I have a beautiful Asian girl."

The hairs on the back of Shannon's neck rose to attention. She reached in her pocket for her pepper spray, finger on the trigger. The man didn't approach her, though.

"I had two. One's dead. Long dead. So beautiful." The man sobbed into his dirty hands. His knit cap and oversized pea jacket hid most of him from her, but even so, Shannon knew most of the regulars from their clothes. She didn't recognize him.

"If you head east on Burnside, you'll find the missions—Gospel Union and Portland Rescue. They can give you a meal. A bed is more of a challenge, but your belly will be full." She kept her distance. Being alone on the streets talking to a strange homeless man wasn't something even she, streetwise and comfortable working with the homeless, felt good about.

"My little one. So pretty. Lost her. Lost her."

Shannon couldn't tell if he was mentally ill, drunk, or both. She remembered the one last packet in her backpack and swung it off to reach for it. Still, she kept her pepper spray in her other hand, on the ready.

"Stolen." He sighed and tilted back his head, looking up into Shannon's eyes.

Her very marrow went cold.

"They took her. Took her from me. Mine. But they took her."

It couldn't be.

Everything in her balked. Daniel. She hadn't laid eyes on him in years. They'd told her he was most likely dead. Even when she'd heard a rumor he might be around, she hadn't believed it. Not really. But here he was, alive and well. Well, at least alive.

"They didn't take her. You threw her away," she hissed at him, but he took no notice.

Shannon wanted to scream at him, thrash him. It was all she could do not to go into hysterics. She whipped around to leave and saw the line of homeless leaning against buildings or sitting on curbs, opening their packets, heads inclined over books, hope or comfort or relief reflecting on their faces. The crinkling dead-weight of the last packet hung heavy in her hand.

If there was anyone else there besides Daniel, Shannon would have offered it to them. Anyone.

Instead, she cinched up her backpack, shoved her pepper spray back in her pocket, and took a step away. Her hot soup, dangling in the bag of her other hand, sloshed as if to remind her of what it was like when she had nothing to eat at all.

And who's fault was that? She started to take another step, but before she could move, her legs betrayed her and turned her back around. Shannon saw how Daniel's eyes transfixed on the packet. His shaky, grime-encrusted fingers reached out toward her.

Always taking.

Shannon tossed the packet at his feet, staying out of reach, and stormed away, anger fueling her as she went up three blocks and came back two, going through an ally here and side street there. She didn't want him following her. She didn't want him knowing where she lived. She didn't want him.

Her father had no business being alive.

CHAPTER 2

Morning dawned after a sleepless night, afternoon approached, and Shannon still didn't know what to do with herself. An edginess she hadn't experienced in a long time rattled her. Daniel alive? In her city? Maybe he'd move on to Seattle or down to California. As long as he went away. Soon.

She'd texted Amber to come over, not knowing what else to do. But even inviting Amber to visit, which usually made her feel secure, didn't calm her nerves.

Shannon itched from the inside out, hyper-alert and displeased with everything. She picked up the dirty dishes from her table and counter and washed them and set them in the drainer. She moved from one side of her 500-square foot apartment to the other, stashing personal things away, moving prints and shuffling papers. After wiping the dust from the cherry wood coffee table, she tossed pillows on the ornate green and gold brocade sofa. Cleaning was therapeutic for her nervous energy.

She told herself she was cleaning for Amber's visit, but Amber couldn't see any of it anyway. Shannon opted to spend a few minutes making sure the floor was clear of obstacles so Amber wouldn't fall and break her neck. Putting everything in its place made her feel more in control of her life. Even if it wasn't true, it at least appeared that way.

A knock came on her door. "Shannon, it's Amber."

Shannon raced to the door, yanking it open.

"What's the SOS? Is Justin okay? Did you break up or something?"

"Not everything is about our love lives." Shannon's dark tone startled her.

"Sorry." Amber used her cane to maneuver to the small dining table that separated the kitchen area from the living room. She pulled out a chair and waved for Shannon to join her.

"I don't want to sit." Shannon tucked her hands into her pockets, feeling reassured and then trapped. She pulled them out and crossed her arms. Nothing felt right. Nothing was right. Her teeth ground out the tension as she fought for control.

"Whatever you say." Amber gave her a patient smile and tipped her head down, starting to fiddle with her phone, pretending to look at it.

Shannon scowled. "You know I think it's creepy when you do that."

"It makes people nervous when I stare out at nothing."

The apps responded with soft clicks and tones as Amber scrolled. She really was handy with all the disabled access apps.

Shannon sat down, shame burning on her cheeks. "Sorry. I just don't know what to do."

"Start at the beginning."

"Daniel's here. In Portland. On the streets. It's not just a nasty rumor."

Amber's fingers fumbled and she dropped her phone against the table. "Oh boy."

"Yeah." Shannon raked her fingers through her hair in frustration, scrubbing her fingertips against her scalp.

"Well, he's alive. That's good, right?"

Everything in her recoiled at the idea. Imagining him having died and leaving her an orphan was much preferable to being abandoned. Even as an adult.

"Right."

"You don't sound convinced."

Shannon couldn't meet her friend's unseeing gaze. The scrutiny proved too much.

"I've moved on with my life. He's got no right showing up and..." Shannon's voice trailed off.

"And being *alive*?"

"It sounds awful to say it aloud." But true. Very true. "I hope he'll pack up and move on, but with my luck..." She stood and started pacing again.

"Wait. He's homeless?"

"Of course he is. What else would he ever be? Why break a twenty-five year roll now? He's hanging out by that church you go to for your support group."

Amber's eyebrows creased and a funny look passed over her face. "Daniel? Of course." Amber put her hand over her mouth. "Shannon. Oh, I had no idea."

"You knew he was there?" Shannon stood, arms akimbo, incredulous.

"I knew there was a homeless man named Daniel camping out on that corner, but I didn't connect that with the rumor you'd heard. I didn't think of your Daniel as a homeless person. Besides, I don't remember what he looks like. I would have been too young to remember. He's been there for weeks now. I guess that corner's his place when he moves through Portland."

"Wait. You mean he comes through here regularly?" The tension in her neck manifested ten-fold, and she tried to rub the burning knot on her vertebra into submission.

"Maggie gives him leftover donuts and coffee every week after our support meetings. She said he's seasonal, like so many of the others. Although, with the tent cities and our warmer winters lately, he could stick around." She blew out a breath. "What a mess."

"Completely."

"Well, why not call one of the shelters? You've got a lot of pull down there. Then he can get some regular meals and clean up."

Shannon's mind whirled at the suggestion. "Clean up? He's not going to clean up. He'd have to want to change, and my father never wanted to change anything about his life. He's exactly where he wants to be."

"No one wants to be homeless. I mean, not really."

"I'm not sure what propaganda you're reading, but there are thousands who do. Including Daniel. He chose it." Her compassion leaked like a sieve from her spirit, replaced with an impervious granite.

"From what you've told me, he's mentally unstable. He's probably not making good decisions because of that." Amber's tone told Shannon she should be ashamed of her feelings.

Hardly.

"And whose fault is that? He could have taken his meds. He could have—" Her voice choked off and she moved to the window, staring out at the Columbia River eight blocks away. The blue-gray expanse dotted with hopeful boaters flowed out toward the ocean, free.

Amber moved over, putting a comforting hand on her back. "He could have chosen to take his meds, and he didn't. And he lost you. I can't imagine how you feel. But if he were my dad, I'd want him off the streets, no matter how angry I was."

Shannon stiffened. "You have no idea how you'd feel. You think your dad was a saint."

Amber backed up. "My dad was a good man."

A snort escaped her before she could cover it. Anger built and swirled into a category five hurricane. Amber's dad had always been off limits—an unspoken barrier.

"What?" Amber's voice revealed the hurt Shannon had inflicted. Shannon should stop. She knew it. But she couldn't. It'd festered for too long now.

"I know Jennifer wanted to adopt me right along with you, Amber. But your dad said no." The pain of it swept along her like an electrical storm. Her life could have been so different. So different. Amber could have been her real sister, not just in affection. Shannon wouldn't have lived out her time in foster and group homes. No one wanted a troubled, angry girl with mental illness and drug abuse in her past. No one wanted her.

"You were still in foster care. Daniel hadn't given you up yet."

"Even if Daniel had been willing to let me go, your dad wouldn't have gone for it."

Amber moved away and sank down on the couch. "I know. After you were stuck in group homes, I don't think I ever begged him for anything like I did for you to be my sister." She sighed. "He had his reasons."

"And I knew what they were."

Amber's face paled. "He loved you in his own way."

"But not as his own. Too colorful for him." She looked down at her tawny arms. "At least that didn't stop your mom from keeping us in touch with each other." Her only balm was Amber's continued friendship. Jennifer had taken her shopping along with Amber for school clothes and supplies. Even after she'd entered permanent foster care, Shannon never lacked those physical comforts as some of the other kids did. The foster system tried—but you couldn't regulate love. She'd have happily lived with her father in tattered clothing if he'd only loved her more than he'd loved himself.

"I don't know what to say." Tears streamed unchecked down Amber's cheeks. With every drop, the guilt of her outburst lanced Shannon's heart.

Shannon came and put her arm around her friend. "It's not on you." She'd been jealous of Amber. For years. But she'd done her best not to let those feelings ruin their sister-ship. Because deep down, that's what they were. What they'd always be. No matter who their parents were.

God gave Amber to Shannon. And vice versa. And God had taken away her jealousy. Or so she thought.

"I'll work this out." Shannon said the words to comfort Amber more than believing them herself. She didn't have a clue how to feel or what to do. Or how any of it would work out.

"Do you want me to find him a place?" Amber wiped at her eyes. "I mean, I could make the calls, so you wouldn't have to."

"Not your responsibility."

"You're always protecting me, Shannon. Why don't you let me protect you this time?"

Shannon started to let down her guard until Amber added, "I'm sure Justin would help, too. What does he think about it?"

"No."

"Why not? He loves you, too. He'd want to help."

Loved her was more like it. "I'm not calling him."

Amber pulled away. "Did something happen?"

Where to start? Not today. "No, I'm just not getting him involved."

A second lie?

"I can see why you'd want to protect him. But if you're in a serious relationship with someone, it's best not to hide things. Especially big things."

"Justin can't understand. He's not like us." Justin always had a family that wanted him. Shannon headed to the kitchen, opened the fridge, and took out sandwich supplies. "Want anything to eat?"

"No. I ate earlier with Ethan. Speaking of..." Amber stopped.

Shannon turned to her, focusing on the warm flush on her friend's cheeks. "What's up?"

"He wanted to know if you and Justin were up for dinner next week."

Shannon could tell this wasn't what Amber was planning to

say. Even before she lost her sight, she'd had an awful poker face. Now, though, reading her was easier than ever.

"I don't know. I'll have to check my schedule." Before Ethan and Amber got so cozy, she'd drop whatever she had going on in a second to have dinner with her Shannon. But lately, it'd felt forced.

She changed the subject. "Speaking of plans, when are we getting out of town? Classes are starting again, and I'll soon be facing those little faces, broken clay pots, and childish outbursts. We never got our road trip this summer."

Not for lack of trying.

"Oh, uh. Soon? When is break over?"

"In two weeks. I thought we'd pack the car and just hit the open road and see where the fall colors take us."

Amber shifted. "What about Mocha?"

"I'm sure Ethan could take care of my cat-nephew."

Nodding, Amber cleared her voice. "Sure. I'll ask him."

Something wasn't right. "Don't you want to go? We need to get more material for your paintings, and I'm itching to head to the Coast range and north. Maybe we'll take in the sights at the San Juan's?"

More shifting.

"Maybe now's not the best time."

"It's the only time I've got." Shannon put down the knife she was plastering mayo on bread with. She stacked the bread with avocados, tomatoes, sprouts, and cheese. Then she added a layer of salt and vinegar chips before topping it with an equally slathered top slice. "What, do you have a better offer?"

Now was the perfect time to go. Daniel could easily disappear while she was gone, and she wouldn't have to think about him anymore. She sat down at the table with her sandwich, picking it up for a big bite.

"Sort of."

Amber's hesitant statement brought Shannon up short. The avocado and cheese fell out, splatting onto the plate.

"What do you mean?"

"Ethan wants us to fly to Boston and spend time with his family. I was actually hoping we'd talk about this over dinner."

"Right." She stared down at her sandwich. Appetite gone, she put it in a container and stowed it in the fridge. The refrigerator door slipped from her mayonnaise-covered hand and slammed closed.

Amber jumped at the sound.

"Sorry." Shannon felt her face heat.

Amber gave her a troubled smile. "Ethan and I have gotten pretty serious over the past couple months."

"Yeah." She leaned against the counter, her insides wrapped in twists of red-hot steel, like a fiery French braid.

"And he's really wanting me to meet his family."

"They were here not that long ago."

Amber cleared her voice. "Yeah, but that's when he was finishing chemo. Now he's in remission, and stuff is better between them. And now, especially..."

"Especially?"

"Ethan's asked me to marry him." Amber's voice was ethereal with happiness and a tinge of apology.

The floor shifted out from under Shannon, and her lungs closed off. Blood pounded in her ears.

"We wanted to share the news with you both at the same time." Amber smiled up at her with tear-filled eyes. "We're so happy." She reached out her hand toward Shannon.

Swallowing hard, Shannon moved and took Amber's hand. She knew all the right things to say, but suddenly she couldn't bring herself to say any of them. Looking down into the radiant face of her soul's sister, her stomach clenched knowing she should be happy for her.

"I'm so glad for you, sweetie." Shannon leaned down and pulled her into a huge hug. One day, she would be.

"Really?"

"Of course."

"I do need more sites for inspiration. But I thought Ethan could help me find some places in Boston."

And there it was.

Amber didn't need her anymore. Even before Amber lost her sight, they'd go on spontaneous treks for artistic inspiration. But no more. Tears stung at the corners of her eyes, and even though Amber couldn't have seen them, Shannon blinked them back, trying to remain in control.

"Great idea." She forced her closing throat to stay open, her tone to stay sunny. "I'll take care of Mocha."

"Oh, wonderful." The relief on Amber's face heaped stones on Shannon's head.

"When do you leave?"

"Next week."

Shannon audibly sighed. Everything in her life was turning upside down. And she was just supposed to let it.

"I feel like I've messed everything up."

"No. You didn't."

"You could take Justin with you." Amber brightened at her own suggestion.

Shannon had to come clean. Each lie tore a new sore spot in her spirit. "Listen, Amb...Justin and I aren't exactly on the same page as you and Ethan. Actually, that's wrong. He's entirely on the same page, but we're not reading the same book."

"You lost me." Amber gave her a quizzical look.

"Justin wants us to get married. He didn't propose, but it's something he's been thinking about. And he wants *me* to think about it." She watched her friend's eyes light up and knew she'd have to pop the bubble fast before plans for a double wedding came racing out of Amber's mouth. "But I told him I don't want that. I've never wanted that." *I can't want it.* That was the reason she'd never allowed herself to date a guy more than twice. It was the reason she promised herself she'd never get serious about anyone. She'd broken her rules, and the damage spread.

"But surely Justin is different. He loves God. He's proven himself. He gets you."

Shannon couldn't help shaking her head. "No. No. It wouldn't work. I can't go there. He knows it. I warned him. He thought he'd change me. Or God would change me. But I'm not going to change."

The variety of emotions playing over Amber's face dizzied Shannon. "Don't feel bad, sweetie. I'm okay. I'm better this way. So is he. Nobody needs this to come home to every night." She motioned to herself before remembering Amber couldn't see her. She sighed.

"But..." Amber started, clearly befuddled at Shannon's misgivings.

"Trust me." She was better. Really. Depending on Justin had made her lose her edge. She'd let down her guard. No. Not when Amber would be with Ethan. Not when there wasn't a choice. She was back to just relying on herself and God—that was the best way to keep from being hurt.

Putting it into practice though? It was a trick she had yet to master.

CHAPTER 3

In the midst of sorrow, wasn't there supposed to be an open window or something to give one hope? Looking out her studio apartment into the drizzling gray September morning, Shannon couldn't imagine the sun or blue sky. All was dismal. And the window was painted shut.

Amber would go to Boston with Ethan. She'd even suggested boarding Mocha. She didn't want to trouble Shannon. But right then, Shannon could use some fuzzy trouble instead of the emotions that battled inside her. Shannon insisted her cat-nephew move in with her. She'd pick him up in a couple of days.

Her finger chipped away at a fleck of paint. She let it fall to the carpet where she ground it into bits with the toe of her boot. The windows rattled as a late summer storm descended over the city. Her cell phone rang.

"Hello?"

"This is Maggie Floros, Amber's birth mom."

Maggie insisted on the clarification, even after these many months. She didn't want to step on Jennifer's toes. After what Jennifer and Amber had been through this past year, Jennifer had to know she had nothing to fear from Maggie. Jennifer was Amber's mom through and through. Maggie wasn't a threat—just an added dimension. Still, Maggie insisted.

Did Amber know what a blessing it was to have *one* mom who loved her, let alone two? That wasn't an experience Shannon would ever have. Jennifer tried. But it wasn't the same. Nice. However, there was always that missing flavor, like when you didn't salt the soup enough. Tasted good—but something was definitely missing. And always would be.

"Hi, Maggie."

"I wanted to know if you could help me with a little problem."

"I'll try." Strange that Amber hadn't given her a heads-up that Maggie might call her.

"Good. Good. You and your Justin work with the homeless shelter? Yes?"

"Yes."

"Do you know if they could find a room for a friend? He's quite ill. I'm worried."

"Doesn't your friend have any family he can turn to?"

"He says no."

"Well, the shelters have a certain protocol. He can't be using, and he can't have an untreated mental illness." She knew that issue by heart. There were services to help, but the person had to admit they needed help in the first place. Then, there'd be hope.

"Do you have a number I could call?"

"Sure." Shannon flipped through some papers on her desk and repeated the number to Maggie.

"Thanks, Shannon. So, you know about Amber and Ethan?"

"Yeah. I'm watching Mocha while they're in Boston."

"I'm very happy for them."

"Yeah." Shannon twisted her earring over and over, wishing the conversation would end.

"And soon, you and Justin will follow?" She could hear the tease in Maggie's voice.

"No. Justin and I aren't seeing each other anymore."

Silence hung heavy on the line.

"Oh. I'm very sorry." Maggie's Greek accent that normally charmed Shannon grated on her nerves.

"It's for the best. You know what? I really need to go."

"Of course. Thank you very much."

Shannon tucked her phone back into her pocket and sighed. Maybe she'd get to work. Her last few weeks of freedom were nearing the end, and she had little to show for a summer off from teaching. Usually, she'd have several hundred photos. Even last year with Amber, she'd taken a lot of shots trying to capture the colors and emotions Amber would later need to reference. But that was no more. She wandered to an antique flat-file cabinet and pulled out her latest prints. There were many of the boats on the river. Those she'd done for contract.

She was in a funk. How had she become so dependent on others? Just because Amber was moving on and Shannon was in between contract jobs, that didn't mean she'd lost herself. She needed to remember who she was, down deep.

Plopping onto the sofa, she grabbed her Bible and read a few favorite verses. Even those fell flat.

Her phone rang again. Justin. It'd been days.

"Can I come over?"

"I don't think that's a good idea."

"I do." His tone told her he wouldn't give up until she agreed. "Fine."

After she hung up, she straightened her apartment and then moved to her portfolio again. All of this was good. Was important. But did it feed her soul?

Where did that come from?

Justin. He always prodded her to find her passion—to be hungry for it. Until recently, her passions had been funneled into Amber and helping her through her sight loss. Helping her recapture her dream of being a painter. And now what?

She flipped through several more shots. The ones that stirred her heart most had to do with the homeless. She'd done a series in black and white for the newsletter of the local shelter. But now, looking back, she'd only given them the hopeful ones. Instead, these were raw, unfiltered, and painful. Their eyes, narrowed in the sun or rain, shot daggers into her heart.

These were the real photos. Pain etched on weathered faces, tears clinging to watery eyes, blackened fingernails grasping their last hope, a desire for more and a fear to try.

She continued to shuffle through, pulling out one here or there for extra study. One of a little girl in a dirty yellow dress caught her attention. She gripped a stained and ragged doll under her left arm. Her eyes and expression were dull and empty. Shannon knew those eyes. She'd seen them in the mirror looking back at her. This girl had seen too much for her age, too. Shannon's life was different than most people's. Even at the youngest of ages. No one else in preschool ever talked about ambulances coming to *their* houses at night to whisk their mother away. Or talked about their fathers standing in the street reading from the newspaper at the top of his lungs until the police came. Or screaming matches where rusty folding chairs flew across the room. Or having no one at home and eating dried ramen for three meals a day until someone remembered her.

No. They made up happy stories about mommies and daddies and babies. They played shopping and house. But Shannon knew. She knew what it was like to smuggle a package of hamburger out of the store inside her jacket, or a bag of frozen vegetables inside her baby blanket. Or a pint of milk in her doll stroller. She knew what it was to have only ketchup and beer in the fridge. To have the aromas of food from the neighbor's house come wafting through their unscreened windows in the summertime, tormenting her hunger while her parents lay in coma-like states with the drug of the month splayed out on their living room furniture. She knew what it was like to be bounced in and out of group homes, until they'd finally taken her away from Daniel for good.

Oh, she knew.

She knew what it was to have her underwear and holey third-hand clothes shoved into a garbage bag while social services barraged her with questions about her parents' drinking habits. To sit alone in peeling yellow-walled, fluorescent-lit offices on hard furnishings and hope this time the family that took her would love her for real.

And she'd been taught to lie. She could lie with the best of them. Yes, her foster parents fed her well. Yes, she felt safe. No, she never had nightmares where groping hands would invade her privacy and more experienced foster kids would try to make her do unspeakable things.

A shiver drove down her back, and she pulled her hoodie closed with the draw strings.

Knocking on her door jolted her back to the present and beat in time with the blood pumping through her ears.

"Shannon? Shannon, you okay?" Justin sounded frantic, his normally stoic voice hitting new pitches. "Shannon?"

"Yes," she croaked, throat dry and tongue stuck to the roof of her mouth from a crying jag she didn't fully remember. "Yes, I'm okay." She stumbled to the oval mirror near her door and pulled back the hoodie to reveal her long, purple hair tangled in static electricity, puffy eyes, and tear-stained cheeks. She grabbed the brush from the stand below and took a few quick strokes, only making it worse. She licked her fingers and blotted her cheeks and wiped them on her sweatshirt. After grimacing at her reflection, she turned away and unlatched the door.

Justin stood there red-faced with perspiration beading across his forehead. "Were you asleep?"

What could she say? She hadn't tuned out like that in a long, long time. Years. Why, today of all days, did her PTSD have to make a reentrance into her life?

"Yeah. Sorry." She chuckled and shrugged before inviting him inside her apartment. She closed the door lightly, not letting the latch catch, and tucked her hands into her pockets.

Justin's eyes scanned her, sizing her up. She hated it when he did that, as if he could see through her. She didn't need that in her life.

"What did you think had happened? I got kidnapped or something?" She watched as his brows narrowed.

"It could happen. Or worse. We work with some edgy people who we don't always know very well."

She didn't need him reminding her of the time she turned her back on that drunk on Front Street. She wouldn't do that ever again. It was a good thing Justin had her back that day.

And there was the rub. She didn't *want* to have him have her back. Did that even make sense? Her head swirled with contradictions and weaknesses. Instead of addressing any of them, she changed the subject.

"Come on in."

"I wanted to apologize for the other day."

"No need." She moved to the kitchen. "Want a drink?"

"Sure. Ice water."

"Out of ice." She pulled out her filter pitcher and poured a glass. "Tasted all freezer-like so I tossed it."

"No problem." He took the glass.

"Do you want to sit down?" Her tone conveyed she didn't really want him to. She hoped he heard it and took the hint. His eyes told her he had, but still he sat and motioned for her to do the same. She did.

"The other day. When I drove away. I was really angry. I've needed some time to cool off and think things over."

"I understand." She cleared her voice as if to say something more, but no words came, so she pressed her lips closed and waited.

"I need you to explain to me why getting married is such a bad thing."

Shannon's teeth ground together to a rhythm all her own as she gathered her thoughts. "It's not a bad thing. Not in itself."

"But it is for you?"

"Yeah. Exactly. It's not for me."

"But living alone, that's for you?"

"Yes. That's for me." Because the alternative was unthinkable. She looked at the pain filling Justin's eyes, and guilt roiled through her. "This is my fault. I'm so sorry. I knew. I've known all along I never—" She bit off a sob. There was no way she was going to cry in front of him. No way. "I should have never let us get this close."

"I know you love me."

"Love has nothing to do with it." She couldn't deny her feelings. She hadn't lied to Justin. Yet. But she loved him too much to let this go any further. There were too many things he didn't understand. Too many things she could never explain or have it make sense to him.

"I know you've been hurt in the past."

He had no idea.

He reached for her.

"Justin. Stop." She put her hand up but instead of heeding her warning, he took her hand in his. She stared down at his large, paint-stained brown fingers intertwining her own tawny ones. The heat from their touch penetrated her fears and worked its way into her blood.

"No." She pulled away. "Can't we just go back to being friends?"

Justin's warm fingers gently tipped up her chin so that she was forced to look into his eyes.

"That's what you want?"

"Yes."

"And you want me to agree to be around you, work with you, spend time with you, and not touch you? Not want to kiss you? Not to want to pull you into my arms and hold you close?"

She licked her lips and lied to him for the first time. "Yes."

Part of her wanted him to get mad. To scream like her parents had. To throw things around. Then...then she'd be justified in doing what she was doing. Part of her wanted him to just storm out and never call her again.

The rest of her hoped he'd agree. It made no sense. It was crazy. But she wanted it. Somehow.

"Okay." Justin's voice reverberated with gentleness. So much so it shocked her. In his deep aqua eyes, she saw a flash of warning mixed with a dare. And something else that scared her more than anything.

Determination.

CHAPTER 4

"You'll—just be friends?" Amber shifted around her apartment, gathering Mocha's toys and food. The skeptical tone in her voice put Shannon on edge.

"That's what I said and he agreed." Although there was still that look in Justin's eyes she hadn't wanted to think about. Instead, she focused her mind on the immediate issue of her cat-nephew and his vacation at Aunty Shannon's house.

Shannon leaned over the growing pile of kitty things on the dining table. This was getting out of hand. "How much does one cat need, anyway?"

Amber seemed to take stock. "He gets lonesome when I'm away. And you'll be working so much that this will take the pressure off having to entertain him all the time." Amber moved to the corner near the couch and picked up a blue folded square that looked a bit like a tent flap. "This is his jungle gym. It pops open into a series of squares and he climbs through it."

Shannon turned to face Mocha, who had leapt to the table and was nosing his belongings with curiosity.

"You've got her right where you want her, don't you, fuzz ball?"

Mocha looked up at her with his golden eyes, did the slow blink, and a contented purr thrummed through the room. *Yep.* She scratched his chocolate-brown head with her nails and he leaned into her hand.

"And how exactly is this going to work?" Amber plopped yet another toy on the table.

Shannon frowned and picked up Mocha. "Good, I think. I mean, I'll feed him and we'll play and nap. He'll get into things he shouldn't and claw at my furniture. What else is there?"

"I mean with Justin."

Oh.

"The same as it's been."

Amber gave her a quizzical look that almost made Shannon forget her friend was blind. "Except for the kissing and the holding hands and the long phone conversations where neither of you wants to say good-bye?"

Shannon opened her mouth to give a rebuttal, but nothing came out, so she shrugged.

Amber's brows furrowed. "I know you just shrugged. I can't see it, but I can sense when you shrug a mile away. This is no shrugging situation. It's dangerous. It's hurtful. For both of you." She moved over and took Shannon's hand in hers. "Why are you doing this to yourself?"

"You know why."

"If you would just tell him, explain it all, I know Justin could handle it," Amber began, but Shannon pulled away.

"That's not his business. My reasons are sound. Besides, as far as marriage goes, I'm a major train wreck waiting to happen." She gathered Mocha's things into two paper bags and tucked the blue-tent-thingy under her arm. "I'm going to take this first load down to my car. I'll come back for the food and Mr. Mocha."

"What about the cat box?" Amber scrunched her nose at the unkempt box in the corner, no doubt realizing she'd forgotten to clean it.

As if Shannon would take that thing in her car? She loved the cat, but that was one side of things that made her wonder if she'd ever move from cat-aunt to cat-parent.

"I bought one."

Amber stopped, mouth agape. "You did what?"

"I figure this won't be the first trip you make back east, so I might as well fit out my place for my fuzzy nephew." Shannon's laughter faded when Amber's smile shifted and she twisted her red-blond hair around her first finger. Something akin to molten lead filled Shannon's stomach. She couldn't bring herself to ask what it meant. It was bad, though. That was clear. Amber only got that look when she was about to say something she didn't want to.

"Listen, Ethan and I..." Amber's voice caught. "We might be looking at apartments in Boston."

Shannon felt all the blood drain from her body, leaving a void space. This wasn't happening.

"He and his parents don't even get along. They're control freaks. He *left* Boston because of them. Why go back?"

"That was before, when he was sick."

Shannon didn't say it, but she knew Ethan was only in remission. His cancer could come back at any time. What would his family do then?

"They've changed. Listen, we're not sure. But..." Tears filled Amber's eyes and she reached a hand out to where Shannon had been. But Shannon moved away. She couldn't be touched. Not now.

"I'd better get these things downstairs. I'll be right back." She made for the door before Amber could tell her anything else. If she didn't tell her, it wouldn't come true. It couldn't. Shannon looked down at Mocha's supplies, all stowed in paper and plastic bags, and flashed back to carrying her own things in the same shape. So many times.

Amber leave? Never mind they'd been together since the age of four. Never mind they'd promised they'd always live near one another. Never mind she didn't know what she'd do without Amber living within twenty minutes of her.

As if marrying Ethan wasn't bad enough. Now this. *This.* How could she survive this?

Shannon pulled the door closed behind her and made her

way down the two flights of stairs to her car waiting outside. She loaded Mocha's things inside. Her mind didn't allow her to think of what could be. Of what might happen. Instead she took a deep breath and headed back, fists clenching and unclenching as she grappled for control. She wouldn't let Amber know how hurt she was. That'd only invite more discussion, and there wasn't any way in the world she could do that now. Instead, she pretended with all her might.

Once back up the stairs, she opened Amber's apartment door and spoke with a carefree voice, even though there was nothing carefree about her. She watched as Amber moved mechanically around the apartment, wiping tears from her eyes.

"Don't leave yet. Please. Let's talk this over."

"I really need to go." Before her emotions got the better of her.

"Worst thing?" Amber's voice turned gravelly with emotion as she asked their old-time question. It was supposed to give them confidence and assurance that things could be worse. That the thing they feared wasn't worthy of their fear.

"Not this time." Because *this*. This was the worst thing. The worst thing ever.

"Shannon?" Amber's face contorted with held back tears. "Don't. Please."

"I can't. Do this. Right now. I can't. Okay?" Her arms crossed her chest, holding herself tight as if to keep back the panic building within her.

Amber wiped her eyes and blew her nose, nodding. No one understood her like Amber. No one ever would. They were sisters of the heart. They'd been through so much. They had survived so many things.

"Let's get you going, Mocha." Amber loaded Mocha inside his carrier and murmured to him, tearfully.

"Be a good boy. And don't try to escape. If you do, just stay in Aunt Shannon's hallway. Don't talk to strangers." Amber gasped.

"And take special care of Aunt Shannon." Tears rolled down Amber's nose and she wiped at them with the back of her hand. Mocha peered through the bars on his kitty-carrier, eyes expectant, nonplussed about his owner's emotional state.

Amber stood, shakily, facing Shannon. "I didn't mean to tell you yet. Not like this. I'm sorry."

Shannon couldn't speak. What she'd thought was an annoying visit back east was turning out to be much more threatening than even Amber's impending marriage. Shannon wasn't just losing her to Ethan. Shannon was losing Amber altogether.

Amber moved toward her, arms out, ready to embrace her.

"Not now." Shannon grabbed the carrier. "Let me know when—" She choked back a sob. Tears gripped her throat as if to strangle her. "When you're home."

"Shannon." Amber's voice was barely a whisper. "Please." She pulled on Shannon's arm, drawing her over. "Nothing has to..."

"Everything will." Shannon couldn't bring herself to say it. *Change.* The word felt like a death sentence. Long distance? When Shannon needed Amber here? What about when Amber needed something? Oh. Yeah.

She had Ethan.

Shannon swept up the carrier and headed to the door.

Her mouth told Amber to have a good trip. But she didn't mean it. At all.

"Good-bye," she thought she heard Amber say, but Shannon closed the door before she lost her nerve. This wasn't how her day was going to go. This wasn't how her life was supposed to play out. They were going to go through life together. Sure, men might come and go, and even stay, but they'd always have each other's backs.

She liked Ethan. He was a good man. He loved Amber, and Shannon wanted that for her friend. She wanted the whole package for her. Nice house, kids, lots of love in her life. And when

Amber had kids, Shannon would baby-sit. She knew she'd never have her own kids, but she'd always planned on having Amber's kids in her life.

Shannon always pictured herself...well, in the picture—not on the other side of the country.

Last winter, when Amber was losing her sight and Shannon stood by her, there'd been no other time in her life when she felt so full of purpose. She could finally be there for Amber the way Amber had been there for her all those years ago. All those sleepless nights. Those terror-driven times when dreams would haunt her even in daylight. Those times when she'd run away to Amber's house to be safe, and Amber would sneak baloney and peanut butter sandwiches to her under her bed until she felt safe enough to return home. Or not to return.

Until today, Shannon always knew she could count on Amber and Amber could count on her. Now she wasn't needed for her day-to-day assistance. She wasn't needed to help her envision her paintings. Or drive her around for groceries. They wouldn't hang out at the coffee shop anymore or go shopping in used clothing stores for outfits they'd never wear. They wouldn't pop into strange pubs and put on fake accents to get discounts on drinks. They'd never get those matching tattoos Amber had always said she'd wanted but when they went into the tattoo parlors, she'd make up an excuse and promise next time.

Next time.

Shannon had only ever had family in bits and pieces—mostly Amber's family, to be honest. After her fourth foster family, she'd let go of that pristine ideal. A bed where she could sleep without fear and a dresser to store her few belongings had sufficed. It stopped bothering her that families on television, or parents of kids in the schools she attended, seemed stalwart, because she had Amber unwavering at her side. She and Amber would be lifelong companions, unlikely twins in the battle of life, the two Musketeers, facing all odds at each other's sides.

You couldn't do that from the other side of the country.

She sniffed and wiped at the tears running freely down her cheeks with the back of her hand.

From now on, nothing was certain. They wouldn't do anything but call often, then occasionally, then sporadically. Then not at all. The texts would wane and e-mails would die off and they'd have nothing to show for twenty-five years of friendship. Nothing but fading memories tinged with the unpleasantness of knowing what could have been.

Mocha mewed worriedly as Shannon drove through the darkening Portland streets, past the homeless shelters and up the hill to her tiny flat.

"Don't worry, Mocha. It's all right."

She didn't know if she was talking to herself or to the cat. But neither of them believed her.

CHAPTER 5

Underneath it all, weren't they all the same? "If you prick us, do we not bleed?"

That was the thought that permeated Shannon's mind as she took photos of the homeless down by the river. They kept their possessions close in dirty black garbage bags, grocery sacks, or rusted grocery carts, lest anyone steal their lives from them. She knew what that was like. Most things were castoffs that no one in "civilized" society would cherish. But to them, a pair of stained, wooly socks would make the difference between safe toes and frostbite.

She focused on an elderly man shuffling up the street, lace-less shoes flopping against the sidewalk. He leaned over a garbage can and withdrew a partially eaten apple. He wiped it on his filthy coat before taking a bite. The red skin of the apple and white bite mark contrasted with his gray, torn coat. They were both damaged and tossed aside. The sunlight hit the side of his face, lighting his deep brown eyes, and Shannon caught the glimmer of life with her camera. His scraggly beard, his weathered, wrinkled skin masked the man and shrouded him in darkness, but Shannon knew there could be light.

Magic Stan and Queen Susie came trundling around the corner, arguing. The spark of disagreement often made Shannon smile—they were so much like mother and son. Stan came around to the front of their green-tarp-wrapped grocery cart and braced it. Susie pushed against him to no avail, and her shoulders sank

41

in defeat. Shannon couldn't hear every word, but the inflection was royal in tone, and his arms shot out in Shakespearean effect as if he were addressing a theatre of eager listeners. She grabbed a photo. *Click* went the shutter on her digital camera. Stan stood in regal authority, his trench coat flapping in the wind, his mouth barking out lines.

"Gentle folk, weeping may endure for a night, but joy commeth in the morning!"

Ah, quoting the Psalms today. She drew closer, capturing the faces of onlookers. Some smiled, some grimaced and walked by, pretending Stan and Susie didn't exist. That was easiest. Homelessness, mental illness, and hunger were too huge for any one person to fix—easier to look away and hope someone else would take care of it. Or blame those caught in the trap—be it of their own making or someone else's. Most people weren't heartless to the plight of the downtrodden, but they felt helpless, so they didn't help.

A haggard-looking woman—eyes sunken in worry, wind-tossed hair, travel coffee mug clenched in her white-knuckled grip—stopped walking as if she'd run into a wall, as if she'd never heard such words before.

"Hear, O Lord, and have mercy upon me: Lord, be thou my helper. Thou hast turned for me my mourning into dancing: thou hast put off my sackcloth and girded me with gladness." At this Stan noticed the small crowd growing, and his voice echoed over the courtyard.

"Let's go, you old fool." Susie Q tried once again to push the cart, but he braced it against the wall and stepped around it, the calling on his spirit overcoming him.

Shannon's legs moved her forward as if pulled by a magnet, slow and sure. She focused her lens on the woman, so captivated, tears welling in her eyes unashamed. *Click.* The light shifted across her face, illuminating her tears, prisms sparkling in truth.

Shannon grabbed another, blurring the focus in the background, sharpening it on Stan and the woman.

Stan took a deep breath, encouraged by the woman's reaction. "To the end that my glory may sing praise to thee, and not be silent. O Lord my God, I will give thanks unto thee forever."

The woman exhaled, color filled her cheeks, and her grip loosened. Her face was awash in wonder.

He bowed, and a few clapped as the crowd dispersed. But not the woman. She wiped the wetness from her face, then reached inside her purse and handed Stan some cash in her shaking grip. Shannon caught the exchange of hands touching—the woman's spotless, Stan's reddened by too many winters on the street, scarred, dirty, and disfigured by arthritis. Neither recoiling.

"Thank you, dear woman." He swept his long arm down and bowed for dramatic effect. Then he reached inside his trench coat and pulled out a tattered green pocket Gideon Bible and handed it to her. "For you."

The woman took the dirty item like a cherished gift, cradling it in both hands, looking wonderingly at it.

"Thank you." Her voice was but a whisper.

And then, all at once, Stan withdrew back into himself, eyes shuttered, head bent, weaving down the sidewalk, urging Susie to continue along, pushing all their most important treasures outside the park. There was something so real and special about those two. Shannon had tried to get them off the streets many times, but it never lasted. They needed mental health assistance. They needed to stick to it after it was offered. There were many organizations to help, but they could only do so much. They couldn't round up people and force it on them. There simply weren't enough workers to go around.

Shannon knew how hard that was from experience.

Her mind wandered to Boston. Amber had been gone for a couple days. Already the sting and emptiness made themselves known, like a rash you forgot about until you were in bed, nearly asleep, and then it would flare and keep you awake, growing in annoyance. Amber had texted a few times, sharing photos Ethan took and funny stories, but Shannon couldn't rejoice with her. The distance grew in her heart, creating a chasm that would only spread wider with time.

Shannon made her way up through the business center and paused to watch a disheveled but clean man lounging on the grass in Pettygrove Park. He read a book—a book she'd handed out last week no less, although she didn't recognize him. Instead of moving on, she grabbed a seat on a faded wooden bench and combed her long purple and black hair over her eyes to shield her gaze. She pretended to focus the camera elsewhere. She didn't want the man to know she watched him. This was the only way she could get completely candid shots.

Even the homeless knew how to put on a happy face.

Shannon framed him in a shot, focusing on the novel gripped in battered, tattooed hands, but before she could take it, he shifted and tucked the book away. He ran his stubby fingers through his hair, tucked in his shirt, and moved toward a group of girls giggling near the sculpted golden fountain.

Her stomach knotted, and she tensed. This wasn't right.

The girls went on alert as the man closed in on them. They moved away, like a group of gazelles out on the Serengeti unsure if they should run from the leopard or not, but then he started chatting with them in friendly tones, and they quieted down.

"I think you dropped this," he said, handing them the book. They faced him, shaking their heads. But he kept insisting, putting on a charade of kindness.

"No, keep moving," Shannon whispered to herself. She gritted her teeth, and perspiration broke out across her neck. She grabbed her camera and snapped photos of the man with the girls. Shannon moved closer, wanting him to notice her, get nervous, and leave.

"You are all so pretty. What's a gaggle of girls doing around here? You must be new, because if I'd seen you before, I'd definitely remember. You want to have some fun? I know this bar."

One girl laughed. "As if. We're under age."

"Oh, now, I happen to know they don't care about that. They are very open-minded. Rules are made to be broken. Good stuff, too. Great music." He licked his lips, eyes glassy and enticed.

Another girl flipped her hair. "We don't drink."

"Never too soon to start. Here's my card." He held out a business card in his sticky fingers. They all just stared at him, disgust in their eyes. "You'll have to excuse my working hands. I'm out here on a break. Then I'm back to it. Takes a lot of man hours to open a club like that." He straightened his gray, well-worn blazer and wiped his hands on his grimy jeans.

"A club?" One of the younger girls brightened at this idea and took his card. But the tallest, if not the oldest, girl stepped in the way.

"No thanks. Let's go."

They started to move away when another crowd of people came through the park. The sight shifted to the surreal as a tour group swooped in on Segways, taking their guide's directions to circle the fountain before heading off over a slight knoll.

Now that man would back off. He wouldn't take the risk. But he seemed to disagree with Shannon's assertions. He pressed them further.

"Could I have my card back, then? They cost a lot to print up, and if you're not going to use it, then I'll find another group of gorgeous young women to give it to. I've got to find just the right ones. Besides—it's only good business sense."

"What do you mean?" The middle girl, red-haired and flush with curiosity, moved closer.

No. Don't do that. Shannon's heart rate soared.

"Everyone who's anyone knows it's the beautiful women that

bring customers into the club at first. All those handsome young men looking for the lady of their dreams. You fit the bill for sure. It'd be a great favor to me. I'll make your food and drinks on the house. What do you say?"

Another group of people in business attire strolled by, taking little notice of what was going on; or if they did see it, they ignored it. What was one more homeless man and a group of young women?

But Shannon knew. It only took one incident to break a girl, to shatter her into so many slivers.

The man, quicker than Shannon would have guessed, reached out a hand and clamped it on the littlest one's arm. "Seems to me she's interested. How about you all come along, too? I'll make sure you get home before dinner. I've got a sweet BMW." He motioned up the block. When the girls turned to look, he moved closer.

"I don't see any BMW." The red-haired girl squinted.

"Just up the block." He chuckled. "Be a tight fit, but I'm okay with that if you are." He waggled his eyebrows at them, eliciting a shy smile from the blonde.

"This is a bad idea." The middle girl hedged and backed away.

"Let her go." The eldest pointed to the little one. "Now."

"Oh, you're feisty." He laughed. "Beautiful and strong. Has anyone told you how alluring that is in a woman? You're going to have all the men eating out of your hands."

The compliment mixed with danger made the girl waver. Unsure, she stepped back. Shannon knew the battle—being admired and thought of as a woman when no one treated you like one was tempting. Even if it was by someone unsavory. The little one squirmed. "I think I want to go home now."

He leaned down and whispered, "Trust me, you really don't. This will be the best night of your life. The start of a new adventure. You like nice clothes? Money? What I'll pay tonight will set you up for the rest of the school year. Everyone will be jealous of you. You'll never be the same again."

Shannon spotted a knife in his hand, but the girls didn't seem to notice.

Her mouth went dry. Hadn't she heard those very same words? She tried to move but couldn't. What was wrong with her? Normally she'd be in the middle of this. She'd take this guy on with no problem whatsoever. Instead, her legs went numb.

Shannon pointed and clicked the camera again, getting more shots, but still she couldn't find her words. The girls seemed to notice her for the first time.

"Can you help us?" The shortest of the four pleaded, voice strained and fearful.

The man turned on Shannon, eyes blazing, locked on her camera.

"What do you think you're doing?"

"Getting shots of the fountain." Her voice croaked. "If you all face into the light, they'll turn out best. I'll get you copies."

Everything tilt-shifted. He came at her hard, shoulder to her gut, knocking her to the ground, breathless. He ripped her camera from her hands and smashed it against the bricks. Bits of black plastic flew into the air and landed around her in slow motion like ash after a volcano. He grabbed her by the hair and wrenched her head around. The girls screamed and ran, calling for help.

"You got a lot of nerve." He glanced up at the retreating girls. "You know how long I waited here for the right ones? How much money you just lost me? Now I got to start all over. Don't mess with me." Spittle flew from his lips and landed on her cheeks. "If I ever see you again, you'll be sorry." His breath reeked of rotted teeth and alcohol.

Shannon's head stung where he gripped her hair, and the bricks below her dug into her back. Still, she had no voice. No retort.

No scream. Nothing but ragged, terrified breathing. Why wasn't she fighting back?

His bloodshot brown eyes crinkled from his victorious grin. And then something dangerous flashed in his eyes. Something that chilled her to her core.

"How about this? You for them? You owe me. You're worth the four of them, easy. Easy." His tone shifted to one someone would use for a frightened animal, but instead of calming her, her pulse raced ever faster. His hand moved down her side and all she could do was whimper.

"No."

"Free drinks, free food. A good time. Real good." He drew out the word *real*. "Lots of money to be made. But I bet you know that already." His mouth was a breath away from hers—and her strength drained like someone had opened a vein.

"Stop." It was more a plea than a command. She'd lost herself somewhere. Where was she? Something split in her mind, and it was as if she was watching it all happen at a distance. A safe distance.

A whistle blew and a police officer beat it around the corner, yelling at the man. The creep pushed off Shannon and her head slammed against the pavement below. Sharp bright lights sparkled through her vision.

Another police officer came around the corner, shouting orders into his walkie-talkie. Then he went to his knees near Shannon.

"You okay, Miss?"

Shannon could do little but stare at him. Her voice hadn't returned yet. From behind him she heard high-pitched voices.

"She saved us. She saved us." The girls were in tow behind a third officer, sobbing. They hadn't abandoned her. They hadn't left her. They were safe. She closed her eyes and felt every nerve in her body return to life as if waking from a dream. Her heartbeat slowed, and she focused on the white puffy clouds passing above her head, gathering and graying at the bottom. There'd be a storm tonight.

"Send a bus." The nearest officer spoke into his radio and checked Shannon over.

"No. Really, I'm okay." She tried to laugh, but it felt foreign to her throat and came out more like a gag.

"Just lay still. There's an ambulance on the way."

"Really," Shannon protested, but she sat up too fast and the clouds spun down around her, mixing with the trees in a blurring whirl, like she was on a merry-go-round, and her brains turned to cotton candy. She clenched her eyes closed and gritted her teeth, which made the dizziness in her head turn to a full-on gale force migraine. The officer put a hand on her shoulder, stilling her, and scooted around to keep her sitting up.

"We have a head wound here. Get the med kit."

Head wound?

She reached behind her and felt a sticky wet spot on the back of her head. Pulling away, she saw red on her fingertips. Shannon rubbed her fingers together, mesmerized by the bright color on her fingers. The prettiest shade of red.

An ambulance pulled up before the officer could make use of the kit, and they loaded her on the gurney. Everything seemed to speed up then, like hitting the fast-forward on an old VHS tape, blurred pictures and lots of static. As they rattled her across the uneven pavement she had only one thought.

"Camera. I need my camera."

The officer ran alongside. "We'll get your information, and we'll need that for evidence. I'm sorry. I think it's toast. But the memory card looks unharmed."

Shannon grimaced as they loaded her into the van, every jolt bringing a new level of pain to the volcanic headache growing exponentially. They hooked her up to an IV and put a warming blanket over her. Her teeth chattered despite its heat.

"Getting shocky. Elevating her feet." The EMT put her legs up on a wedge cushion, and her focus improved.

Her camera destroyed. How could she afford a new one? Not on her salary. It had taken her years to save for that.

"Miss, should we contact anyone to let them know you've been taken to the hospital?"

Should they?

Who would come? If she called Justin, he'd read more into it than she wanted. And Amber was gone. Was there anyone? Mocha. He'd be hungry.

"My cat."

"You have a cat?"

"No. Not my cat. But..." Shannon couldn't remember what was so upsetting. Nothing made sense.

"I'm afraid I can't call your cat." She could hear the smile in his voice, but it just made her angry.

"Not *my* cat."

"Got it. You rest. We're almost there."

If she could reach the Sharps container next to her, she'd thwack this guy. Why didn't he listen to her?

"Amber."

"Your cat's name is Amber?"

"No. I need Amber." She tried unsuccessfully to remove her phone from her pocket, fingers fumbling and stiff. Amber was gone. Soon forever. She'd never be able to count on her again. Not like before.

"Got it. No worries."

Shannon knew this guy didn't have a clue.

"She's my friend. Mocha's mom." Her words mushed together.

"Your cat's mom?"

How had this guy passed the EMT exam?

"Are. You. Serious?" The last three words ground out against her teeth, and she faded away.

CHAPTER 6

The smells and sounds of her hospital room brought Shannon back to the present, back to the pain, back to the fear sleep helped her evade. Much to her dislike, and shamefully equal pleasure, she found Justin sitting at her bedside, looking panic-stricken, his face white and eyes pinched at the corners.

"Thank God." He scooted his chair closer, taking her hand in his. "You had me worried."

The pounding behind her light-sensitive eyes forced them to close. "I'm okay."

"You nearly weren't."

In all reality, she knew he was speaking from a place of concern. But she didn't care. She didn't need to be chided. "Neither were those girls."

Justin didn't respond at first. He was thoughtful like that—considering every word, playing out scenarios in his mind before acting on impulse. So different from her. Sometimes this attribute made him appealing, manly, powerful.

Not today.

"That guy was dangerous. He had a knife. The police found it next to you. Do you have any idea how that could have ended?"

"Yeah. Actually, I *do*."

Justin quieted. She waited for him to ask "how?" Maybe this was the moment it would all come out naturally. This was the moment she would explain to him why she'd never get married or have kids or be fully dependent on anyone. Ever.

But he didn't.

"I'm just grateful you're okay."

Another opportunity lost. *For the best.*

"I need to rest." She really did. Everything spun around her, and she could feel herself being drawn away, sinking into the pillow.

"I'll be back later." He brushed her temple with his lips and let himself out of the room before she asked how he'd found out she was there in the first place. By then, though, it didn't matter, because darkness was her friend, and it pulled her safely into its embrace before another thought ran through her mind.

The phone rang on her stand. It didn't sound like hers. It sounded like an old-fashioned one ring-ringing her awake.

Her eyes opened to the apricot-colored molded phone on the hospital stand near her bed, and the present reassembled itself.

Lifting the receiver, she pulled the bulky handset to her ear. No wonder she'd hated talking on these things. Texting was a much more natural way for her to communicate.

"Hello?" Shannon's voice sounded thick, medicated. Her tongue stuck to the roof of her mouth, unwieldy.

"I can't leave you for a day. Are you okay? Justin called me. I'm coming home."

"Amber?"

"I'm flying in this afternoon. Justin is picking me up."

"What?"

"I'll be there at four. You rest. Don't worry about anything."

"Wait. No." She couldn't seem to gather her thoughts enough to make a good argument.

Neither of them spoke for a moment.

"No?"

Shannon ignored the hurt in Amber's voice.

"It's not a big deal." Her mouth felt lazy and her brain like pillow fluff.

"As if," Amber scoffed.

"Really." Shannon fiddled with the loose-weave yellowish bedspread draped over her legs.

"You have a concussion."

News to her. Why did other people always know more about her than she did?

"People get them all the time." No wonder her head felt like someone popped it off and put it back on again with a plunger.

"I'm worried about you."

"I'll be okay. You stay with Ethan."

"Too late. Plane ticket is bought."

Shannon sighed. A strange happiness filled her and mixed immediately with guilt. Amber still loved her as much as ever, but Shannon didn't want her to mess up her vacation with Ethan. Not much anyway.

"I'm going to have to get used to doing things on my own—I might as well start now." Her words slurred like she'd been drinking. She took a deep breath, focusing with all her might. "It'll be good practice." As much as she was trying to convince Amber, she was also trying to convince herself—because right then, if pushed, she was pretty sure she'd burst into tears.

"I don't like it."

Shannon released a strangled chuckle. "Justin won't let me out of his sight for long." Which was an issue unto its own.

"Okay."

Part of Shannon felt a keen disappointment, the other relief.

"Oh, I know, my mom can help." Amber sounded hopeful.

"No." Her head pounded harder.

"My mom loves you. Both of my moms love you. They can check on you. Make you food. Well, my mom will probably bring you take-out and Maggie will bring reheated frozen dinners. But it'll be food. I didn't get any cooking skills from either of them, I'm afraid."

Shannon couldn't help laughing for real that time. She might not have a mom of her own, but those ladies did a pretty good job mothering both her and Amber. And they were both atrocious cooks.

"Fine. See? I'm in good hands. I don't need you."

That didn't come out right at all. It had snuck up out of some store of residual anger she'd put a tight lid on last week. The problem with things that snuck out is they were unplanned. Genuine, but harsh and unnecessarily painful. Like acrid smoke pooling under the lid of a pan forgotten on the burner, just waiting to set off the fire alarm in your apartment.

"Oh."

"You know what I mean." Shannon shoved the bitterness back where it belonged. The voices in her head taunted her: *You don't need anyone. Show her.* Deep down, she knew it wasn't true—but the pain of being tossed over for Ethan lingered. Still, she hadn't meant to say it. *Ever.*

"Right. We'll talk later."

The click in the earpiece alerted Shannon that Amber had hung up on her.

Crud.

Why couldn't she be mature about this?

It hurt so bad. Her head. Her heart. It was hard to tell which one hurt worse.

The nurse came in, followed by the doctor. They'd keep her another night, and then release her in the morning if she had someone who could keep an eye on her.

She did, she lied. *Again.*

She'd forgotten how easy it was to lie. Once she started, the floodgates just opened and poured forth.

Justin came by a couple hours later with flowers and a sack

of Burgerville cheeseburgers. Her mouth watered. He wasn't playing fair.

She hardly thanked him before she opened the sack and devoured the first one.

Justin sat back, pleasure in his eyes.

"I'm surprised you bought this for me," she said between ravenous bites.

"One can't live by tofu alone."

"I've never heard you say *that* before."

"Well, I'm doing a lot of things I never thought I'd do lately." He gave her a significant look with his aqua-colored eyes. He fiddled with his eyebrow stud, something he did while pondering.

She didn't question the statement, but continued devouring the heavenly meal once encased in crinkly brown paper. After the second one, she lay back, sated.

"Can you put the other two in the fridge at the guest station with my name on them?"

"Sure. Can't have anyone else pilfering your burgers."

"Exactly. Put hands off in bold red and underline it." She sighed. "I'm getting out of here tomorrow." He needed to know she wouldn't be there. She'd be fine on her own.

"No problem. I've asked for the week off."

Shannon frowned at him. "What for?"

"You can't be alone with a concussion. You've got to have someone watch out for you for a couple days."

"So, you're staying with me?"

"Of course." The answer appeared obvious to him.

"In my apartment?" Not big enough for two. Just enough for her.

"Yes."

"Have you seen my apartment?" Sarcasm, her best defense and offense. A weapon to be wielded sometimes in strips or small piercing cuts. Today it was wide swaths.

"I'll bring a sleeping bag."

Good. Because her couch was more of a love seat, and he wasn't sharing her bed. Although the thought of it sent a warm feeling over her for which she hated herself.

"Fine. Amber put you up to this, didn't she?"

Justin's eyes filled with hurt. "No. Can't I think of ways to take care of you without Amber's help?"

Well, she was really racking up the points today, wasn't she?

"Of course. Sorry."

"Maybe it's a good thing Amber is considering moving."

Oh? For once he appeared to have said exactly what he was thinking the second he thought it. Bad subject to start with though.

"What's that supposed to mean?"

"Maybe if you don't have her to lean on, you'll look around and see she's not the only one in the world that wants to take care of you."

Her jaw worked. "I don't need anyone to take care of me."

His eyebrows rose. "The doctor begs to differ."

"Aren't you on a roll?"

"What's that supposed to mean?"

"Mister never-makes-a-decision-without-hours-of-planning-and-detailing suddenly says what's really on his mind. Well, you're wrong. Relying on Amber isn't the reason I don't want to get married, and her moving isn't going to send me running into your arms."

Again, he didn't ask. Instead, he went on the defense.

"What's wrong with making careful plans?"

"It doesn't suit you." She motioned to his piercings, tattoos and blue-tipped hair fashioned by a prohibition cut—long on top, brushed back, sides shorn.

"I'll have you know I planned out each of these so I didn't regret any of my choices. You could take a lesson there."

That did it. She'd only told two people about the unfortunate tattoo of a man's name on her hip that she'd regretted from week two. She was sorry Justin had been one she'd taken into her confidence.

"Leave."

Justin's eyes widened in regret. He put his hands up in surrender. "Wait."

"Go. I'm tired." She curled into a ball, back to him, and closed her eyes.

Seconds later she heard the door slide closed. She sighed and turned back over, only to find him still sitting there, staring at her. Only now tears welled in his eyes.

Her own eyes filled in empathy. She'd never wanted to hurt him.

"Don't shut me out."

She heard the *please*, even though he didn't say it.

And for the first time since she'd let Amber into her life, as scary as it was, she agreed.

CHAPTER 7

Shannon didn't feel comfortable having Justin stay with her. He'd reluctantly left her on her own after she agreed to have him call her every hour and wake her up. Or make sure she woke up. In retrospect, maybe not the best plan, but giving him a toehold in her life again was much different than letting him into her apartment. Into her daily routine. Seeing her with bedhead and sleep-crusted eyes. Yeah. No one needed to see that.

She buried her face in her pillow and heard the lulling purrs emanating from the snoozing brown lump curled next to her head. Mocha had been very patient with the wake-up calls and only too happy to bring her the occasional toy in the beginning. But by four A.M., even Mocha had tired of the phone and had peered at her through slits of annoyed yellow-green eyes.

As she ran her fingernails over his soft head, he curled into a tighter ball, refusing to wake fully. Just as well. At least one of them would get some sleep.

Shannon climbed from the bed, head pounding from lack of sleep as well as the concussion. She dared a glance into the bathroom mirror and found a pale face, eyes ringed in dark circles, and matted hair. Grateful she hadn't needed stitches, she showered and washed the blood from the back of her head, being careful not to touch the butterfly bandage. The image of the attack formed behind closed eyes, the man screaming, spittle flying from his enraged lips and landing on her face.

Or was that another time?

The sting from shampoo hitting her wound and the cold water cascading over her body shocked her back to the present. She couldn't figure out why the water went cold so quickly. It didn't usually do that. Maybe she needed a new water heater?

Once out of the shower, though, she saw from the clock she'd been in there for forty minutes. Could the concussion make her doze off like that?

Unsettled, she dressed in sweats and baggy shirt, waiting for Justin and lunch. Mocha still lounged on her bed, but she resisted the urge to join him. Instead, she found a spot on the couch and looked out over her balcony at the Portland horizon.

Her phone rang, making her jump.

"Hello?"

"Are you okay?" Justin's voice sounded strained, worried.

"Yes. Just waiting for you."

"I've been out here knocking for five minutes."

She looked at her phone. Another chunk of time lost. Getting up, she let Justin inside. His eyes scrutinized her.

"What's going on? Were you asleep?"

"I don't think so." She looked out the window and saw the sun was in a much different position than before. Time shifted around her in slow motion.

"Come on in." She waved him to the chair to sit and she resumed her vigil on the couch. She bore up under his scrutiny, pretending all was well—but his doubtful expression told her otherwise.

"Are you okay?"

Could she tell him? No. "Yeah. Just didn't get much sleep."

He came over to her. "Let me see your eyes?"

She looked up into his, getting lost for a moment, before she raised shields. He cupped her cheek with his warm palm, squinting and looking back and forth, measuring. Nothing romantic there. But when he took his hand away, a chill washed over her face.

"Your pupils are the same size now. That's good."

"Can I sleep now?"

Justin pulled a square of paper from his pocket and unfolded it. "Yes. Oh." His cheeks went red.

"What?"

"I guess I could have let you sleep two to three hours." He chuckled. "Sorry about that."

"Ugh." She flopped back against the couch, and regretted it instantly. "Ouch." Her hands moved to her head, cradling it.

"Better not do that for a while."

"No." She grimaced, opening one eye at him. "I guess you're off the hook now."

"What if I don't want to be?" She couldn't read his expression.

"Um." She hated how unsettled he could make her.

"Just teasing." He tucked his hands in his pockets and shrugged.

He wasn't. At all. But she felt awful about yesterday, and the whole crushing him thing.

"I really appreciate that I can count on you."

He grinned. Bonus points.

Justin moved over to the fridge and opened it. "Wow."

"What?"

"You've actually got food in here."

She crossed her arms and pulled up her knees. "I keep a full pantry."

He shot her a questioning look, but she didn't elaborate. She watched him open her cabinets that were also fully stocked. Even after all the months they'd been together, they'd hardly hung out at her place—so her apparent preparedness caught him off guard. When you grew up with little, and you weren't sure when or if you would eat again—you got used to stocking up on sale items and putting things away for "in case."

"Your cans are alphabetized." His eyes were wide in amazement.

"Yeah?" How else would you have them? They were also cycled by expiration date. "I'm not like Amber—never planning for the worst."

Justin shot her a look and she shifted from one foot to the other, afraid she'd revealed too much.

"Although, I've taught her a thing or two about organizing since her sight loss."

That elicited a wide grin of appreciation. "You never cease to surprise me. That's one of the reasons I..." He broke off what he was going to say next, and turned abruptly away, taking a glass from the cabinet and filling it with the filtered water at the sink.

Shannon felt her breath catch. She'd never had anyone outside of Amber tell her they loved her. Not and really mean it. Until Justin. And now she'd made him feel like he *couldn't* tell her. She clenched and unclenched her fingers, pinching them to keep concentration. Shannon could feel herself slipping—to where she wasn't sure—but it felt familiar and frightening.

After putting the glass down on the coffee table in front of her, he sat in the arm chair. He rubbed the wood of the arms and fiddled with the velvet arm rests.

Shannon's shaky hand reached for the glass.

"You okay?"

"Super tired is all." She raised an eyebrow at him, letting him know it was kind of his fault. "I'll be fine after resting a couple days."

"I really am sorry. If you would have let me stay here, I would have felt safer about it all."

"I know. Thanks for respecting my wishes."

Justin nodded.

She watched the way the sun lit the angles around his eyes, the shadow and light playing over his features. Her hands itched to take a photo. Then she remembered.

"Oh, no."

Justin started. "What's wrong? Where do you hurt?"

"No, I'm okay. But what am I going to do without my camera? That creep smashed it to bits."

"Will the school let you borrow one?"

"They don't have any of the same quality. That—" She caught herself—"jerk. If I ever see him again..." She stopped. After her performance yesterday, whatever she'd say was an empty threat. What would she do? Freeze and let him maim her, or worse?

"I hope they keep him in for a long time. Soliciting under-aged girls—probably initiating them into the trade. And attacking you. Wielding a knife." He counted off the offenses on his fingers. "Knowing our justice system, though..." Justin shook his head in disgust.

Shannon pursed her lips in thought. "Yeah, ten to one, he's already out. Guys like that have reserves wrapped up in drug-selling buddies and crooked lawyers who know how to manipulate the system. There's almost no stopping them."

Justin's eyes widened. "You mean he might be on the streets already?"

"You know, for someone who appears streetwise, you know very little about the way things actually work out there."

A frown creased his brow. "I know how it is with the homeless. I'm less familiar with drug-dealing pimps."

"I'm glad you don't know." Again, she didn't elaborate. She waited to see if he'd ask. He didn't. She wasn't sure how much she would have shared even if he had.

Someone knocked on her door.

Justin checked his smart watch and smiled. "I'll get it."

"I'm not expecting anyone." She immediately went on alert, her heart beating faster, eyes darting for exits. Maybe she'd hide in the bathroom.

"Don't worry. She's friend, not foe."

Shannon frowned, waiting for the door to open wide enough

so she could see who it was. Mocha darted out from under her bed and raced past Justin's legs.

"Oh, no! Catch him." Shannon shot up from the couch and a shift of weight, like one of those tipping birds, rushed from her head to her toes and back again with pounding pain. Wincing, she dropped hard onto the couch. She closed her eyes, breathing deep until the room stopped spinning. When she dared open them, she sighed in relief that her spell appeared to have gone unnoticed.

"Bad kitty." Amber's familiar voice chided Mocha. He mewed like a kitten.

What was Amber doing here?

Amber came around Justin, holding a contrite and purring kitty, his head rubbing contentedly against his owner's chin.

"Nice catch. He hasn't tried that even once since he's been here." Shannon's voice sounded scratchy from the strain. She hoped Amber missed it.

"Hey you. You sound done in." Amber's eyebrows scrunched together in worry.

So much for going unnoticed. Amber used her cane to maneuver into Shannon's apartment.

"I'm going to go run a couple errands. If you ladies need anything, let me know." Justin gave Shannon a warm smile before he shut the door.

"What are you doing here?" Shannon had been explicit. As much as she wanted Amber to come home, she didn't want to be *that* friend. The one who would manipulate and cajole and get in the middle of a relationship out of jealousy.

"Where are you?"

"I'm on the couch."

"You really do sound awful." Amber waved the cane in front of her until she found the couch. She leaned down and gave Shannon a gentle hug. Then she pulled Shannon up to her feet. "Come on, let's get you tucked into bed and I'll grab a nap on the couch. I couldn't sleep at all on the flight. Every creak and groan from the plane, not to mention the complaints from aging passengers in my row, kept me from dropping off on the way here. I forgot my ear plugs." She led Shannon by her arm through the small kitchen/living room to the area behind a Japanese paneled shoji screen where her queen-sized futon bed waited.

"I still don't know what you're doing here." Shannon felt herself being tucked in, fluffy comforter wrapped around her like a luxurious hug. She loved her comforter almost as much as she loved her form-fitting pillow.

"Where else would I be?"

"But what about Ethan?" Shannon's eyes closed of their own volition.

"I'll fill you in after we get some sleep." Amber patted Shannon on the back. Shannon heard her checking to see if the blinds were open and closed them. Then she heard her closet open and Amber rustling with the bedding.

The aroma of coffee and toast woke Shannon. She peeked past her squinted eyes to see that it was still light out. Her stomach rumbled in anticipation of food, and she sat up out of bed. Glancing at the clock, she saw it was six. But the light looked funny outside.

"Is that breakfast or dinner?"

"Hey, sleepy head," Amber answered. "It's breakfast. You were out cold. Don't worry, I made sure you weren't in a coma a few times."

"That's comforting. I don't remember. You must not have tried very hard."

"You're alive, aren't you?"

She slipped on a sweatshirt and zipped it closed over her wrinkled T-shirt and headed to the bathroom. Amber had eggs cooking on the stove, fruit diced in dishes, and was heavily buttering the toast.

"What, no PB and B?"

"You didn't have any baloney, or I might have."

Shannon stuck her tongue out at Amber. "I'm sticking my tongue out at you," she spoke past it.

"Thanks. Special. Very mature."

Shannon laughed for the first time in a week and moved to the hall to use the bathroom. She washed up and tried to use her brush before she remembered the gash on the back of her head.

"Ouch." She extricated the brush from her hair and just did the bangs and sides. Her black roots were coming in, pushing out the violet and blue. She'd have to wait until her wound was healed, though, or that would bring her a new level of pain.

She washed up her face and brushed her fuzzy feeling teeth. By the time she came out, Amber was sitting at the table listening to her phone read a book and sipping coffee. She'd eaten some of her toast.

"Thanks for waiting."

"Like my dad used to say, 'Like one animal waits for another.'"

"Good old dad." Shannon took her fork and poked around her eggs, pushing them from one side of her plate to the other as quietly as she could. Her fork scraped the plate with a screech.

"What? Looking for shells?"

Shannon felt heat shoot to her cheeks in shame. "Well...yes."

"I've taken several cooking courses now. I've learned to feel for shells. It makes cooking whole eggs tricky. But I'm very good at scrambled and omelets."

Amber took a liberal bite of eggs as if to illustrate the point.

"Okay. Sorry." Shannon took a tiny bite and, after not finding shell, she took another. If there was anything that would make her throw up, bits of crunchiness that were where they shouldn't be would do it. Like sand in her sandwich at the beach. Or scales from fish.

Her stomach roiled at the idea and she shoved all the visual images from her mind and concentrated on bites of toast and sips of black coffee.

Laced with bitter grounds.

"Um. Bracing." At least the crunch of coffee didn't set her teeth wrong. She pretended it was chocolate covered espresso beans.

"Too strong?"

"You try."

Amber picked up her mug and took a sip. A happy expression crossed her face. "Just right."

Shannon's mouth fell open. Just as she was about to call Amber on her declaration, Amber choked.

"Oh, just kidding. This is super chewy. Sorry." Her lopsided smile made Shannon laugh.

"You know what? Who cares? You'll get there someday." She picked up the mug and toasted to that day.

"And you'll always be my best Guinea pig." Amber winked.

"Does Ethan eat your cooking?"

Amber's nose wrinkled. "He says it's incredible."

"Oh, girl. He's got it bad."

Amber's cheeks went pink. "I think we both do."

Then the remembrance that Amber was probably moving away struck Shannon in the gut again.

What was she going to do without her best friend?

CHAPTER 8

Breakfast finished quietly after that. Amber probably sensed something was off, but she wasn't peppering Shannon with questions.

Shannon excused herself, took her dishes to the sink, and grabbed clothes for a shower. She was in and out fast.

"You next? Or do you want to head back to your place?" As she sat on the couch, Shannon towel-dried her hair, cautious to miss the cut. It was a matted mess back there, but still too tender to do anything about it.

"I thought we could hang out a bit longer. Sound okay?"

"Yep." Sitting back against the couch, she closed her eyes and listened to Amber wash the dishes. She must have dropped off because she woke to find the apartment still and a blanket over her. There was a note on the table.

> S~
> Grocery store for kitty food. Back soon.
> ~A

Looking at her phone, Shannon saw three hours had passed. She had no idea when Amber had left. As if on cue, Mocha leapt into her lap.

"Hey, you." She scrubbed his head. "Your mommy went to get you snacks." Mocha purred approvingly. She'd rather enjoyed his company over the last few days. It was nice not being alone. Coming home to someone—even a kitty—was comforting.

Misgivings about putting off Justin filled her mind. And then memories replaced them, as if speaking to her. Each one dashed a dream and confirmed she'd made the right choice. She sank into a darkened well filled with crushed hopes and bitterness.

She used to feel like hope was an enemy that played tricks on her—but as she grew, she realized she'd been putting her hope in circumstances, not God. She'd get excited about a new teacher or new foster home or new caseworker. Maybe this time it would live up to her expectations, and a new hope would well in her heart. But within weeks, days, and sometimes even hours, those hopes would be pulverized.

Kids *did* find good foster homes and get adopted and were loved. Just not her.

Drifting to her bed, she lay down, pulling up the blanket and curling into a ball. Her eyes shifted from the slatted window above her head to the rice-paper shoji screen separating her bedroom from the rest of the apartment. She counted the square panes on the screen, trying to empty her mind of negativity, of hurt, of abandonment. All the things that weighed on her and pinned her down. Especially false hope. What a dangerous enemy false hope could be.

Shannon tried not to be hopeful in general things. She tried not to count on anything. Except God. Somehow, even in the middle of all the pain of loss and abuse, she knew He was there. With her. Through it all.

Some of the most painful memories weren't the neglect—but the betrayals by those she trusted. Like Amber's dad. Every time he'd call her *kiddo* or *sweetie* Shannon's hope rose.

Her mind shifted as she remembered the night Amber and she had hatched the plan. They'd created the perfect scenario of cleaning the house and making a dinner for two. Like in the *Parent Trap*—which at that point had been their favorite film—two sisters, one cause. Then, when the moment was right, they would ask Russ and Jennifer to adopt Shannon. Of course, in their childlike starry minds, no adult could ever turn down anything with a cleaned house and a meal.

That's how it was in the movies.

But Russ hadn't taken the bait, and Amber and Shannon were told to let it go.

How could a nine-year-old, longing for love and approval, just let go of her dreams of a perfect family? It was like asking her to stop loving dessert or puppies. Or wanting to be loved for who she was, not who she had to pretend to be.

When she returned to her foster home that same night, it had been in utter chaos, with a new sniveling arrival, police officers, and the caseworker. All the kids ducked out of the way until her foster mom had put them to bed—or rather sent them off and expected they'd do what they should. One of the older boys snuck into Shannon's room and had climbed into bed with the eldest girl. They giggled and carried on. Shannon stuck her fingers in her ears.

Her foster mom, Willa, was very kind, but disorganized and overly trusting—which was nice if you were worth trusting. With the new kid, it brought the total to three boys and two girls. The boy got out of the girl's bed and headed to Shannon's. She snapped her eyes closed. She could hear his breathing, an annoying adenoid-infused snuffle, and he stood there for what felt like a long time.

Shannon held very still, pretending to be asleep. Her heart raced, and she was sure he must hear it. She kept her eyes relaxed and closed, but her arms and legs tensed. It wouldn't have been the first time an older kid tried to hurt her—but they'd never succeeded. She reached under her pillow with slow, imperceptive movements and wrapped her fingers around her pocket knife.

Technically it was more of a dining utensil with fold out fork and spoon, but it did have a push button to open. She'd used it before to good effect.

"Leave her alone." The girl sounded jealous more than protective.

"Nah, I'm not into her. Although she's pretty enough. I saw her playing with a necklace last night. I think it was gold. Does she have any more good stuff like that?"

"How should I know? I don't watch her." Her voice showed her disgust, then worry. "You better head back to your room."

He stood still, towering over Shannon a few seconds longer. "Yeah."

He'd left, and Shannon heard her roommate drop to sleep. Just as she was about to let herself relax, the boy came back. He started rustling through her things in the drawer assigned to her. She wasn't worried—what little of value she had was in a black plastic bag stashed under her bed. And her most important belonging, a necklace from her mother, as well as a few dollars in cash, was in a zipper sandwich bag taped in between her mattress and the frame. She'd learned that from a kid a few years back. No one had ever found her stash yet. *Please don't find it.* She risked a peek through cracked eyelids and almost screamed when the boy, on his knees, clamped a salty, sweaty hand over Shannon's mouth.

She squealed and struggled against him, her lungs burning for air. Her heels dug into her mattress trying to gain leverage, but they kept slipping.

"Take it easy," he hissed. "Listen, I know you have jewelry and maybe some money. I seen it." He pushed her hard against her mattress, his other arm trapping her shoulders. "You're never in any trouble, and you look cute and innocent. I got a plan that will help us both out. You give me your money, and I'll leave you be. You start finding bits and pieces around the house, loose change, rings, earrings and things like that in the couch, money foster-mommy leaves out and you happen to see? When you go to that rich girl's house and her folks leave things around? At school? I need money. I get money and I leave this dump and don't come back. You like that idea?" He let up on his hand against her mouth and she gasped for air before he clamped it back down again.

She nodded.

"You give it all to me, and I'll go on leaving you be. You understand me?"

Shannon nodded again, against his hand. He slipped a hand up under her shirt, and she began to sob.

"And if not?" He showed her what would happen.

Her sobs grew louder, and he pushed his other hand down harder against her lips.

"Shut it." But at least he stopped touching her.

Tears dripped down Shannon's cheeks.

"We got a deal? Unless you want me to come back."

Shannon shook her head violently.

He sneered. "Then you know what to do. As much as you can gather. Got it?"

A distant slam and Amber's voice was calling to her. Shannon blinked and felt the pound of her sore head and heard the ringing in her ears—like when a gun goes off and you're deafened for a few minutes. You can't even hear your own screams.

She wasn't in foster care. She was in her bed. Relatively safe. Her hand was under her pillow, gripping a comforting clump of fluff. Not a knife. Just her pillow. Shannon released her grip, and the blood tingled back into her fingers. She breathed slowly to calm her heart.

"Shannon?" Amber called. Paper bags crinkled and thudded onto her dining table. "Shan?"

Shannon winced at the bright sunlight cutting through the slats over her face.

"I'm here. I was asleep." But she hadn't been. She'd been transported away, reliving something she'd kept a tight lid on for over twenty years.

She mentally shoved the lid back onto the memory's container.

She'd nail it shut, super glue it, duct tape it—whatever it took. She wouldn't let that out again.

"Oh, good. I was worried for a minute." Amber unpacked the grocery bags.

"Your note said cat food," Shannon accused as she sloughed around the screen, her blanket over her shoulders like a shield. She counted three stocked bags and one more still in the pull-cart. She rubbed her eyes, trying to block out the flashback that had come over her so suddenly.

"Well, you don't have snacks for people, either."

"I do, too." She forced a smile.

Amber shook a box of cookies and held up a package of baloney. "Proper snacks like these?"

"No. Just healthy ones." Although, peanut butter and baloney sounded very comforting just then. It wouldn't taste half as good as it did when she was a kid. *Probably.*

"Now don't get all judge-y on me. If we're going to do a sleepover, we need to eat garbage."

Sleepover? Had she agreed to any such thing? Justin must have orchestrated this. She'd talk to him later.

"What about Ethan?" They still hadn't talked about Ethan and Boston. Although Shannon didn't really want to dredge it up right then, they'd have to.

"He's fine. He's with his folks, still."

"He didn't come back too?" Shannon shifted on the couch and curled up. "Bring me cookies."

"And milk?"

"That's a given."

"Truth." Amber opened the fridge and poured them a couple cups of milk and brought the cookies over to the coffee table. They were proper cookies, too, with huge chunks of chocolate and macadamia nuts. You had to break them in half to dip them in the glass. Amber took the chair, curling her legs under her as she sat down.

They dunked cookies in quiet, both lost in thought. Shannon watched one cookie soak the milk and the little corners sag and break, falling useless into her glass.

Amber's words broke the silence.

"We weren't there for an hour before they started in on Ethan to do something sensible and retire and move back in with them. Since he's dying." She put finger quotes around the word dying.

"But he's in remission."

"His grandmother and mom were quick to mention how that might not last and he should live his best life now."

"I hate that phrase. Best life now. Like you were saving it up for later? And besides, what a horrible thing to say."

"Exactly. I didn't know how much more I could take. And that best life now garbage? Frankly, heaven is going to be way better than this, right?" Amber swiped a hand in front of her eyes.

"Exactly."

"Anyway. Justin called, and I had a panic attack and Ethan suggested that I go home, and I hate to say it"—she leaned over and whispered—"*I was relieved.*"

"That I got bonked on the head?"

"No, dummy, that I could come home. It's romantic to think of moving, but Boston is huge. And my work and Mom and you are here. And that makes *this* home."

Shannon sniffed and wiped at her eyes with her sleeve.

"No crying allowed." Amber took her hand. "Sorry if what I said worried you."

Shannon wasn't sure what to say. Relief washed over her.

"Are you sure about your decision? You were only there a couple days."

"Absolutely."

Amber's tone of finality brought Shannon up short. Something wasn't right.

"What aren't you telling me?"

Amber sighed loudly, her shoulders sagged, and a defeated look filled her eyes. "I'm not sure where to start. But things didn't go exactly as planned."

"Well, this can't be good." Shannon sat up straight, alert and waiting for Amber to continue.

"It's probably nothing."

"Spill." Why didn't Amber just tell her what happened? Unless she was moving for sure—she just couldn't admit it to her. Shannon waited for the worst.

Amber sighed. "I don't know."

"Well, I don't like it—so stop it." Shannon fiddled with a popped seam on the couch. The poor thing was aged, but it fit her in all the right places. She didn't want to get a new one. Ever.

They sat in quiet, both thinking, until Mocha ripped by with a fluffy stuffed toy, startling them both. They jumped and spoke at the same time, "It's Mocha's fault."

Mocha dropped the toy, mouth agape as if they'd shocked him with this accusation. Then he turned, flicked his tail, and sat, back toward them, licking his paws in complete indifference.

"My word. What an ego." Shannon tossed the toy across the room. It landed with a quick squeak. Mocha moved to his haunches and did a tushy-shake before pouncing upon it.

"Did he go for it?"

"Of course."

The tension broke between them. Amber spoke. "I've had to lean on you so much for the last year. Way more than I ever wanted to."

"That's what I'm here for." Shannon didn't follow. Isn't that what they'd always done?

"I just..." She stiffened in her chair, maybe expecting the worst.

Shannon could see the fear in her eyes. "I just never want to use you up. Or lose you."

"As if." Shannon snorted. It was the most ridiculous thing she could imagine. "We're sisters. Nothing you go through is going to change that. I'm always here for you. Always."

Amber visibly relaxed, eyes watering with emotion. "I'm always here for you, too."

A ray of sunshine broke through the partially opened blinds, casting a golden hue over a slice of the room. Shannon watched the dust particles float like snow on the breeze. Her fingers itched to take a photo. She used her phone, satisfying the urge. A lightness filled her spirit until another question formed.

"Wait a minute. Is that why you were willing to move to Boston?" Shannon watched as Amber's cheeks pinkened.

"Maybe. I don't know. Mostly it was because I thought it'd be good for Ethan."

"But now?"

"I think it would be really bad for him. And you."

Shannon shifted in her seat. Her headache was threatening to come back. She rubbed her neck, trying to find a more comfortable position as they continued to talk.

"So, let's review. You backed away from *me* to save our friendship, and you were willing to move to Boston because it'd be good for *Ethan*."

"Yeah. I guess that's it."

Shannon laughed. "You're stupid."

"Nice." Amber growled, reaching around near her, fingers searching.

"What are you looking for?"

"A pillow to throw at you."

They laughed for a moment and then Shannon asked, "What about you?"

"Huh?" The quizzical look on Amber's face was priceless. So

often she spoke or acted before thinking. Shannon thought first before acting. They were a good balance.

"What do *you* want?"

"I wasn't thinking about me."

"Obviously."

"That's pretty salty."

"But true."

"I want to stay. You're here. My work is here, my mom and Maggie are here. Although," she said, breaking off and making the iffy sign with her hands. "The balancing act between them is pretty tricky sometimes."

Shannon guffawed. While Jennifer had accepted Amber's birth mom, Maggie, rather quickly, it was clear over the past year that she still feared losing her adoptive daughter's affections. It was jealousy of a type and guilt, too, that she had the privilege and blessing to have raised Amber. Meanwhile, Amber tried to treat them equally, but Shannon couldn't tell if that was enough.

"Ethan's here." Shannon reminded her.

At that, Amber's countenance changed. "I hope so."

"Are you ever going to tell me what happened in Boston?"

CHAPTER 9

Amber zipped and unzipped her jacket's side pocket. "The plane ride there went really well. I was excited by all his descriptions, the history. It sounded amazing—until we landed." She let out a sigh.

"You couldn't picture it."

"Exactly! He talked so fast—I felt all floaty like a hot air balloon being directed here and there but I was really adrift. I never found a place I could tether to. I had no anchor." She reached out for Shannon's hand. "You and I speak the same language. I love Ethan, but..." Amber's voice trailed off.

"I get it." She watched her best friend, knowing this was just the top layer of the stratosphere.

"Then you decided to go and try to get yourself killed by a pimp." She pushed Shannon.

"Don't change the subject. Besides, what else is new?" Being streetwise didn't change much. There were always dangers. Familiarity lulled a person into dropping their guard, that was why she was careful who she chose to put her trust in. The fewer, the safer.

"And then there were his parents."

Shannon's protective instincts went on red alert. "What'd they say to you?"

"It wasn't the words so much. But I got the distinct feeling I was an interloper. They have this idea of who Ethan is, or should be, and who he should be with."

"Not you?"

"Not someone blind and needy."

"Okay, ouch. Listen, I've never once thought of you as needy."
Amber brightened at Shannon's words.

"They made a huge deal out of telling me where to step in the
house, how to be careful around their precious furnishings and
plants—like I was a clumsy helpless oaf."

"Who uses the word oaf anymore?" Shannon nudged Amber's
knee.

"Shut up."

Shannon waited a minute before trying a more pointed question. "How did Ethan take that?"

"That's just it. He *caved.* He let them label me and put me in
their box. It felt like he handed them the packaging tape. Before
I knew it, he was making excuses for me and telling me they'd
catch up with me later in the day and saying I probably wanted
to rest after our long trip. As if. If I wanted to rest, I would have
said so." Amber chewed on her lip, something she only did when
truly frustrated. "Ethan, of all people. He's a blindness counselor!"

"Everyone has weak spots. I'm sorry." Someone had to say it.
Obviously, Ethan hadn't.

"When Justin called, I knew I needed to come home—for you
and for me."

"What about Ethan?"

"He's got to experience the coddling and overprotectiveness
on his own without me pointing it out."

"Now who's salty?"

"Heh."

"Good girl." Shannon agreed. "I mean, if a blind person can
see it..."

Amber kicked Shannon in the shin. "Snarky."

They tried laughing about it, but Amber quieted, a look of
despair on her face.

"Don't worry, Amb. He'll figure it out." The certainty in Shannon's voice surprised her. She actually liked Ethan. He was good for Amber, and vice versa. Shannon hoped he realized it before it was too late.

An idea popped into Shannon's head.

"You know what this means? We need to order in and celebrate. First concussion. First leaving boyfriend in Boston. First facing off with said boyfriend's parents and winning. What will mark the occasion best? How shall we drown our sorrows?" Their life-long habit of celebrating firsts took precedence over all else. Triumph or trial—it must be marked.

"Ice cream from Star-Crossed Cup and Cone?"

"Oh, she goes straight to dessert! How about burgers from the food cart down the street, and then ice cream? Because I haven't eaten properly in three days—and I want that ice cream to stay in my tummy."

"Fine. Burgers. With extra cheese."

"Definitely worthy of extra cheese. And extra ranch for the fries?"

"Lots of ranch. Lots." Amber said under her breath, "Ethan hates ranch."

As if on cue, Amber's phone rang. Ethan's warm-timbred pre-recorded voice sounded over her speaker. "Ethan calling."

"I'll go get the food. You talk to him." Shannon patted Amber's shoulder.

"Are you sure you're able?"

"I could use the fresh air. I'll be back in thirty." She slipped on her black, thick-wedged high-heeled Doc Martens and pulled on her bright orange pea coat over her PJ top and leggings, buttoning it closed and flipping the hood up to cover her matted hair. She grabbed her wallet, reusable grocery bag, and keys, pulling the door closed behind her.

Living in the heart of downtown, she had the best of food within a few blocks. After picking up the burgers, she headed to the ice cream parlor. It was more of a hole-in-the-wall, but the lines would wrap the block in the heat of summer. Even now, at fifty degrees, there were ten people ahead of her.

She ordered and gathered their things together in the grocery bag with Day of the Dead heads and flowers all over it, and headed back to her apartment. She felt lighter than she had in months. Even with the slight pounding of her wound, life felt...hopeful. Amber and Ethan would work stuff out. Justin would be...Justin. And everything would go back to normal and life would move on. Nothing had to change.

As she turned the corner, her legs stiffened, and she came to a standstill when she saw him. There was Daniel, leaning against a building. Somehow, she'd forgotten all about him. She'd pushed him from her mind—erased the possibility from her brain.

That's the thing she often forgot.

Brains were tricky.

CHAPTER 10

Rivetted, Shannon watched as a priest passed Daniel, stepping around his legs as if he were a fallen branch on the sidewalk. Then a group of women in crisply pressed business suits passed, one covering her mouth and nose with her sleeve. They said something derisive—she couldn't hear the words but recognized the tone. Deep inside, their treatment of Daniel hurt, awakening a familiar ache. Following the women, a group of teens went by, jabbering and staring at their phones. They nearly tripped over his belongings and then did trip over another man squatting nearby. The man cursed, and the teens laughed.

Her legs engaged, and she crossed the street, going up the block, planning on passing him by.

Daniel's head sagged against his chest, collection cup in hand, asleep against the brick church building. He'd never know she came by. She should keep moving and say nothing. The image of him asleep on their old couch in their old house, yellow and brown diamond afghan over him, filled her mind. She remembered slipping in between him and the sofa on sleepy Sunday afternoons, and he'd tuck the cover under her chin and they'd fall back to sleep together.

She pushed back against the memory and started to move when the aroma of hamburgers in her bag tugged at her nose. How long had it been since he'd eaten properly? As angry as she was with him, she didn't want him to suffer. She just needed to protect herself. She couldn't let him in. She stepped back and stared down at him.

Dirty blond hair peeked out from under a blue, frayed knit cap. It framed a face once full, now sunken. His puffy army-green nylon coat encased him like a sleeping bag. His jeans were worn with holes on the knees and thighs, revealing red long underwear. His boots were army issue, and duct tape covered over worn spots to keep out the rain. The laces were tattered and knotted—more knots than lace, really. Behind him were three black garbage bags and a brown duffle bag.

Daniel had nothing that wasn't within reach. He used to have a wife. He had a house. He had a little girl that adored him—her hero. Now he lay wasted on the sidewalk, alone and cold. What made a man with everything throw it all away? How did he live with himself knowing what he'd given up? Did he ever think of that? Or was surviving day-to-day all he could handle?

A police officer walked past behind her, tipping his head to Daniel. "Don't worry, he's harmless."

"That depends." She didn't elaborate, and the officer didn't ask questions but kept moving on down the street. She counted ten more homeless on this street alone. They were trying to pass a no squatters law in Portland. Businesses were happy, and the homeless were indignant. Where were they supposed to go?

Where indeed?

As she was deep in thought, Daniel had woken up and was looking at her. His open stare made her jump. She covered her error quickly by holding out the bag.

"You hungry?"

"Yes." His watery blue eyes, tinged red from cold and the elements and probably one too many hits, crinkled at the corners. "You have any change?" He held up the cup.

"No. But you can have my hamburger." First rule of reaching

out to the homeless was not to give cash for their habit, but to render physical aid.

"Oh my. It's been a long time since I ate a hamburger." He didn't reach out expectantly as he had the first time she'd seen him. This time he was unthreatening. Like any normal, drug-addicted homeless person at the end of themselves.

After burrowing through her bag, she pulled out her own burger and her fries.

"It's got the works."

She remembered that Daniel liked the works. Every now and then when he was on his meds and sober, they'd take their food stamps and buy something substantial like hamburger. When they did, he'd get a tomato, an onion, and a small block of cheese. He'd made *the works* sound like something phenomenal. To her six-year-old self, it was like delicious magic. Especially when she was starving.

"No point in eating a hamburger with nothing on it. Then it's just meat and bread." He chuckled at his own joke. A joke she'd heard at least twenty times. She almost smiled, and then anger lanced through her, unexpected, like touching hot wires on a broken bulb. She winced from the pain of it. Shannon had plenty of days with only bread and no meat. And sometimes no bread either.

Her fingers clenched protectively around the hamburger, as a sudden unwillingness to go any further with this ruse washed over her. And then—as if a power outside herself took control—she handed over the tightly wrapped burger and paper cup of fries to Daniel. His eyes filled with a softness she'd not seen in years.

"My, oh my. It's been a long time since someone was so kind." He tucked the fries in his knapsack. "Saving those for later. Don't think I don't appreciate them. The burger will rot, the fries won't." His words were like a mantra reminding him to be careful.

He'd done that, too, hadn't he? Little sayings that seemed to make no sense to her as a kid, repeating them over and over. "Brush your teeth three times and you'll have three times less cavities," or "Mind your Ps and Qs" when she'd been naughty. What did that even mean? Several choice phrases filtered through her mind.

On his manic days, he'd repeated one phrase in particular, "It's not happening, it couldn't be happening, it's not happening," while he sat and rocked in the corner, knees pulled to his chest, or paced through their apartment screaming at the top of his lungs.

On those days, Shannon would hide under her bed or go to the park and stay there until dark. Tim's Corner Mart, wasn't it? She hadn't thought about Tim's in a long time. Guilt tugged at her. She'd always promised herself that she'd go back and make amends. She owed a debt there.

Daniel's voice drew her back to the present. "It's good." He chewed it slowly, as if enjoying every bite of a gourmet meal. She felt small in his presence, like a time machine transported her and she was nine.

"I'm sorry. What kind of gentleman am I? Do you want half?" He handed up the hamburger, but Shannon shook her head.

"I've got to go." For a moment, she considered telling him who she was. The sentence felt bulky and stale and stuck her tongue to the roof of her mouth. And then she decided she should probably never see him again. Only, the confidence she'd felt with that decision a week ago was missing this time. Something inside pulled at her to see him again. But what good would it do? Nothing could change Daniel until Daniel wanted to change. And even then? He'd been a drug addict and alcoholic practically his entire life. Nothing could change that. It was embedded in his DNA.

"Thanks again for this kindness." He crumpled the wrapper into a ball and tucked in into his jacket pocket. It was then she realized she'd stood over him as he ate the whole thing. How creepy of her. Her brows knit in question, but he didn't explain.

"Okay then."

"Can I ask you a question?" He sat up straighter against the building.

"Sure." She suddenly felt the urge to run fast and hard—to anywhere.

"Do I know you?" His blue eyes questioned hers, looking at her like she was a puzzle to be put together. The edges were forming, but the middle was missing.

Her heart raced. "No. You don't know me." It wasn't a lie. He had no clue who she was anymore. Besides, he hadn't recognized her yet, and he wouldn't likely.

"Well, thanks for this. It made a dull day brighter." The light in his eyes faded, and he gave her a nod before tucking back into his jacket.

She nodded and turned back toward her apartment. At the food cart she bought a second burger for herself before heading up the stairs.

Each step up the stairwell felt like one step closer to something frightening. Stairs. Peeling paint. Roaches and spiders. Flickering lights. The sweet, smoky aroma of cigarettes and pot. Where was that? She stopped moving and closed her eyes. Another foster home? No. No. She remembered now.

It was one of the places Daniel would buy drugs. He hadn't been home for two days. She'd followed him a couple times before, without his knowing, because she worried about him. He always told her to tell him where she was going. He never told her though. And this time, he'd not come home. It was the first time he'd stayed away so long.

The fridge was empty, except for ketchup, and she was on her last sleeve of saltines. She used hot water from the tap and mixed it with the ketchup to make tomato soup, but it wasn't right. Too sweet. Too watery. She'd crumpled most of another sleeve of saltines into her bowl to make it thicken, but that made it worse. She ate it anyway. There wasn't anything else.

The house felt empty without her dad—especially after her mom had died, though she was home little enough before she'd overdosed. Shannon had pulled on her too-tight tennis shoes and wrapped a thin blanket around her shoulders because her winter coat had disappeared. Later she'd find out he'd traded it and other pieces of decent clothing for a fix.

As Shannon took each step up, she seemed to shrink in size, losing five years, then ten, then twenty. She stepped past garbage and puddles of unknown liquids. She heard sounds of moaning and crying and laughing. She went to the door she'd seen her daddy enter and knocked. No one answered, so she used the cold doorknob. She could see her reflection as a shadow on the dirty handle.

The door squeaked on heavily painted hinges, past rust and warp, and gave her a glimpse inside of bodies, tumbled and sagging over the floor and cushions. She looked at each one, not finding her father. Then she went into a bedroom and there he was, on a dirty mattress, rubber cord wrapped around his forearm, red marks streaking his skin.

Shannon called to him to wake up, and he finally did. His eyes took her in and he pulled himself together.

"Why are you here? You should be in school."

"It's Sunday. I'm hungry, Daddy. Please come home." She pulled on his grimy hand, trying to get him off the floor and back home.

Instead, Shannon's hand met her own familiar doorknob, and the shock of it pulled her out of her mind and back to the present. She was twenty-six, not six. She was safe in her apartment building. She looked behind her. There weren't roaches or garbage or urine soaking the halls.

As Shannon inserted the key to her apartment door with shaky fingers, she could hear heated words—Amber and Ethan arguing over the speaker phone. She stopped and waited in the hall and hoped the ice cream wouldn't melt. When the voices went quiet, she unlocked her door and went in, pretending she hadn't heard anything.

"I'm a little worried about the ice cream—I was waylaid—I'll just pop it in the fridge and we can start the celebration." She gave Amber a sideways glance.

"Add first big argument to the list." Amber sat down at the table, dejected.

"I'm sorry."

"Yeah. It's like he's a different person when he's with his family. Insecure, unable to stand up for himself. I don't like him like this."

Shannon put the burgers on the table.

"Only one order of fries?" Amber pulled them out of the bag.

"Oh, yeah. I gave the other away."

Hopefully Amber wouldn't ask to whom. She didn't. She just set the remaining order between them.

Shannon smiled. "Eventually, he'll see it. Don't give up on him."

"I'm not giving up. I'll fight for this. But I'm not going to try and convince him of anything. I don't want to be pitted against his family, ever."

"How'd you get so savvy?"

"Years of watching my mom and my grandma go head-to-head, I guess." Amber took a big bite of her burger. Then she slathered ranch on the fries.

"What happened to the other fries, again?"

No more lies. "I saw Daniel. I gave him a burger and my fries. I just forgot to get more for me."

"That's awesome. Have you seen him a lot?"

"No. And let's not go there."

Amber frowned. "I'd give anything to spend time with my dad again." Amber didn't mean it as a dig, but Shannon felt the sting anyway. They finished their burgers, and Amber moved to the fridge and hunted around the freezer.

"What are you after exactly?"

"My pistachio cream."

"To your right. There you go."

Amber grabbed both cup-sized containers. She went to the correct drawer and pulled out a spoon. She waved a second one at Shannon.

"Sure." Shannon wasn't hungry. But she gave up trying to get Amber refocused.

"I just wish you'd give him a chance. It might be very cathartic."

"That's because you had a normal dad. Even your birth dad sounds amazing and self-sacrificial. You don't know what this is like. Not being wanted. Never being enough."

"I know my dad let you down."

"He did. But that's not got anything to do with this either. If I'd been white, I'm sure he would have loved me."

"Shannon..."

Shannon put her hand up to stop her before realizing Amber couldn't see the gesture. "Amber, you're my sister where it matters most. But I can't pretend your dad's attitude about race didn't matter. Or that your parents couldn't have tried harder. It just wasn't meant to be." She was ten times as strong as she would have been if she'd been adopted.

Ten times as broken, too.

"Okay." Amber let the subject rest.

"Changing the subject, remember Tim's Corner Mart?"

"Was that by the green house or the yellow house?"

"It was the yellow tri-plex."

"By the park." Amber swigged her soda.

"We spent a lot of time hanging out there."

"Yeah. Ice creams on hot summer days. Good times."

"You and ice cream." Shannon snickered.

"I have my priorities straight." Amber took a bite of her pistachio-cream. "Why do you ask?"

"It came to mind when I was talking to Daniel." Shannon took a bite of her own ice cream, swallowing a large lump of frozen cookie dough, creating an ache all the way down.

"I think Daniel sounds good. Maggie says he sounds healthy enough. Last week she gave him a winter coat and some wool socks. They've had some good talks."

Guilt rose inside. And a strange kind of jealousy.

"Have you talked to him?" The tension in her own voice startled her.

"Only in passing."

"Don't tell him who you are. Or who I am."

"I haven't. But don't you want to just see how things are?"

"No. I don't want him to know where I am or *if* I am. That's not a road to take."

Amber started pushing her spoon around in her ice cream, no longer taking bites. She could say more by saying nothing better than anyone Shannon had ever known.

"What?"

"I'd hate to discover someday that this was a God-given opportunity for you both to reconcile."

"Can you just trust me that it's better this way for me?"

Amber looked up at her with such intensity that if Shannon hadn't known better she would have sworn she was staring into her soul.

"What if it's not about you?"

CHAPTER 11

The corner grocery mart sat in a square, two-story building across the street from a weed-ridden park. Children played on paint-peeled equipment. What was bright yellow and red and blue in days gone by was now crusty and orange from rust. They had been getting there even when Shannon was little. She could almost feel the splinters of metal digging into her hands and see the metallic stain as she rubbed the soft center of her palms. She closed her eyes, listening to the tell-tale squeak from the swings echoing in the background over the top of the traffic from the nearby overpass.

She and Amber had spent many hours playing here under the watchful eyes of Jennifer. Whenever a bully or unsavory person approached them, Jennifer would stare them down or intervene. What Jennifer didn't know was on every other occasion, Shannon would play there alone, unchecked. She'd lie on her tummy on the swing seat and put out her arms, pretending to fly, watching the ground under her blur back and forth. A wood chip was a house, a pebble a car, the carpenter ants the people.

She was free, untouchable, like the birds of the air, landing only when she wanted. Always alert and ready to take flight at the slightest hint of danger.

Shannon faced the market, preparing herself for the encounter to come. Yes, she'd been a child, and there were extenuating circumstances. But that didn't erase her responsibility.

The light cast bright on the exterior, glaring off the sidewalk and blinding her as she crossed the street from the park. Glancing up, she could see the apartment over the market had a FOR RENT sign in the splotchy, mildew-covered window.

As she pulled open the front door, it slid screeching over the cracked pavement, and she stepped back in time. No longer nearly twenty-seven, but seven. And very hungry. Shannon walked down two narrow aisles that carried only one brand of each item. One kind of cleanser, one kind of dish soap. One kind of soup—Campbell's chicken noodle with extra noodles, her favorite. She ran a finger over the macaroni and cheese box and remembered taking one from the shelf and slipping it under her shirt.

Opposite the staple food shelf was a snack rack, holding a large variety of candy, gum, beef jerky, and chips. Next to it ran the freezer section sporting a small section of frozen TV dinners. Alongside that was a refrigerator compartment encasing off-brand baloney and hotdogs, cheese, eggs, and milk. These were the basics of every low-income family's diet. Surprisingly, she discovered a fresh fruit section stocked with red delicious apples, mandarin oranges, and bananas. Mixed in were some bags of baby carrots.

She came around the corner and caught sight of where they specialized—beer and cigarettes. Of those, there seemed to be no end. Next to the counter sat a plethora of chewing tobacco and pepperoni sticks.

And all of it like time had taken a photograph and saved it for this very day.

"Can I help you?" And older man, scruffy and unshaven, wearing a shabby flannel shirt tucked crookedly into his well-worn jeans, addressed her from the front counter. Lottery tickets, cigarettes, and breath mints framed his position. He could have been the man who owned the store from her youth. If so, time had not been kind. She was about to ask, but instead, an entirely different question came out of her mouth.

"How much is the apartment for rent?" Where had that come

from? She had no intention of moving. She'd come to make amends and pay penance. But as her mind balked, a clear vision of Daniel splayed on the sidewalk, filthy and freezing, mocked by passersby, flashed in her mind.

"Five hundred, all utilities included."

"How big is it?"

"Not big. Good for singles. One room, kitchenette, and a shower with toilet."

It was three miles from her place. Close enough for him to walk to a job downtown—if he could keep one. Far enough they shouldn't cross paths.

"Can I see it?"

The man eyed her. "Seems kinda lowbrow for your type."

Looking down, Shannon saw her new jeans, dress boots, and matching jacket. She stifled a laugh. If he'd only seen where she'd come from—that room upstairs was probably well above anything she'd lived in until recently.

"It's for a friend." She put out a hand. "I'm Shannon."

"Bill." He shook her hand. He went to the front door and affixed a clock-face sign set ahead 15 minutes in the door's window and locked the door. "We're not too busy in the afternoon, but I gotta take precautions against theft."

A chill swept over Shannon. *Remember the reason you're here?* She'd address that soon enough.

He motioned for her to follow him through the back exit and around the side of the building to a door that opened onto a one-level stair. Three mailboxes were at the foot, aged and painted in high-gloss white like everything else. The thickness of the paint, and the peeling spots here and there, made her wonder about lead content.

Shannon followed Bill up the creaking wood stairs, bracing herself to catch him as he teetered on each one. His knee joints crackled and snapped like Pop Rocks. She took a breath of relief as he made the next floor.

Three doors, like a four-way stop, met them at the top. He motioned to the far left. "That one's mine. I keep an eye on things." His tone sounded a warning. She couldn't blame him. Rent laws had just passed in the city—if you evicted anyone without cause, you had to pay moving fees to get rid of the tenant. It was making all the low-rent owners nervous.

He pulled out a ring of keys and unlocked the far-right street-side apartment. The door scuffed back over the aging gray and blue flecked linoleum. As they entered, Bill closed the door and next to it was the bathroom slider. Inside was a toilet and shower. At an L to it in the main room was a small, one-hole sink, a tiny enamel-covered metal counter with two cabinets over it, and a two-burner stove. Under the lower shelf was a small hotel-style fridge. The far corner was edged in windows. Under the windows, in the corner, was a yellow laminate dining table with two metal chairs, each with yellow cushions. The full-size bed was directly across from it. And along the near wall, down from the bed, was a closet.

It could easily fit into her current apartment twice over. But it was much better than the street. She walked to the window and looked out over the park. From this vantage point, she could see the roof of the apartment she and her dad had lived in all those years ago.

"How are the drugs in this neighborhood?" The last thing she wanted to do was deliver her father into a safe-looking place more treacherous than he'd left. You expected to keep your guard up on the street, but not in a nice little neighborhood like this.

"You looking to buy?" His voice dripped with disapproval and disappointment.

Shannon spun on her heel. "No. I don't use. I need to know that there aren't any readily available. I need to keep my...friend...safe."

Relief covered his features and he shook his head. "No, ma'am. Neighborhood watch helps keep an eye on things and reports all that sort of thing to the police. They've been real supportive of our little community. Been well over two years since such troubles."

More and more places in Portland were turning to that. Getting to know their neighbors again and watching out for each other. The city didn't have the budget to do it all, so they'd dug in. Things were improving.

"If I pay the rent, can my friend, who is down on his luck, stay here?"

"I need first and last and a security deposit for the mattress and furniture. I know it isn't much, but it's still costly to replace."

"I understand. I'll also need a favor." She took out her business card and circled her cell. "I'll need you to call me if you feel like something is off with him."

Bill frowned. "This fella okay?"

"He's had a lot of problems. He's not dangerous. But I'm worried for his health."

Bill tucked the card into his shirt pocket. "I can do that." He cleared his throat. "I'll hold the apartment for twenty-four hours."

"No need. I'll fill out the paperwork and give you the down payment today." She was certain Daniel would agree, if even for a month. He might be selfish—but if memory served, he knew a good thing when he saw it.

She wasn't sure how she could afford another five hundred a month—especially when she needed to replace her camera. But she'd try. If he was off the streets, then she wouldn't have to worry about him. Or cross paths with him unexpectedly. Or feel guilty.

Shannon was most of the way home before she realized she hadn't done what she'd intended. Amends would have to wait. For now.

CHAPTER 12

S hannon shuffled around her apartment. She wasn't sure what to do next. She'd rented an apartment for a father she wanted nothing to do with. She hadn't paid back the store owner for all of the things she absconded with as a child. And she didn't want to tell Justin anything about either one.

Being back in her childhood neighborhood had brought up a lot of old memories, most of which were scary or uncomfortable. Taking care of herself for most of her life. Being left alone without food in the apartment, without knowing where her parents were, had been frightening. No. Terrifying was a better word.

She went to the sink and picked up an old dish rag and began wiping down her counters and straightening scant containers and putting away dishes from the rack—what little there was to put away. She didn't like things left out. She didn't like things showing. A salt and pepper shaker and garlic salt sitting next to the stove were the only apparent seasonings. A mixing spoon and a spatula stood in a metal perforated container. She pulled her toaster oven out away from the wall, saw a few crumbs, and wiped them clean. Then she dumped out the toaster. When every speck of dirt she could find had been wiped away, she turned around to the rest of her apartment. But somehow everything was already in its place. Her bed was made, and the cushions on her sofa straightened. The few magazines on her coffee table were also found just right.

Maybe lunch was in order. She went to her cabinets and opened them. Staring out at her were alphabetized cans of vegetables and tuna—and packages of Asian noodles. Nonperishables. And up in the far right-hand corner, rather out of place, sat a backpack. It was purple with lime-green and sky-blue stripes across the bottom.

Shannon's shaky fingers reached up for it and cradled it down to the counter. Her heart pounded as she unzipped it. She hadn't looked inside in a long time. When she had moved from place to place, she just kept it zipped closed—safe. But now her fingers laid back the flap and she looked inside. She removed two shirts rolled in a tight tube, a pair of jeans—rolled same, several pairs of wooly socks, and underwear. Most of the items too small for her now. There was a baggie of trail mix and some energy bars. Probably stale or rancid by now. Underneath those a packet of papers—her birth certificate, her social security card, and a loaded debit card—sat securely encased in a Ziploc bag. Next to that, another Ziploc with an envelope inside. It opened with a crackle, and she fanned the money inside—three thousand dollars.

Her breathing came in gasps as her mind rushed with images, feelings from old fears raking up and down her spine. Shaking from head to foot, she tucked it all back inside and replaced the backpack in its cubby but didn't close the doors. She backed away from the cabinet and tripped over the area rug. She landed soundly on her butt, her teeth rattling at they clapped together, making her head wound pound like a sledgehammer against her skull.

It'd been so long since she'd needed to run. After Amber's dad died, she had decided to stay around and be there for Amber. She'd moved many times since then, staying nearby. Without giving it any thought, she'd moved her backpack, too—keeping it ready for someday. Apartment after apartment, she would stash it in a cabinet easy to reach but hidden from others. No one knew about her go-bag. Not even Amber.

Amber would have taken it the wrong way, like she was ready to leave town at a moment's notice. Like Amber wasn't reason enough to stay in one place. She wouldn't ever understand the need to disappear.

As she stared up at it sitting on the upper cabinet shelf, it seemed to mock her. What did she have to run from these days? She was employed. She was financially secure. She didn't live with anyone abusive, a drug dealer, or drug addict. She wasn't wondering where her next meal was coming from. And yet, at her core, there was the deepest fear that one day someone would find her, and she would have to run.

Where these thoughts came from she wasn't sure. Her heart continued to race, and sweat trickled down her back in between her shoulder blades. She shivered.

Her eyes blurred, and suddenly she was four and curled up in a little ball in the corner of her room, cloaked with her favorite blanket. Daniel came racing into her room, eyes wide, the whites showing brilliantly in the darkness. Flashing red and blue lights shone through her bare window.

"Is it Christmas again?" Her little heart filled with hope. Christmas never had treats or toys. No one in the house but her seemed to realize there was a holiday. Shannon only knew because her teacher told the class and had them make cards for kids who didn't have a family. Shannon had taken one and stuck it in her backpack. On Christmas she gave it to herself with a handful of melty peppermints she'd scooped from the bowl on her teacher's desk when her back was turned.

"We've got to go. Grab your things. Where's your go-bag?"

"I don't want to go anywhere. Don't make me go. I want to stay with Mama." Mama was sick. She'd been on their couch for days. "Unless Mama is coming, too?"

"That can't happen, don't you see? It's too late for her now." He raced back and forth in her room, grabbing things and then dropping them. "Too late. Couldn't save her."

"What do you mean, Daddy?"

"We just got to go, we got to go." Daniel sobbed. "Too late, too late." He shoved a fist against his mouth and stifled a sob. "They're coming. They're coming. We've got to run. They'll take you, and I'll never see you again."

Daniel began ripping blankets and clothes from closets and cupboards and shoving them in plastic bags. Shannon watched in horror as her stuffed animals were knocked around and her dolls were kicked to the side.

"I want my dolls," screamed Shannon. "I want my teddy bear!"

"There's no time for that." He wrenched Shannon from the floor. "Please, just do as I say." Shannon's insides went cold.

The front door banged open, and men started shouting. Shannon tugged her hand from Daniel's and crawled under her bed and covered herself with the blanket. She heard Daniel yelling and struggling. And then the house went very quiet, except for footsteps coming toward her.

"This one's alive." Strong arms wrapped her blanket around her and lifted her. A voice spoke into her ear. "Keep your eyes closed, kiddo. We've got you. Just keep your eyes closed."

But Shannon hadn't kept her eyes closed. She opened them, peeking out from the folds and seeing the sprawled form of her mother on the couch, eyes open but unseeing. She looked cold. And alone. Shannon's mouth formed the word *mama*, but nothing came out. She reached for her, but the man carrying her whisked her into the frigid dampness outside. Rain spattered her exposed legs, and she tried to see past the flashing bright lights to the screaming man in the police car that was her father. He beat on the safety glass of the backseat window and screamed her name.

All Shannon could think was that she wished it was him on the couch.

• —————— • • • • —————— •

Loud knocking on Shannon's apartment door alerted her, bringing her back to the present. The apartment was dark, and her head was pounding. She was sprawled out, face against the floor. The scratchy sisal rug pricked against her cheek.

"Just a minute," she croaked out, pushing up off the floor. Her voice made her headache worse, and she clenched her teeth against the pain. She felt the back of her head. The butterfly bandage seemed okay—no blood. She got to her feet and turned on the lights in the kitchen. The contents of her go-bag were scattered across the countertop. An old flannel shirt and jeans had been tossed on the floor, the trail mix scattered, and the money strewn.

Had she done that? She didn't remember doing that. Was she alone? Her eyes darted into every corner of the room, and she dashed to the bathroom, switching on the bright vanity light, shining into the darkness, and saw nothing but an empty tub.

The knocking on her door turned to a sharp incessant rapping.

"Hang on, I'm coming." Her mind tried to put the pieces together, to remember where she was and who she was. *When* she was.

She opened the door a crack. Why she didn't check before she opened the door to see who it was she didn't know. It wasn't like her to be so unguarded. Outside stood Amber with a quizzical and worried expression on her face.

"Are you okay? I've been out here for ages."

"I'm fine. I was just napping." Or passed out.

Amber started to move forward and bumped into the door.

"Are you going to let me in?"

Even though Amber couldn't see the mess, she could trip over it.

"Everything is really messy in here right now. I don't want you to come in. And fall." Her last words were stilted and stuttering.

Amber focused on Shannon, listening. She always knew when something was wrong.

"You're not answering my texts. You're not answering my

phone calls. And now that I come all the way over here, you're not going to let me in?"

Shannon opened the door. Maybe it was time to take someone into her confidence. Maybe now was the time to try to explain everything.

"Okay, come on in. Be careful, let me lead you." Shannon took Amber around the piles of mess.

"What's going on?" Amber's shoe kicked some of the papers.

"I'm not even sure where to start. It happened after I knocked my head. I'm having flashbacks."

"I thought you'd gotten past all that."

It *had* been years since Shannon had experienced anything close to what she was living through right now. Back then, though, her thoughts hadn't taken her away from life like they were now.

"There's a lot you don't know." Shannon helped Amber get situated on the couch and picked up the money and clothes.

"But we've known each other forever—practically our whole lives."

Shannon didn't even know where to start. How could she explain this to Amber in a way that she would understand? Even though Amber had been adopted, Shannon didn't think she had ever been misused or abused by any foster parents. In fact, until she lost her sight, Amber had led a rather charmed life. She didn't know what it was like to fight for everything. To be afraid all night long. To be hungry. To see your mother dead...

"I don't know how to explain all these things to you, Amber. I don't know how to describe it. Every time I start to think about it, my mind goes fuzzy and thick."

"We've always been there for each other, haven't we? There's nothing you can say that will make me think differently of you."

Shannon hoped Amber meant what she said, because she was about to tell her everything.

"Do you have anywhere else to go tonight?"

"No. Mocha has been fed. And Ethan isn't returning my phone calls. You have a lot in common that way."

"Harsh." She swept the last of the trail mix into her hand and tossed it in the garbage. With the exception of the backpack still being on the counter, everything was back in its rightful place.

"What do you mean he's not returning your phone calls?"

"Well he *is* busy with his parents. I know it's wrong of me to want him to choose me over them I know it's unreasonable. And I don't really want him to. But..."

"You want him to see his parents for who they really are." Shannon's voice lowered, but Amber didn't seem to notice.

"Exactly. They keep treating him like a child. They don't know the things he's overcome. They don't know the life he leads here. He's needed by his clients and, well, by *me*."

"Sometimes," Shannon hedged, "it's not easy to hear negative things about your parents." Amber's eyes narrowed in consternation.

"What's that supposed to mean?"

CHAPTER 13

Y
ou never want to hear anything negative about your father."
Shannon sounded accusatory, but she couldn't help it.

"I know he wasn't perfect." Amber shifted uncomfortably in her chair.

Shannon snorted. Amber's face paled, and Shannon regretted her words. "I'm sorry. This isn't on you."

"You can't blame him forever."

Oh, she could have. But years ago, she'd brought the issue before God. She'd never understood why God couldn't have used Amber's family to get her out of harm's way, to become her own family. But He hadn't. It was above her pay grade to figure out what good it came to. She was whole, or close to it, and had become a productive member of society. She avoided drugs and alcohol. She'd stayed away from abusive men—for the most part. She'd broken all the boundaries for someone who'd survived what she had. An outlander. Maybe knowing it could be done, being the object of proof that you didn't have to follow in your parent's footsteps, was the point of her life? Shoot, being an object lesson was better than it not meaning anything at all. And late at night, she worried about that. The waste of all her suffering.

"You never gave my mom a chance. And my dad, he meant well. He just had no idea the world was such an ugly place."

Unlikely. Not when he had made himself part of it. Maybe it wasn't right that Shannon put it on his shoulders, but the what ifs bore through her mind, not listening to reason.

"I know it's not fair. You can't know how it hurt, though, Amb." Tears threatened, but Shannon wasn't a crier, so she swallowed down her emotions. How could she explain to Amber what her father's words and decisions had done to her?

"I hurt, too. I wanted you to be my official sister more than anything in the world, but he just wouldn't budge. My mom even begged him."

This was news to Shannon. Would that have made any difference to her little-girl heart if she'd known? The clock couldn't be turned back now to find out.

And as if someone changed the channel on the television, images filtered in across her eyes.

Mr. Kirk stood staring down at Amber and Shannon with a mild scowl on his face.

"But daddy, there's a bad boy at her foster house and he wants to hurt her."

"Amber, that's enough. Don't make up such stories. You know we've talked about this before. This isn't the time and it just wouldn't work. There are extenuating circumstances you both can't understand at this age."

Shannon's stomach tightened. She'd been on her own almost from birth. What had made her hope that Mr. Kirk would want her? Her own father didn't. Her mother died to get away from her.

"It's no big deal." Little Shannon turned to go, the bitter taste of bile in her mouth. She had to get out of there. Now.

Amber tugged on her arm. "No, tell him. Please, he'll help you."

Shannon's stomach twisted, and she turned back to Mr. Kirk for one last plea.

"The boy told me if I don't steal money and jewelry, he'll hurt me. A lot."

Mr. Kirk's face went crimson, and he pulled Shannon roughly to the side, fingers tight on her arm. "What a thing to say in front of my daughter. I don't want her thinking about those kinds of things. How dare you." His fingers tightened as if he could squeeze the ugliness out of her, and Shannon started to cry.

"Won't you help me? I won't eat much. I can do all the chores. I'll do anything." *Please.*

Jennifer entered the room, her protective-mother-radar on high alert. "What's going on?"

"Some nonsense. A wild imagination and poor parenting." The vice released from Shannon's arm. "I think we need to limit Amber's play time for a while."

Shannon knew what that meant. She'd crossed a line asking for help. She should have known better. You could only count on yourself in this life.

"I need to go." She picked up her backpack.

"Hang on." Mr. Kirk tugged her backpack from her shoulders.

"Don't. You don't have a right. It's mine." She pulled back, her nails gripping it like she was hanging from the side of a cliff.

"Russ, really, you shouldn't."

Russ looked at his wife. "After what she's just told me?" His hands wrenched it from her grip and dug through her things. He pulled out jeans and a T-shirt, some socks and a plastic bag with a necklace and bracelet inside. The only things she had left of her mother.

"Where did you get these?" He held up the baggy.

Shannon had reached her limit. She snatched the baggy and shoved it deep inside her pocket. Then she stuffed her clothes back inside the pack and zipped it closed. She glared at Mr. Kirk through her tear-filled eyes.

"Don't you ever touch me again. Don't ever touch my stuff." She glanced at Amber. "You're my best friend, Amber. But I won't be back."

Jennifer gasped. "Please, Shannon, help us understand. I want to help."

Russ shook his head. "We're not getting involved in that,

whatever it is. I've told you for a while I didn't think she was a good influence. Now she's got Amber and you all worked up over nothing."

Shannon didn't bother trying to explain anymore.

She *did* go back, she couldn't really stay away from Amber. But every time she entered their house, she felt like a liar. Mr. Kirk would ask her if she was fine, and she'd always say yes. He would get a satisfied look in his eyes that made Shannon want to scream.

She never visited Amber with the expectation of hope again. Amber's parents never asked why she was so quiet, why she was so thin, why noises startled her. No one checked on her status at the group home, and she ran away twice more before she found a place she could survive.

Sadly, it got easier when Mr. Kirk died from a heart attack a few years later. She'd cried at the funeral—but not for the reasons Amber or Jennifer thought. She'd cried for Amber—because whatever kind of person Mr. Kirk was, he loved his daughter dearly.

People were complicated. Her Sunday school teacher told her that at church. They had layers of good and bad. What had Jesus said though? *If we, who were evil, knew how to give good gifts to our children, how much more would their loving and good heavenly Father give them?*

"Shannon?" She felt Amber's gentle hand on her cheek, cool and comforting. "Shannon sweetie?" Amber's fingers wiped the tears from Shannon's face. "Shannon?"

"What?" A haze lifted from her eyes as they adjusted to her apartment. It was like going to the movies when it was light out, and after it was over, it was dark. The shift of time made her dizzy.

"Where am I?"

"Oh sweetie. It's bad this time, isn't it?"

It was all Shannon could do not to sob as her friend pulled her in for a long hug.

Amber had no idea.

"How long?"

"Weeks." Shannon took a shuddering breath. "It's been ages since my last flashback flare. But lately it's like I can't think of anything else. I thought it was gone forever. But then..." She broke off.

"Then I told you I might move and Daniel showed up. Not to mention getting attacked."

"That guy was a thug." Shannon's tone dismissed Amber's comments.

"It doesn't matter. I think it's flipped a switch."

"Maybe." Shannon didn't know if it was that easy. Could a cascade of stress trigger her PTSD? She'd had lots of stress over the last year. Justin entering her life, Amber's losing her sight. Ethan. For some reason Ethan's appearance made her equally happy and angry.

"It's like I'm reliving my childhood. All the pain. Your dad not protecting me." Shannon choked off a sob.

Amber knelt by Shannon's side and took her hand. "I never realized. I didn't see it that way. Oh, sweetie." Amber's tears dripped on Shannon's jeans. "What my dad did left you in such danger. I'm so sorry. Can you ever forgive me?"

Shannon let her hand trail down her friend's head to her back and rubbed it in a circle. "It's not on you. You can't take responsibility for what he did or didn't do."

"I could have tried harder to convince him. Knowing that you suffered because of me..." Amber stopped, unable to go on.

"I never blamed you. And somehow, I need to quit blaming him and forgive him. I just can't yet."

"But this is eating you alive."

"I think it's more than that. It's everything." Shannon's voice was barely a whisper.

"You need to get back with your therapist." Amber tipped her head up and wiped her cheeks.

"What? No." Shannon put her hand up to block the idea. "It's been too long. I have the tools she taught me, I just need to employ them." She pushed back from Amber, and her angsty fingers reached to straighten things before she froze, realizing there wasn't anything in her whole place out of order just then. She stuffed her thwarted fingers into her pockets.

"She's surely forgotten all about me. Or moved her practice. No."

"She'll have your records. At least call her. Right now, the waves are lapping at your ankles."

"And they'll soon topple down over my head?" Shannon shivered. There'd been a time, before she knew Jesus fully, that she'd stood in the waters off the coast and thought about letting the tide carry her off to solace. The sand had shifted beneath her toes, mesmerized her, rushing in and out until a sneaker wave—a wave that came out of nowhere—knocked her from her feet. The water closed over her head and tugged her out to sea.

She'd sputtered and choked on salt water as it burned down her throat, and she'd lost her footing. Not knowing which way was up or down had made her cry out for help to Jesus—and He'd been there, so real. She'd found herself suddenly on all fours on the sand, soaked, chilled, and filled with the heavy certainty that God was real, and He wanted her around. For what, she didn't know. Over time, she'd learned though. And now Jesus was real through and through for her, her savior in every way.

Amber's voice pulled her back, keeping her present.

"It's like a tsunami, sweetie. I don't want to see you there again." She patted the coffee table for Shannon's cell and, after finding it, handed it to her. "Call."

"Now?"

"And please let Justin know what's happening."

"What? No. Why?"

"Because whether you like it or not, he loves you, and he deserves to know. Those closest to you need the opportunity to keep you safe." Amber put an arm around Shannon's shoulder. "You know I'm right."

"Maybe."

"Soon."

"Don't push." Shannon felt her anger rising, but she found her therapist's number and dialed.

CHAPTER 14

Shannon sat in the waiting room at her therapist's office, doing her best to ignore the other patients. The office was on the thirteenth floor, and if she had been superstitious she might be nervous. For some reason, when you'd survived really bad things, superstition didn't ring true anymore. Just like monsters in the dark—she knew them by name, and they were way worse than her imagination.

She cast her gaze through the huge glass panes and scanned the taller and shorter buildings surrounding them. It had been years since she'd been there. Down below she could see the food carts. People milled around like she was playing a Sims game. She could almost see little green diamonds over their heads, or maybe red ones. Because they'd be hungry. Her stomach growled. Maybe she should have gotten something to eat?

One of the shorter buildings had a garden-top penthouse apartment. The trees and grass were manicured perfectly. A small garden edged the pathway. She wondered what it would be like to have your own private yard on top of the world like that. Independent and safe; self-sustaining.

The faux leather chair squeaked next to her. A rather unkempt fellow with a partially tucked plaid cowboy shirt sat four seats over, shifting from side to side, scrolling through messages on his phone. His belt rubbed on the plastic chair back, making squeaking sounds. A slender young man came in carrying a Styrofoam container. Shannon looked around to see if there was any DO NOT EAT signs in the office. There weren't.

The receptionist made a pleasant sound. "That smells amazing." Her eyes twinkled at the young man. "Where did you get that?"

The man grinned at her. "At the falafel cart downstairs."

"I love that place. Did you ask for extra hummus?"

"I didn't know I could do that. Next time I will for sure. Let me know if you'd like something, I could get it for you."

Shannon wasn't sure if flirting with the patients was professional or not. Or counting on the young man to bring her food. She tried to tune out the receptionist and the man as they discussed every detail of his meal. Her stomach growled, and she shifted in the chair to hide the noise. She really should have eaten before she came.

To get her mind off food, she scanned the rest of the room. Another woman, older in years, appeared quite uncomfortable. She moved two seats down from the young man, put her hand over her nose, and pulled her coat closed with the other hand.

The unkempt man, who must've been in his early seventies, continued to poke at his phone. His bushy gray hair fell over his forehead, and he brushed it back. "I can't remember how to work this thing." Shannon looked away so he wouldn't think she was willing to help. He seemed to be talking to himself though.

Suddenly the phone started to sound a ring, and she realized he'd put it on speaker.

"Hello? Hello?" echoed a woman's voice.

He frantically started pushing the buttons. Then he put it to his ear.

"Can you hear me? It's me, your loving husband. Yeah, I'm in my doctor's office."

Shannon thought that was sweet. Somebody loved the unkempt man. It made her happy for him.

"Yeah, Hawaii is great. But I wish you were here."

Shannon's ears snapped to attention. *Hawaii?* She hadn't meant to listen but how could she help it? She looked over toward the young man and the receptionist to see if they noticed — they appeared oblivious. He was offering her bites of his falafel. That was unsanitary. Gross. Shannon shivered and stared down at her hands, trying to shut everything out.

Her hands felt prickly as she watched them clenching and unclenching. She dug her fingernails in to try to draw her attention and calm her heart. This is the last thing she needed. Weird drama.

"Yeah, my knee replacement went great, I'm sure the doctors can sign me off soon for travel. I only have a couple more rehab sessions. That's where I am now."

Oh, that was the mistake. The man thought he was in his rehab office. Shannon leaned toward him to correct his misunderstanding, when the charge nurse came out and said, "Mr. O'Donnell?"

Mr. O'Donnell stood up quite steady. "I have to go, my love, they are calling my name. I hope to be home soon. Paradise is empty without you." He snapped his phone shut and slipped it into his pocket on the way down the hall to his appointment room.

Well, there went that theory. Maybe he really thought he was in Hawaii? The wind whipped past the building, startling her as the windows rattled and rain pelted the glass. That would take quite some imagination to believe that they were in Hawaii. And to believe you were recovering from knee surgery.

The falafel man had seated himself and was eating his food with smacking gusto. Shannon tried not to look—or listen. Her eyes met those of the older woman. They bonded in that moment, and a smile crossed both their faces at the same time. Shannon knew this wasn't the place to make friends, or even small talk. But for some reason she was drawn to her.

"I'm not sure why they let people bring food in here," whispered Shannon.

"I'm sure I've never liked it," the woman responded. She leaned

111

toward Shannon, put out her hand but pulled back equally as fast and tucked it into her pocket.

Shannon understood. They were in the counseling office, after all. Shannon gave her a gentle smile.

"My name is Shannon." Shannon gave her a small wave.

"My name's Rae."

That seemed to be the end of it. Neither wanted to give away too much. They sat in companionable silence—or would have if the man eating hadn't been in the room. This was the most still Shannon had been in quite a while. The falafel man threw away the garbage and left the room. Shannon's eyebrows went up in question at the receptionist.

"He comes in here almost every day just to eat his lunch. I think he's lonely." She shrugged.

A sense of guilt washed over Shannon, and she shifted in her chair. She shouldn't judge people so harshly. That wasn't like her.

Rae was called back for her appointment with another therapist, and Shannon found herself alone. She closed her eyes and listened to the gentle sway of the Muzak playing overhead. Her ears caught the tune of something familiar. She started to giggle as she recognized "Welcome to the Jungle" by Guns N' Roses. Axl Rose had no idea his music would be turned into a peaceful jingle. And then her smile faded.

How had she ended up here? Her mind wandered to her homeless friends. What made her so different that she got treatment and others didn't? Queen Susie and Magic Stan only needed medication and they could be off the streets. No. It was probably more difficult than that. They were a pair. And even though she was the one giving away her things, somehow, they were the ones to encourage her.

Her hands ached as she remembered the loss of her camera, like the loss of a limb tingled in ghostly memory.

Shannon might not have her camera, but she still had the photo memory card. She needed to get it back from the police officer. That day had ended bad, but something special had happened with Stan and that woman. She needed to witness it again.

Some days she wanted an easy answer for everyone. Even Daniel.

The rain whipped against the building again, startling her. Everything seemed to shake her these days. Daniel was out in the storm. He didn't know she found him a place to stay that was warm and dry and safe. She hadn't figured out how to get him there without saying she was involved. Maybe she was punishing him. She just couldn't tell him who she was yet. Maybe she never would. She closed her eyes. *I'm sorry, God, I don't know how to do this.*

As always, when she felt out of control, she made lists in her head of what could help. Like if she had a plan, all would make sense and be well. She needed a camera. She needed to get prints made. She needed some jobs to make money, or she would lose both their apartments before Daniel moved in.

Maybe he could live with her? No. Not a chance.

How long had it been since she lived with her dad? She'd been sent back to him repeatedly only to be removed to foster care permanently by the time she was ten. As an adult, she'd investigated if she could sue the state for returning her to an unfit parent. It would take several lawyers and more money than she could ever hope to have in order to bring such a case. She never could figure out why the state kept returning kids to their damaged parents, past when it was reasonable. There should be a three strikes law for parents that couldn't take care of their children. Let them live safely elsewhere. Let someone adopt them while they were adoptable. Let someone love them.

By the time you hit puberty, you were damaged goods. All of the babies got adopted. There were waitlists for babies.

"Shannon?"

Shannon looked up to see her counselor waiting in the hall for her with a worried expression. Had she tuned out in the waiting room? She needed to get a grip.

Dr. Corey hadn't changed much in ten years. Her blond hair was a bit grayer, but still pulled back in a ponytail. She still wore her cable-knit cardigan with the big macramé buttons. Maybe she was like Mr. Rogers—his mother had made him identical sweaters for each year's show. Dr. Corey kind of reminded Shannon of Mr. Rogers—soft-spoken and kind, never a harsh word for anyone. Accepting.

"Are you ready?"

Shannon wasn't sure if she was ready or not, but she was sure more than ever that she needed to be there.

Once settled inside Dr. Corey's office, sitting in a big squishy chair, Shannon felt every muscle relax, like she'd been cued to do so. Dr. Corey moved around the room, switching on a fake flickering candle and turning on a little water fountain in the corner. The water trickled over the rocks. Dr. Corey turned down her desk lamp and spoke in a soothing tone.

"It's really good to see you, Shannon. How have you been?"

"Not too bad. I'm working for the inclusive art school downtown. I teach photography." She crossed and uncrossed her arms as the tension returned ten-fold.

"I've seen some of your work in the galleries around town. And a few in the coffee shop not too far from here, I think? They're very insightful pieces. You should be proud of the things you've accomplished."

Dr. Corey had a way about her that put even Shannon, who was not ever at ease with anyone, into a comfortable state.

"I appreciate that." It was then Shannon remembered again she didn't have a camera anymore.

"What's that frown about?" Dr. Corey motioned toward Shannon's face.

"My camera was broken the other day." Shannon took a deep breath and let it out with a shudder. She felt tears forming.

"Was this during the event you left a message about?" Dr. Corey flipped through some notes on her lap.

"Yeah, it was."

"Why don't you tell me about it?" Dr. Corey picked up her pen and started to write some notes on her file.

Shannon went on to describe the event. How she stopped the man from accosting the young girls. How he turned on her and she'd fallen. About her head wound and her camera. When she finished, Dr. Corey was extra quiet. Shannon looked up to see what caught her attention. Dr. Corey's expression filled with surprise and admiration.

"You saved those young women? That's incredible!"

Shannon shrugged.

"And is this when your PTSD flared?"

Shannon hadn't thought about that. "I guess so. I think it probably started after my fall."

Dr. Corey frowned at her. "You mean after he attacked you?"

"I hit my head."

"Describe it to me please." Dr. Corey wrote in her notes again.

"Once I started to get in the way of that creep he turned on me and came charging. He grabbed my camera. We slammed into the ground and somewhere along the line I hit my head."

"Did you hit your head, or did he throw you to the ground and that's when you hit your head?"

Shannon had to think a minute. What had happened? Her hands opened and closed, clenching and unclenching. She watched the blood flow in and out, flashing pink then tan and pink again.

"He grabbed my shoulders, and he pushed me hard on the ground. I guess he slammed my head into the concrete." She reached back around behind her to feel the lump. It was still sore.

"That must have been terrifying. Did you press charges?"

"Of course, but he's out already."

"Do you feel safe?"

"I'm not sure why you're making such a big deal out of this." She crossed her arms.

"Because a sex trafficker attacked you in the middle of the park. And you were injured and hospitalized because of that attack. It is a big deal."

Shannon kept her lips pressed together and didn't respond.

"Let's try a different tact. You remember your breathing exercises?"

Shannon nodded.

"Why don't you do a few minutes now? I'll check you for your posture and make sure you got all the steps."

Shannon breathed evenly in and out. In and out again. She listened to the sound of her own breathing, the rhythm, the tone. She listened to her heartbeat. She felt her fingers relax and then she relaxed her arms and her toes and then her legs. She sagged sideways in her chair, feeling comfortable.

"Shannon?"

Shannon's eyes sagged open. She hadn't realized how tired she was.

"How do you feel?"

"Relaxed."

"Let's talk about the tuning out. List all the incidences you remember. Give me the dates to the best of your ability."

"The first one was in the shower after I...after the attack."

"Why do you think it's so hard to admit you were attacked?"

"I'm on the streets all the time. I'm supposed to be better than that."

Dr. Corey leaned forward. "Better than what?"

"Some weak and inexperienced girl. I grew up on those streets."

"But this time you were worried for other people's safety.

Couldn't that have something to do with it? Anyway, living on the streets doesn't mean you don't feel afraid. Does it?"

"I guess not."

"We'll touch on the subject again later. When is the next time you remember tuning out?"

"I'm pretty sure this has something to do with my concussion."

"Possibly, but tell me anyway."

Shannon went on to list the times Amber and Justin had trouble getting her attention in her apartment. Now that she was counting, there were more than she realized.

"Nothing else?"

Shannon felt a tickle of memory. "Actually before. Before the attack. I got caught up in a memory."

"About what?"

"My childhood. Being alone in my apartment. Being hungry. Raising myself."

Dr. Corey flipped through old notes, page after page, until she stopped. She underlined something.

"You were raised in foster care, weren't you?"

"Like that matters."

"We talked about this before, Shannon. Many foster families are very loving. Most are."

"If you say so."

"None of yours were?"

"No. Well—there were a couple. They never stuck it out with me. I was too much for them."

"You were too much? What does that mean?"

"I was bad. I ran away. I didn't want to be there."

"What would they do?"

"Give up on me. Move me. Leave me."

"Is that what happened with Daniel?"

Dr. Corey's mentioning Daniel put Shannon on alert immediately, and her hands went hot and sweaty. Perspiration dripped down her neck. The air in the room stifled her. Her stomach turned with nausea.

"Can I have some water?" Her voice shook and cracked.

Dr. Corey rose and went to a little cooler in the corner of the room and pulled out a bottle of water. She cracked the lid off before handing it to Shannon. Shannon had several sips. She took a shaky breath, and the tension eased.

"I didn't mean to upset you. We can talk about Daniel next time."

"No, this is okay. I'm all right. Might as well get it over with."

Dr. Corey smiled. "Yes, by all means let's get it over with."

Shannon chuckled lightly, and then her countenance darkened. "He's back, you know. Did I tell you?"

"No, you hadn't told me that. How long has it been?"

"A long time. And I didn't approach him to tell him who I was. And I don't want to. All he's ever done is disappoint me. When I was little they gave me back to him a handful of times. He blew it every time. I wish he'd given up early. It was so selfish."

"Does your father have mental illness?" Dr. Corey began to flip the pages of Shannon's chart with her nimble fingers as she searched for old notes.

"Don't we all?"

"Funny. But if he couldn't take care of you, what was he supposed to do?"

"Then he should have given up. He should've quit trying. Maybe someone would've adopted me."

"I think you're forgetting that he loves you. Most parents want to raise their children. Even if they aren't able, there's a desire deep within them that tells them to try."

"Real love means putting someone else first. It means living sacrificially."

"Do you think Daniel knows how to love someone sacrificially?"

A very clear image of Jennifer and Russ Kirk came to her mind. Loving smiles on their faces and arms open to her. It was an old dream she needed to put away forever. A fantasy that never happened. She shook her head to clear the picture, like shaking an Etch A Sketch, to erase the memory for good. The dark lines and highlights filled in with gray sand. Their smiles warped to scowls of disappointment. Then they were gone.

A voice interrupted her thoughts. A little girl was begging. "Please, I'll be good. I'll clean the house. I can do lots of things. You'll see."

"One daughter is enough," Russ patted her head as one did with a dog you wanted to dismiss.

"Can we talk about it? It would make me and Amber so happy." Jennifer pleaded with Russ.

Shannon continued begging, her desperation growing. Her fingers clung to Jennifer's pants, and they curled into the fabric, making her knuckles ache and burn.

"Don't make me go back. I'll do anything." Shannon's sobs grew panicky. She felt fingers around her waist hauling her back as she lost her grip on Jennifer. She could hear Amber crying in the corner, begging her father to reconsider.

But what happened next? Was that even a real memory? No, that had been her dream—more like a nightmare. One that revisited her many nights.

"Shannon? Can you hear me?"

Shannon felt a warm hand on her shoulder and she startled from her chair.

"What?"

"You've been tuned out for several minutes. Don't worry, you are safe."

If she couldn't keep her head straight with her counselor, how was she going to do it outside in the world? Let alone continue teaching her students. School had only been back in a couple weeks. She didn't recall any upsets during class time, but what if she wasn't even noticing? Would she let down her kids? Shannon sank back in the chair. Maybe she should move into the office, or just hire Dr. Corey to follow her around for the rest of her life.

"Sorry."

"There's nothing to apologize for."

"Now what?"

"Let's take this one step at a time, okay?"

What did that even mean?

CHAPTER 15

Shannon stood outside her school for several minutes staring at the doors—their gaping dark eyes staring back at her. After she'd finished classes for the day, she had gone outside to walk the perimeter of the parking lot while she got up her nerve for what she had to do next. She'd made it through the day, once again with no mishaps. Hopefully. None of the students mentioned anything was amiss. Fear of revealing her weakness to them gnawed at her.

The principal, Brandon, had office hours now. She took a deep breath, about to do something she hated, but one glance at her bank balance told her she must.

As she entered the long, carpeted hallway, that familiar sense of belonging to something good washed over her. She loved this school and the kids. She loved being part of something that would encourage young artists and give them an outlet. She didn't want to lose this or them.

Her mind slipped to middle school and her photography teacher. He'd assigned her to the school paper, and it was then she felt the first tingle of promise and connectedness. Taking candid shots of sports events and music competitions. Going on assignment to see plays with reporters.

Then entering contests and winning prizes for something she loved. What a concept. If it hadn't been for her art teacher, though, who showed her how to use the darkroom and gifted her with supplies that her foster family refused or couldn't pay for, she wouldn't have found her niche. Or her escape. And that became her salvation—well, that and Jesus.

Shannon had always known Jesus. She didn't know how she knew God was real when there was no earthly reason for her to know such things—her parents never spoke of God except in expletives. But she'd always spoken to Him—not like the praying she'd seen on television, pious and solemn, on their knees. Shannon would just talk to Him. Like a person. And as she grew older, she knew Jesus *was* a person and understood her better than anyone else. Especially since the ocean incident. That's when He became less of an ethereal emotion and more tangible.

He'd planted something in her heart that enabled her to trust Him. She didn't know, even now, why all the bad things that happened did happen, but Shannon knew nothing was wasted with God—He was able to make something good out of the hardest, most awful of circumstances.

Her prayers didn't get direct answers, exactly, but she knew in her heart she'd been heard. Jesus would provide a neighbor with food. Or Jesus would lead her teacher to get her a winter coat. Most of all, Jesus helped her feel like she wasn't alone—even when Daniel left her on her own for days or was checked out on drugs. Jesus was with her.

Shannon's mind filled with the image of a scary man chasing her, and her heartbeat increased. She clenched her eyes against the memory. She did her breathing exercises, she focused on relaxing, she tried to count—but it still barreled in.

She'd been with a neighbor girl at an old arcade a couple of miles from home. Tori had been left on her own a lot, too. And since Daniel was gone, she felt no need to stay at home when Tori knocked on her door and asked if she wanted to hang out. They'd walked blocks and blocks and had ended up in front of the arcade. But the arcade was a place where rich kids wasted quarters on electrical lights and sounds. She had no such luxury.

"I don't have money to play any games." Shannon backed up, wishing she'd stayed home. She didn't need any reminders of how the other side lived and where *she* belonged.

"No big deal. I know the owner. Come on." Tori entered the arcade filled with older teens and sketchy looking adults. The lights were off, and the machines glowed red and orange and yellow in the darkness. The sounds of crashing cars, shooters, and arcade game jingles saturated the air. Tori turned and shouted at Shannon.

"What?" Shannon couldn't hear her. Tori leaned in close and yelled in her ear.

"I said he's in the back. Come on." The girl pulled her by the arm into a dusty workroom with television monitors actively watching the filled arcade. There were several open-backed machines, and a man working over one of the electronic boards on his desk.

The balding man scowled up at her friend. "What?"

"Can we clean some screens for tokens?"

The scowl deepened. "I guess that'd be okay. The morning shift guy walked out on me, and the place hasn't been cleaned in a couple weeks. It's getting ripe out there." He turned to the shelf behind him and grabbed two bottles of cleaner. He started to hand them to the girls and then pulled them back out of reach.

"Five bucks of tokens for each of you, but you have to do the bathrooms."

Shannon felt uneasy. She hadn't wanted to clean anything. She thought this would be fun.

"Deal." Tori jabbed her elbow into Shannon's ribs.

"Sure." Shannon gasped, rubbing her side.

The man handed over the bottles of spray cleaner and two rags. "The cleaning supplies for the toilets and sinks are in the cabinet inside each bathroom."

Shannon wasn't worldly, but she knew cleaning all the machines and the bathroom was a lot of work for five bucks—of tokens no less.

A thought occurred to her. "Can I have my pay in cash?"

The man snorted. "A businesswoman in the making, huh? Fine. Cash or tokens."

Shannon followed Tori back out into the game room.

"What did you do that for? I was going to talk him up to seven bucks of tokens when we were done."

"I need the money." That's all Shannon would say. The fridge in their house was empty, and she'd eaten the last ramen noodle pack for breakfast. Her mouth watered. What kind of world did she live in where ramen noodles made her mouth water?

Tori shrugged and went to work cleaning the screens. Shannon moved to the other side of the arcade, cleaning the machines that didn't have any players and then went to the more popular games and waited in between matches. The place was overwhelmingly male, but there were a few girls playing. No one wanted to wait until she'd wiped the screens clean.

"That's all Asian chicks are good for." One boy sneered at her and spit a loogie on the screen. Shannon stood up as tall as she could for ten and stared him down. "Go get a paper towel from the bathroom and clean it up." She sprayed cleaner over his spit and the rest of the screen. "Or you'll have the whole place mad at you."

He called her a name, but she didn't relent. She left it unwiped and stomped off to the next one. When her side was done, she headed to the bathroom and discovered Tori already entering the women's bathroom.

"Hey, why do you get the women's bathroom?" Shannon had had enough. She wanted her money and food—and to go home.

"Because this was my idea. The next time you figure out a way to make some money, *you* get to choose who gets to do the dirty job." Tori left her staring at the men's room door.

Shannon knocked. No one answered. She opened the door and called out. "Anyone in here?"

No one answered back, so she entered and locked the door

behind her. The room held a stall with no door, a urinal, and a sink. Toilet paper was strewn across the floor, wet and sticky, as well as dirty footprints and a substance Shannon couldn't—and didn't want to—decipher. The sink was running, and the soap dispenser was empty. She turned off the tap and faced the urinal. The acrid smell of urine overpowered her, and she gaged, quickly pulling her shirt up over her nose.

She turned to the cabinet and breathed a sigh of relief that there was a mop inside. She pulled out the cleaner and sprayed it liberally over the floor, and into the toilet in the stall. By the time she was done scrubbing, mopping, and refilling the soap, she was disgusted by boys. But at least you could tell she'd been there and it smelled tons better.

A knock on the door startled her. "Just a minute," she called.

She washed her hands three times before leaving. As she opened the door, a tall, scruffy-looking younger man stood in her way with a menacing look on his face.

"What took you so long?" The man pushed past her. "What are you doing in here anyway?"

"Cleaning this disgusting place. You're welcome, by the way."

The man whipped around and pushed her shoulder into the wall before he turned his back to her and started to unzip his pants as if he'd been alone.

"Nobody asked you to," he growled.

Shannon rubbed her arm. She didn't like the tone of his voice or that he'd acted as if it were normal to have a girl in the bathroom with him. Instead of one of her retorts, she ducked out and raced to the manager. She wanted her money, and she wanted to go home.

"Can I have my money now?"

"I have to inspect your work." He snorted as if he'd made a joke. He left the back office and went around inspecting the games and checked the bathrooms. She followed him, staying safely behind. When they got to the bathroom, the other man was gone.

"I guess it's good enough."

Shannon held her tongue.

The manager went to the token machine and turned a key and started to draw out tokens.

"You said you'd pay cash."

"You get more value in tokens." He continued counting. Tokens wouldn't buy her food, and she needed that a whole lot more than video games.

"Please, mister. I really need the money." She put on her saddest face and looked despairingly up into his bloodshot eyes.

The manager chewed on his cheek as he thought. "Okay. But only three bucks."

"That's not fair. You said five."

"I said five in tokens." He closed the machine and started digging in his pocket.

"Five." Dashing the sad act, she put her hands on her hips and gave him her most intimidating glare.

He narrowed his eyes at her. "Fine, kid. Four bucks. But don't count on me doing this again."

He held out four dollars to her. Shannon took it. "Don't worry, I won't be back."

Shannon moved to the door and felt someone tug on her arm. She clenched her fist, ready to fight, but it was only Tori.

"Where are you going?"

"I'm outta here."

"I thought we could play some games and hang out." Despite how she'd treated her, Tori actually sounded disappointed.

"I gotta get home. My dad will be wondering where I am."

"Hardly. Your dad is probably off with my mom. They won't be back before Monday, I bet."

Shannon didn't like the implication, even if it was true. She pulled Tori closer. "Keep your voice down. I don't want to end up back in foster care."

"Fine. But don't leave me here. It's not safe for either of us to head home alone."

"I don't have any tokens."

Tori handed her five tokens. "You should have gotten these anyway. He's a big jerk."

Five tokens were spent faster than Shannon could have realized. The games were fun and distracting from her hunger, but once the tokens were gone, she became ravenous. Various meaty and fried food smells wafted over from the McDonald's across the street.

How long had it been since she had a decent burger? Shannon moved to the door and saw the lit golden arches sign boasting two cheeseburgers for a dollar. *Two.*

"You leaving again? I still have a ton to spend." Tori motioned to the huge jangly bulge in her jeans' pocket.

"I'm starving."

Tori gave her a disappointed look. "I get it. Okay. See you later."

Shannon's stomach sank, worried about walking home on her own. She looked past Tori's head and saw the grumpy guy from the bathroom in the background watching them. The hairs on her neck prickled to attention.

"Careful of that guy." She motioned toward him.

Tori turned, and the man moved off. "Who?"

"Never mind. See you."

"See you." Tori melted back into the darkness of the arcade and Shannon moved to the sidewalk and crossed the street. Inside the McDonald's, she ordered her two cheeseburgers. The woman gave her fries and a drink, too.

"I just wanted the special. Not the fries and drink." She needed to make this money last.

The woman behind the counter studied her. Shannon shifted from one foot to the other.

"It's fine. We're going to close anyway, and I'd just throw them away." The woman bagged them and went to the fry area and dumped a couple others in the sack, along with a five-piece McNuggets.

She handed it off to Shannon and Shannon handed her a dollar.

"Don't worry about it, kid. I'll cover it for you."

Shannon looked down at her ragged clothes. Her shirt and jeans were stained from cleaning the bathroom.

"I don't need charity." She started to take the hamburgers out of the sack.

"Hey, kid. Look at me. I'm seriously going to throw all that out, and the pop doesn't cost us more than twenty cents. It's cool."

Even at her young age, she knew pity, but her brains told her she might not have food again for a while and to take it.

"Thanks." She looked over the counter. "You got anything else you don't need?"

The woman laughed. "There you go. Let me see." She came back with a Filet-O-Fish and a Big Mac.

"Seriously?"

"Yep."

"Wow. Thanks."

The woman pulled out a larger sack and packed it carefully, tossing in plenty of napkins, ketchup, and dipping sauce.

Shannon's eyes filled with tears as the woman handed her the drink and she saw it was a chocolate shake. Shannon hadn't had ice cream in months. Maybe over a year. A sob broke from her closely watched barrier.

"Hey, it's cool. Don't worry."

Shannon couldn't stop crying—until the woman said something that stopped the dam fast.

"Are you in trouble? Do you live around here?"

She wiped her cheeks with her free hand. "Oh, yeah. I'm fine. Just tired. Thanks lady."

"Chellie." She leaned over the counter and whispered so that her workmates in back couldn't hear her. "I usually work evenings. If

APRIL McGOWAN

you're in a jam, you can come back about this time in the evening. I'm the night manager." She winked at her. "I can't promise it'll always be so much, but there's usually one or two items left over."

A smile broke over Shannon's face ,and she felt the tears start welling again. She had to get out of there.

"Thanks, Chellie."

Her prayer that morning came back to her. She'd prayed to God for food. She thought that God had provided the four dollars—and He had. But this was a windfall. If her dad was home, she had enough to share and to save for a few days.

Shannon pulled the bag close, protecting it like a treasure, and headed out of the restaurant, turning for a final wave of thanks to Chellie. As she tromped home, she felt lighter and better than she had in a long time. Her stomach moaned as the aroma of the food wafted up at her, but something in her told her to wait.

It was a good thing, too.

CHAPTER 16

Night fell over Portland like a foggy wet blanket, and the chill in the air settled into Shannon's bones. She pulled the hot bag of food closer and hoped it'd still be warm by the time she got home. The yellow lights from the streetlamps guided her way up one street and over two blocks. She had a few to go when she heard the buzz of a bike chain coasting up behind her. Shannon walked faster. "It's not much farther," she told herself. "You're almost home."

The cyclist sped past her and went around the corner.

"Silly. It's just someone on their way home, too." Her voice sounded echoey in the foggy air. The night sounds of traffic from the freeway faded to a stillness. She'd not felt so alone in a long time. The fog created a sense of quiet stillness, like snow. No crickets, no cats, no rustling bushes, nothing moved.

Shannon moved on across the next street, hearing only her footsteps until the whirring click of a bike changing gears traveled through the gray mist toward her. The squeak of brakes directly behind her made her jump to the grass to get out of the way.

"Hey there. A sweet thing like you shouldn't be out here all alone. Can I keep you company? You look like someone who could use a little company." It was the grumpy guy from the arcade bathroom. He touched her shoulder where he'd hurt her earlier. She shrank under his touch.

Fear contracted her throat. For some reason a lesson from her animal science studies came to mind. *Don't make eye contact and keep moving forward. Don't run or they will chase you. Get to a safe place and call for help. Making noise scares them off.*

Shannon gulped down her fear and kept moving.

"Hey, pretty. I asked you a question. It's plain rude not to answer." He smiled and made a sound like a strangled chuckle. Shannon rushed by him. He rode his bike off the curb, then circled back and came up behind her again, then again from the front, like a collie herding sheep.

And still, she kept moving.

"Looks like you made out pretty good tonight. Want to share?" He motioned to the over-full sack she carried. For some reason, his being after her food made her more frightened than she'd been. She needed this food.

"It's for my...my parents. They are waiting for me." Her voice stuttered as she exaggerated the number of people who waited at home for her—having more than just her drugged father felt more secure. Like maybe he'd worry if more than one person might notice she'd disappeared.

"Well, that's great. You know, you shouldn't be out here at midnight all alone like this. It's not safe. You never know who might come upon you. Why don't I go with you and talk to your parents about that?"

"No, that's okay. They haven't felt good, so I picked up dinner."

"That's really nice. No worries. I'll escort you home. It's the gentlemanly thing to do." He grinned at her and reached for her again.

She shot around him and moved up the street, walking as fast as she could without running. Her eyes darted from one darkened house to the next, hoping and praying for a light on a porch or in a window. She finally found one and raced up the sidewalk to the door.

"I'm home now. Thanks." She put her hand on the door handle, waiting for him to retreat.

"Good. Go on in." His smile slid sideways into a sneer. Somehow, he knew she was bluffing.

Shannon prayed that the people inside would be kind and help her. A million ideas raced through her mind. They would want to know why she was out so late, too. They'd ask why her parents let her go alone to McDonald's so far away. They might call the police.

Shannon knocked on the door.

"No key?"

She knocked harder. No one came. She dashed off the porch and ran to the next house, banging on the door. The man snickered and followed on his bike, all the while riding lazy circles on the sidewalks and driveways. Her heart was a walloping hammer in her chest, and with every beat her adrenaline surged like electricity pumping through every vein and artery.

Her hands shook, and knuckles stung from rapping on the doors. His bike got closer and closer, like a shark tiring out and circling his prey. She tried six houses until finally someone opened the door. When she looked over her shoulder, the man had vanished.

"What in the world?" An older woman clothed in a robe and slippers stared down at her. "Is there a fire or something?"

"No, ma'am. I'm sorry. I'm on my way home and this man was chasing me and I was scared." Oftentimes the truth was the best policy. Not this time, though.

"What man? What are you up to?" The woman craned her head over Shannon's head, scanning the street for trouble. "Harold?" she hollered behind her, "call the police. There's a child out here." She looked down at Shannon. "I don't know what's going on here, young lady, but you should know better than to bother people out of their beds. Do you know what time it is?" She started to draw Shannon into her house by her arm, but Shannon wrenched out of her grip, afraid of the police and of being put into foster care once again. She ran zig-zagging up the street and around the corner. She heard the bike and the resonating sound of the man's laughter and gulped in panic. Between her hunger and lack of oxygen, spots swam before her eyes. If she passed out, he'd have her for sure.

She should have waited at that last house for the police. The dead sureness of that thought bore into her mind like a corkscrew digging into a stopper. She booked it as fast as she could up two more blocks, and all the while the bike sounded closer and closer. She thought she heard him chuckle. She reached her own door, pulled her chain necklace free and stabbed the key she kept there into the door lock.

"Hurry, hurry, hurry." The key rattled and fumbled in her quaking fingers. The bike's brakes screeched to a halt behind her and she heard the rattle of frame and chain as he dropped it on its side on her lawn.

"Nice house you have. If it's really yours this time. I think I'll come in. Meet the folks."

"Hurry. Oh, help, Jesus." The key slipped in and she was inside, deadbolting the door behind her as fast as she could. She turned on all the lights and closed all the curtains. She darted to the backdoor and bolted it, shoved the table against it and sank to the linoleum.

The smell of the food caught her attention. She'd haphazardly dropped it as she'd come in and it lay by the front door, spilling out of the sack. The milkshake had tumbled free of its lid, and she watched as it pooled and melted into the golden shag carpet.

Shannon grabbed a towel from the sink and crawled to the mess, trying to be quiet and keep out of sight of the windowsas best she could. She wanted to salvage all she could of the delicious shake. Tears flowed freely down her cheeks. She heard a creaking on the porch outside, and her breath caught in her throat. One step then another. Shannon shoved her fist against her mouth, stifling a scream.

Talk.

The word came unbidden to her mind. Talk to who?

Talk.

And talk she did. "Dad? Hamburgers are here. How's mom doing?" Her voice sounded alien and shrieky. If the man thought she wasn't alone, he'd leave. She took tiny breaths, trying to control her fear. What if he broke in? How could she stop him? Her eyes darted to the phone on the wall, but she knew it was dead—her father hadn't paid the bill in months.

Steps overhead thumped, a glass broke, and someone was crossing the floor upstairs. Terror washed though her. How had he got in so fast? The footsteps thumped, coming down the stairs to the living room. She needed to hide, but her mind froze, she couldn't think straight. Hunger, fear, and sheer exhaustion wore her to desperation. Shannon was about to scream when she saw her dad stumbling down in front of her.

"Where've you been? You scared your mother and me near to death." Daniel's blond hair was matted and dirty, his T-shirt torn and stained, and his sweatpants hung loose on his emaciated frame.

A strange numb feeling filled her legs, and she faltered, relieved to see her father and not the man. The outside porch step creaked again, and she heard the man's steps retreating and the rattle of the bike taking off.

Shannon launched herself into Daniel's arms, sobbing. "Oh Daddy, I'm so glad you're home. I was so scared."

Daniel sank to his knees. "Baby girl, what is it?"

Shannon said a prayer of thanks that her father wasn't strung out at that moment. "I went with the neighbor girl to the arcade and on the way home this—" She gasped for breath—"this man chased me. I was so scared."

Daniel's grip on Shannon tightened. "Baby. No. I'm so sorry. We shouldn't have left you on your own. But why did you go out so late?"

She swallowed hard and looked up into his confused face. She gaged his alertness, his ability to understand. Maybe this time he'd hear her. "I didn't have any food."

He'd heard her but was still confused. Daniel sank to his knees, still not understanding. "But we just went shopping."

"Daddy, that was three weeks ago." Shannon's voice was just a whisper. "I didn't know what else to do."

"But Mom went out yesterday and got groceries. She got you that macaroni and cheese you love. We even have real milk to make it with this time instead of just water..."

Shannon took her father's face in her hands. "Dad, Mom died six years ago. Remember?" Her dad's illness and drug use affected his memory. Sometimes he remembered easily. Other times, like now, it didn't go over well.

"Dead? No. How can that be. Oh, no." Tears trickled over his unshaven face. "Dead. That's right. I forgot."

"I'm sorry, Daddy." She hated to hurt him.

"*You're* sorry? Oh darling. Oh, baby girl." He pulled her back into his embrace. "I wouldn't hurt you for the world. Your mom would be so sad to see us like this. My beautiful Mayuree." He refocused on her face, brushing her hair back behind her ear tenderly. "You look so much like her. That's why we used her name for your middle name."

"I know, Daddy," she responded, but he didn't seem to hear her.

"Mayuree means beautiful. And Shannon means little wise one. My beautiful and wise little one." He pulled her closer, burying his face in her neck. "What am I going to do? What are we going to do?" His voice cracked, and Shannon felt him shaking and crying. And as wise as he said Shannon was, she didn't have any answers.

CHAPTER 17

A child's laughter shattered the memory, and she was back at the school with classrooms filled with little people and their dreams and imagination. Shannon rubbed at her eyes and took a shuddering breath. She'd forgotten how close she and her dad had been. She'd loved him—and he her. Not enough, though, for him to put her needs first. She reached out and steadied herself against the wall, touching the concrete block and cool surface, grounding herself in the present.

She was here to beg for much more than hamburgers and French fries. She'd better get on with it.

Shannon passed by the classes on the way to Brandon's office, seeing the students hard at work, creating their little hearts out. This was an immersion school. So many schools had cut their budgets for the arts that their private school was in high demand. There was more to an education than the technical side of mathematics or science. To be well-rounded, you needed to find that other side of yourself that created, that connected you to your Creator.

Shannon knocked on Brandon's door, and he called to whoever it was to enter.

"Hi, Brandon. Do you have a minute?"

Brandon's fuzzy white eyebrows rose in surprise. "Heavens, yes. How are you? We were all horrified when we heard about the attack. Thank God you're okay." Brandon got up and pulled a chair over by his desk before he sat back down to his meal.

He took a heaping bite of tabouli salad and motioned for her to sit. "You don't mind if I finish my lunch, do you? I have a class in a half hour and this is the first break I've had today."

"Please, go ahead. In fact, if you need me to, I can come back another time that's more convenient." The comforting idea of escape rose in her chest—maybe she'd put this off until another day after all.

"No, no. Go ahead. How can I help?"

She steeled herself inwardly and took the plunge. "During the attack, my camera was destroyed."

"That's awful." He took a gulp of his homemade smoothie from a canning jar. It filled the room with the aroma of peaches and ginger—how something dark green and lumpy could smell of peaches, she wasn't sure.

"Yes. Unfortunately, I don't have the money to replace it. I was wondering if I could borrow one of the school's cameras until I've done enough jobs to purchase a new one."

Brandon's lips pressed together and disappeared behind his full beard.

"That's not something I can make a decision on without the board's approval. You know we've had bad experiences in the past, and those cameras are for student use only. Their tuition goes to pay for the use and upkeep. You've seen the contracts we make them and their parents sign."

"Of course." Shannon's heart sank. She knew it was a longshot, but because it had taken so much out of her to even come and ask, she'd let her hopes rise. *Okay, God, now what?*

"Have you considered taking on more freelance work?"

"I have, but I can't if I don't have a camera. It's a catch twenty-two."

"Ah." Brandon continued to eat. "I might have an idea. The school needs a new brochure." He pulled a folder from a pile on his overcrowded desk. Several slips of paper fell out, along with sample brochures from several design companies.

"You know how to use layout software, right?"

"Yes. I'm not a commercial artist by any means, but I do make my own flyers for my showings and Amber's stuff. Rafe has employed me many times." Shannon pulled out her phone and flipped open a file that held photos of some of her posters before handing it to Brandon.

"These are good." He gave her phone back to her.

"Thanks."

Brandon made some notes and shuffled them all into the folder.

"I want something for this fall, something eye-catching and personal that shows how much we value our students and their families. We want to show the inclusiveness of our program, talk about scholarships and outreach to poorer students. Portland is growing, and I want to reach out into all avenues of our city in a new way."

"Have you considered doing a neighborhood party?"

"We haven't done one of those for years."

Shannon's mind started to reel. "What about an open house? We invite the neighborhood, sure, but also invite prominent families in the area. We could focus advertisements in districts that have recently cut their art programs. Really push the aspect of creating a well-rounded student in today's charged climate. Talk about the arts in relation to increasing emotional intelligence." Something else sparked in her mind. "What about an outreach for disabled students?"

"Now you're talking. You're hired."

"Seriously? How much were you willing to pay the others?" Shannon blanched at her own forwardness. Sometimes she could really put her foot in it. She was about to take it back when Brandon waved her off and smiled.

"You get a description and mockup of what you think you

can offer, do a fast layout and some quick pictures of what an art program for the disabled might look like, and I'll get it before the board this weekend. I put the bids of the others in there so you can see what that looks like. Frankly, I'd rather hire in-house for this anyway. You know me. You know my high expectations, but you also know we want to keep this authentic and available. It needs to be realistic, and these other places just didn't get it."

"Not only do I get it, I believe in it."

"Perfect." He put out his hand and shook Shannon's warmly. "Even if they don't go for the idea of expanding to specialty classes, I want us to look into that for the years to come. There are many children with autism and physical challenges who could benefit from our school—I don't want to lose that idea."

"I'll make sure to put an emphasis on that. Do you think you could give me any money up front once the board approves? I still won't be able to do the work if I don't have a good camera."

Brandon's eyes narrowed at her for a split second before he reached down next to his desk and unlocked the school safe. He lifted out a camera bag and handed it to her.

"This is mine. I want to loan it to you with the understanding that if anything happens to it..."

"It will be coming out of my check."

"For a long, long, long time." He chuckled, but she could hear and see the seriousness in his joke.

"Got it." She opened the brown faux-leather bag and looked inside at the camera. "Oh my gosh. Is that the Mark 5D?" Shannon's camera and lenses were worth a few thousand dollars, but the Mark 5D body alone started at three thousand dollars. The bag was full of lenses, batteries, a light meter, and flashes. "I don't think I can take this, Brandon."

"I know you can't. But you *can* borrow it. Show me what you're worth, Shannon. If you do a good job, I can make recommendations for you for other commercial projects. And feel free to use the camera for your personal use. The sooner you make enough money to replace your stuff, the sooner I get my camera back."

"I'll only do this if you create a contract between us. Make a tally of parts and pieces, and I'll sign it and agree to my responsibility." She handed the heavy camera bag back to Brandon.

Brandon nodded slowly in appreciation. "You are a person of high integrity, Shannon. Come back tomorrow after classes and I'll have the contract and the equipment ready."

Shannon left the school and headed to her car, relieved the meeting went better than she expected. She put the key in the ignition; her hand froze as she watched a group of kids cross the street at the light. One of the boys fell, and his parent picked him up and got him across before checking the crying child's knees just as the light changed and a speeding car zipped by where the boy had just been. Close call.

She remembered what it had taken for Amber's grandmother to have her driving privileges revoked. Several near misses and then hitting that tree. She'd clung to those keys harder than she had life. Even after she'd hit the tree. And children were precious to her. What if Shannon checked out and ran that light and hit that kid? A shudder coursed through her. She didn't dare drive.

She leaned back in the car, the heat from the sun beaming down on her, radiating from the black dashboard, stifling her. She turned the key and rolled down the window before turning it off again. Birds twittered in the trees lining the parking lot, the freeway nearby rushed with cars, sounding like a river at this distance. She could start taking the bus. Or Uber.

That didn't solve the problem she faced right then, though. How to get her car home, and how to get to her psychologist appointments.

If it had been two years ago, she'd call Amber. But Amber counted on her now. Well, until recently. She wiped a drip of sweat from her brow and stared at the dash, watching the mirage of heat lines warble the view through the windshield. She reached out and touched the dash, the heat tricking her skin, so it felt cold at first before the burn caught up with her nerve endings. She held it there for as long as she could and then pulled it away, feeling the relief. It refocused her mind.

"Well, now what?" She could leave her car in the lot and hope that no one would vandalize it before she could get it towed home.

There was a simpler answer, but she didn't want to consider it. Several solutions came to mind, and she dismissed them all. She'd have to do it, even though everything in her balked and told her to do anything but what she was about to do.

Shannon tugged her phone from her pocket and scrolled through her contacts before hitting the call icon.

Justin answered right away.

"Hey you. I haven't heard from you in a couple days. How are things going?"

She'd not told Justin what was going on with her head, her emotions, or Daniel. The subject of Daniel would have to wait. Right then it was all she could do to admit she needed his help.

"Things have been simpler."

"Are you okay?"

"Technically. I'm at the school."

"Me, too. Just finished my class."

"Did you drive?"

"No, I took my bike today. The chill this morning told me that the nice weather is about to end, and I wanted to get a good ride in after work."

Shoot. She didn't want to inconvenience him.

"Something wrong with your car?"

You could say that.

"Me. I'm what's wrong with my car."

"I don't get you."

"It's a long story."

A tapping on her car roof made her jump. Startled, she saw Justin waving down at her. He'd walked outside while they were talking.

"Bye."

"Bye," she responded to her phone and hung up, waving it helplessly at Justin.

"What's the deal?" He frowned. "Are you okay? You look done in."

She pressed her fingers to her temples, trying to gather her thoughts. Shannon didn't even know where to start—she just knew it was time to let Justin in a little bit more. Or a lot more.

"It's a long story."

Justin's eyes softened. "I'm available for a long story." He opened her door and put his hand out for her.

She took it.

CHAPTER 18

Justin and Shannon sat on the curb under a tall stand of eucalyptus trees at the edge of the parking lot. The medicinal aroma mixed with fall smells and reminded her of childhood colds and one particular foster mother who had been elderly and very kind. The wide green leaves clapped in the wind, like birds taking flight. The embankment behind them and the brush and trees created a quiet spot, isolated from the otherwise busy street.

She told him about the PTSD. She told him about seeing her counselor again. She shared about tuning out—but not all the details. He rested his crossed arms on his knees and listened to every word. Occasionally he'd look worried, but he didn't interrupt.

"That's it, really. The episodes catch me unaware, and I don't think I should be driving."

Justin tilted his head on his arms and looked thoughtfully at her, his aqua-colored eyes assessing her. She loved his eyes and the way a stripe of color in his hair matched them perfectly. They were like a calm, deep Pacific sea at the moment, but she'd seen them flash dark and stormy when he was protective of someone or sparkle like the waves with flecks of sun playing over the surface when excited about an idea. But always there was a kindness and a goodness there—his eyes were the first thing that attracted her to him. And right then, they were what told her she could tell it all to him, and her story—her very self—would be safe with him.

"When did this all start happening?"

She looked into his eyes again, weighing her options. Her hands were cold as she interlaced her fingers together. Was she really going to do this?

"I know it's hard for you to trust people. But I hope you know by now that you can trust me." Justin untangled her fingers and took her hand in his. The warmth enclosing her hands melted her misgivings.

"It's just really hard for me. It's not that I don't trust you." She stared out at the street and watched cars go by, and busy people on their way home after work. A man and a woman held hands and laughed together. They look so confident and comfortable.

"I don't know how to explain it. It's easy for me to take photos of people and reveal their emotions—it's not easy for me to share mine."

"If you're not ready, it's okay. I'm in no hurry. Just know that when you're ready I'm here."

Shannon leaned her head against Justin's shoulder wishing she could tell him everything, but for some reason the words stuck in her throat. They continued to sit next to each other in silence, as the traffic died down and the people thinned out. The sun began to set. She realized they'd been sitting there together for nearly two hours. She hadn't checked out. Instead, she'd been at peace for the first time in a long while.

"I grew up not trusting anyone."

"Except Amber." He whispered into her ear playfully.

"Right. Except Amber." She grinned. "I think when you grow up with someone like we did, it's easier. You know for sure they'll stick by you through it all because—"

"Because they have already."

"Exactly." She took a deep breath, readying herself for this next step in their relationship, but before she could start he changed the subject.

"Want to take a walk? I'm getting pretty hungry."

"Of course, you are. You haven't eaten for at least an hour." She jabbed her elbow in his ribs.

"Can I help it if I like food? I'm a growing boy." He patted his stomach. He ate more than anyone Shannon had ever seen—and he never seemed to gain a pound.

He stood up and pulled her to her feet. They kept holding hands as they crossed over the now-quiet intersection and headed to the waterfront. They stopped by a food cart and ordered fully loaded gyros and a couple blackberry kombuchas. They ate at a picnic table near the river while they watched the seagulls play on the wind and some kids with kites fighting the cross drafts. Clouds were rolling in for that storm Justin told her to expect, and the sunset cast an orange-red shadow.

Shannon had a few bites left of her gyro, but Justin was done.

"You full?" He motioned to her food, eyebrows up in hope.

"Back off. This is mine, dude." She knocked against him, and he put his hands up in surrender.

"I'm just checking."

"Your parents must have gone broke feeding you."

"My mamá knew how to cook masses of delectable Mexican food on a small budget. Still does." He smiled and closed his eyes.

"Are you dreaming of your mom's tamales right now? After you've woofed down your extra-large gyro and begged for mine?"

"If you ever came over for Sunday dinner, you'd be dreaming of her tamales, too. Or her sopes con carne topped with tomatillos, homemade pickled carrots and crema. Mmm." She watched his expression shift to one of bliss. Justin's gastric track had moved him into another dimension.

Shannon felt the dig about Sunday dinner. He'd asked her to family dinner on more than one occasion, but spending time with his family would take their relationship to a level she didn't want yet. Yet? She used to think never. Maybe after today...maybe after today the decision would be made.

"Next time buy two for yourself." She took a huge bite and made appreciative noises. "Mmm."

Justin's stomach growled loudly, and Shannon burst out laughing at him. He grinned in embarrassment.

"See? Proof. I'm not a glutton, I'm just starving."

Shannon glanced around and saw an ice cream cart. "Want a scoop?"

"Triple please. And toppings."

"Sheesh, man." She nudged his shoulder.

He shrugged, helpless.

They decided on sundaes—his ginormous with every topping, and hers one scoop with hot fudge and whipped cream. Amber always accused *her* of having a bottomless pit, but she'd never seen this side of Justin.

"Hey, I figure you need to know what you're really getting into here." He laughed.

"Like needing an additional job just to keep you fed?"

His eyes twinkled in triumph, and she felt the barriers she put on their relationship crumbling.

They turned back to their table, but the kids had taken their spot to work on their kites, so they found a place on the grass.

"Thanks for all of this." Shannon spoke after a long time.

"It's good food."

She laughed. "I mean, the listening ear. And also for being my backup driver. I'll need a lift to my psych appointments." The last two words came out in a whisper, afraid he'd hear and run, but equally hopeful that he'd stay.

"Just get me your schedule. It's seriously no problem. I can hang in the waiting room." He studied her face and must have seen her fear. "Or not."

"Sometimes I'm not really ready to chat after I see her. It's all hard things."

He frowned. "I know I'm distant from all that. I had both my parents. I wasn't tossed around in foster care."

"You never lived on the streets or had a dad with bipolar," she volunteered. *Baby steps.*

Justin went very still. "No. I didn't. But my mom's parents were a train wreck. That's why we live out here away from family. I guess listening to her stories gave me a foundation to listen to other people's."

He'd never mentioned that before.

"No one in the family understood it because my grandparents put on a good show for the neighbors and everyone—keeping up appearances and all that. You know how tight family is in my culture. It was horribly hard to leave. But my grandpa was an abusive drunk at home, and my folks never wanted me exposed to that. So, it meant having everyone else in the family treat us like the bad guys. Being on our own for holidays. Making friends our family."

"Sorry."

"It is what it is, right?"

"Right."

"I figure God works stuff like that out and it changes us."

"Or ruins us." Where had that come from?

"You really believe that?"

"No. Not really. I think if we give over the hard things to God, He can use it to shape us, and then we can help other people. Nothing is wasted if we give it to God."

He kept his eyes focused on her. "But sometimes it's hard to understand why He lets it happen in the first place?"

"Yeah. Sometimes." She'd trusted God through so much, she didn't often let her mind go there. But on occasion, it couldn't be helped. She knew God could do anything. He was all powerful—and He was entirely good. Why didn't He make her dad behave, or keep her from being hurt?

"I try to remember that God loves the people that hurt us just as much as He loves us. We're all broken on some level because of sin in the world. I don't think I'd want to be made a puppet any more than He'd like a puppet of His creation worshipping Him because He forced them to."

She looked down at her melting ice cream. The chocolate was pooling with the other toppings and making mud. "Big thoughts." She swirled the mud together.

"Sorry."

Shannon reached out and put her hand on his arm. "No, it's okay. I've never doubted God loved me, or that He was with me. And I don't get why my parents had to be the way they were. I guess someday I'll be with Jesus face-to-face and then I'll see clearly. But I do find myself wondering what my life could have been."

"I'll be praying for you about that." He put his hand over hers.

When Justin said that, it wasn't like when other people said it as a way to end an uncomfortable conversation. Instead, he meant it. Every word. They sat in quiet again, watching the sun finish its descent. A few homeless people wavered by, asking for change. Justin pulled a couple supply kits from his backpack and gave it to them. One was grumpy, the other appreciative.

"Did I tell you my dad is in town?" What a way to break *that* into their conversation.

"No. Is that a good thing?" Justin didn't jump to the positive and this gave her confidence to continue.

"I don't know yet."

"Is he staying with friends?"

"Funny story, that. Have you seen that homeless guy that lives by the church where Amber has her support group?"

"Yeah. Maggie gives him coffee and donuts. I told her that's risky, he might feel like she's becoming more familiar and trespass, but she said he's harmless."

"He is, pretty much. As long as you're not depending on him to raise you."

Justin's eye color darkened to where she couldn't see his pupils. "This man is your father?"

"Good old dad." She shrugged and looked down at her sundae.

"Are you going to find him a bed at the shelter?"

"I'm preparing to move him into an apartment to get him off the street. I've already signed a lease. I just have to get him there."

"Just tell him. He'll be glad to be off the streets for a while."

"You'd think so."

"What does that mean?"

"In order to stay off the streets, he's got to take his meds, clean up, get sober, and get a job. He's never cared enough about anyone or anything to do that before." *Not even me.*

"Maybe he's changed?"

Shannon chuckled lightly. "*Maybe they'll change.* Do you think there is any other sentence so overused as that one?" She saw his countenance fall. "I don't mean to be a downer. I've waited my whole life for that sentence to be true. Just once. About anyone."

"You don't think people can change?"

"I think they, with the help of God, have the capacity to change. Do I have a lot of evidence of that happening? No."

"Then why help?"

"Why help what?"

"Why spend all those hours on the street taking photos of the downtrodden, handing out packets, reaching the hurting?"

"Because it's my job as a Christ follower to care for the suffering. What they do with that care is up to them."

"Does your dad know about the apartment yet?"

"No. He doesn't even know who I am."

"Once you tell him, you'll see, he'll change."

Justin, forever the optimist.

"I'm not going to tell him."

Justin's eyes narrowed at her in confusion.

And this was where they were going to have a problem. Because she wasn't going to tell Daniel who she was. If he wanted to change, he needed to do it for himself. She wasn't going to risk being hurt. Not ever again.

CHAPTER 19

The coffee shop wasn't as busy as it normally was. Many tables were open, so Shannon chose one close to the front for Maggie to be able to find her easier. At least, that was how Amber liked it. Shannon figured like mother, like daughter. The lack of customers also made it quieter, and Shannon needed peace. After trying to explain her stance to Justin for over an hour, and having given up, she felt worn—like she'd run a race uphill for days. Her arms and legs ached inside, and fatigue wore on her like sandpaper over a rough piece of wood.

Maggie Floros entered wearing her cheerful expression and optimistic energy, tapping her white cane along the floor, searching for counter bases and table legs. Shannon got up with the intention of guiding her over to her spot.

Maggie called toward the counter, "Kalimera, barista." Shannon smiled at her Greek greeting.

"Morning, Mrs. Floros."

"Ya, Krista. How does the day treat you?"

"We're doing well. How about you?"

"As good as can be expected." Maggie's eyes crinkled.

"Triple shot bitter mocha with whipped?"

"Perfect. Also, a cookie." Maggie pronounced cookie like cookey, making Shannon giggle.

"The regular for Mrs. Floros," called Krista.

Maggie turned toward Shannon. "I know that laugh. Greetings, sweet Shannon." Maggie reached out, and Shannon took her hand.

"Good morning. Thanks for meeting with me."

"We don't have many moments together, do we? Amber usually leads the conversation. I'm glad to have some time to chat."

Shannon led Maggie by the arm to their table. Maggie felt for the chair and the table top with her hands, tracing the outline and the top like a craftsman searching for blemishes, before folding her cane and taking a seat with a peaceful smile on her face. Maggie seemed unflappable and exuded a warmth that always put everyone around her at ease.

Shannon didn't know how she did it, losing her husband and her sight so soon after arriving in the US and then losing her daughter to state custody. But instead of being crushed, she flourished. And now God had brought Amber and Maggie back together again.

Justin's words of advice from the day before echoed in her ears. She needed to ask Maggie what she thought of Daniel's condition and moving him to an apartment. Not that Maggie was an expert on the homeless, but she was an expert in dealing with the brokenhearted as a blindness support group leader. And Daniel was practically living at the church right then.

The barista brought over Maggie's order. "Here you go, my dear."

Maggie beamed. "Smells wonderful. Thank you." Krista laid her coffee at twelve o'clock and her plate of cookies at three. She put a stack of napkins at nine.

Shannon knew the drill but was impressed with the care being shown. Krista saw her watching her and offered an explanation.

"My mom's blind. That's how Maggie and I met."

"She takes very good care of me." Maggie patted Krista's arm and Krista squeezed Maggie's hand in thanks. Then Maggie turned her attention back to Shannon.

"Well now. Did you get a coffee?"

"Yes. I'm enjoying it with a bagel and cream cheese."

"Oh. I love the cream cheese."

Shannon had to grin at how she'd surrounded herself by people who loved food as much as they loved life.

"I suspect you've got something on your mind, yes?"

Maggie was like her daughter, not much for small talk. They liked conversations of purpose.

"Actually, I do. You know that man who squats outside the church meeting hall where you hold your support meetings?"

"Ya, Daniel. Such a kind man. Confused sometimes, though. Probably from low blood sugar. Much heartbreak in his story."

Shannon didn't respond to the latter part. "Yes, that's him." She wasn't sure how to proceed. Amber would eventually confide in Maggie about Daniel because of her worry. She might as well get it out there.

"I'm worried about him. He doesn't look good."

"Ah, no. Most of the homeless don't." Maggie was waiting, her face expectant. "What makes him a special case, though? I like him very much, but I'm not sure anything I do will change his circumstances. Although, donuts and coffee, and a bath and clean clothes have done much to improve his current condition and made him more pleasant to be around."

"You got him a bath and clean clothes?"

"The church has an old shower in the basement he's used several times, and I went to the thrift store and found him some clothes. I washed his sleeping bag and got him a water bottle." Tears filled Maggie's eyes. "He's had a rough time."

Guilt filled Shannon. Maggie had done more for her father than she had. Until now. And she seemed to have chatted with him enough to know a bit of his story.

"Do you think he'd be averse to having a place to live?" Shannon knew full well that many homeless believed they were safer and better off on the streets. They felt like it gave them control over their situation. It was backward thinking, but it made sense to them.

"No. Not at all. I've asked the church if they know of anyone with a room, but it's very hard to trust a stranger in your home."

"I've gotten him an apartment."

Maggie sat up, expression alert. "That's going the extra mile for your fellow man, for certain. If you don't mind me asking, why does Daniel rate so high? I've not known you to speak to him save one time. By the way—" She grinned, nodding in approval—"he's spoken of nothing than the beautiful girl who gave him a hamburger. From his description, was it you?"

Shannon's stomach roiled, and she felt like her bagel was reassembling itself in her digestive tract. One bit of the story would demand the rest be told, like taking one step on a steep hill of gravel and sliding all the way to the bottom before you knew what was happening.

"Daniel is my father."

Maggie's face showed shock and surprise.

True to her word, it was clear Amber hadn't said a word.

"He doesn't recognize you? He often talks of his wife and child."

"No. He hasn't seen me since I was ten. He was arrested for neglect, and I was taken by social services for the last time." It'd been two months after the arcade incident. Daniel had actually tried for a couple weeks. He'd found odd jobs and bought groceries, paid the water and electricity bill... But then his depression hit, and he turned to his old solace–drugs. He'd disappear for days at a time, leaving Shannon in terror that the bad man would return.

Her mind clicked like someone putting a new round-reel into a View-Master, and she was lost in a memory.

She spent the days at school, teased for not having lunch—she'd say she'd eaten it already—or for having dirty hair. She tried to use dishwashing soap for laundry and shampoo, but it wasn't as effective as she'd hoped, and it gave her terrible dandruff.

She went to the office and asked to be added to the free lunch program, but the woman said she needed her parent's signature on a form. She'd forged her father's signature, but they had it on record from registration and told her she shouldn't lie and steal food from those that really needed it.

Tears filled Shannon's eyes as she looked at the school secretary. "But I do need it."

"Then have your *father* sign the slip." The older woman held out the form again. "Bring it back tomorrow—signed properly." The woman crossed her arms, waiting for Shannon to leave.

Shannon spied the teacher's lounge through an open doorway and saw a cake and some other baked goods as well as apples. Her mouth watered.

"Yes, ma'am." Shannon turned to go, and the secretary went to answer the phone on the other side of the counter. Shannon ducked low and slid into the lounge. The room was empty. An honor box sat on the table, full of money for donating to one of the teachers on maternity leave to get her a present. Shannon thought of the water bill, soon to be turned off, and scooped the money up and stuffed it in her pocket. Then she slipped the bread and some apples into her jacket, zipping it tight. Her fingers shook with guilt, but the will to survive had overridden her morals in the moment.

Instead of leaving by the office door, she headed to the window on the other side of the room, opened it, and looked down. It was only six feet, but it felt higher. She pushed a chair over to the opening and was about to drop down when she saw the refrigerator. She glanced at the clock, hoping no one would come, then opened the fridge. Inside was a container of milk. It'd been so long since she'd had any that she gasped at the sight. She opened her purple backpack and slipped it inside. She grabbed several people's sandwiches and a container of margarine. The lunch bell sounded, and she knew she only had seconds before she'd be found.

Her heart pounded as she reached the window, climbing onto

the chair once more. She put one leg over the edge and then the other and lowered herself down. Except, she couldn't. Her backpack was lodged against the window catch, leaving her legs dangling.

Kids passed by the door in the hall and she heard noises in the office. The teachers would be in there any second. She pushed and pulled and shifted. The door opened, and two teachers entered, arguing about testing results. Shannon's heart raced as she gave one more push.

Like the piece of meat that shot out of a choking man's mouth she'd seen in a movie, Shannon shot from between the window panes and landed with a thud on the ground outside. Her ankle twisted under her and she fell into the rosebushes, hiding her from the cars driving by.

"Ow." Thorns snagged at her hands and face and tangled her hair, and her ankle screamed with pain. She shifted and rolled out, leaving long scratches on her cheeks. Little drips of blood rolled down onto her jacket. She looked up at a grating sound and saw a teacher close the window, all the while complaining about where the banana bread had gone.

Shannon held her breath and sat as still as possible. Cars whizzed by, and older students walked down the sidewalk to the corner store. She pushed herself along the school building until she was completely hidden behind bushes. She'd wait until the school bell rang and the kids went back to their classes.

She took stock of her injuries and felt a wetness seeping across her back. Slipping off the backpack, she saw that the milk container lid had popped off when she landed on her back. She dug around the bottom of the milky bag, found the lid and secured it back atop the container. Looking inside, she bemoaned the loss of several glasses of milk. She quickly decided she couldn't salvage any from inside her dirty pack. Instead she turned it upside down and let the contents soak the ground. Her binder, books, and homework were saturated.

"Why?" her voice croaked softly with emotion. She choked back her tears of frustration. Just as her emotions were about to get the best of her, she heard shouting and the words, "We should call the police."

They must have noticed the money was gone. And maybe the food. She realized she hadn't the time to wait until lunch was back in. She took a corner of her shirt and spat on it before wiping the blood from her face. Then she pulled up her hoody, secured her pack and waited in between stragglers and climbed from the bushes. She crossed the street and darted in and out of pods of kids walking back from the store, eating candy bars and drinking soda—two items she considered delicacies. Her ankle burned, but she didn't dare limp or draw any sort of attention to herself.

She kept her head down and walked up alleys, ignoring the barking dogs. After fifteen minutes, she snuck in the back gate of her yard so no one would see her enter her house. Then she unlocked the back door, locked it behind her, and sank to the kitchen floor.

Her shoe felt tight, so she slipped out of it and peeled off her milk-soaked sock. The skin was purple and swollen by the bone, but when she flexed it, it didn't grind or cause her extreme pain. Probably a sprain. She took off all her clothes and dropped them in the washer. She used a bit of dish soap and started the load that had been building for the past week. Then she hopped up the stairs and decided to take a bath. Under the bathroom sink, alongside a partially empty first aid kit, was a bag of Epsom salts—crusty and solid. It must have gotten wet from the leaky pipe under there, because it was in a mass of sticky crystals. She hit it with the palm of her hand and loosened some, dumping it in the water. Then she sank down and soaked until the water went cold then bathed with the dish soap. How she missed shampoo and regular soap!

After she dried off, she pulled on some sweats and one of her dad's T-shirts. She sat on the steps of the stairs and let herself down one at a time, like a toddler. Then she hopped to the freezer and pulled out the ice tray. Most were evaporated, but she got enough to wrap in a towel and put on her ankle. She refilled the tray, returned it to the freezer, and sat on the couch, going through the food.

Taking the lid off the milk carton, she gulped down four big swigs and then put the lid back on. "Gotta save that." She took the plastic wrap off the banana bread and broke off a few bites. She wanted to eat the whole thing, but knew she'd probably throw up if she did. There were cookies and donuts as well. After the milk spill, she was doubly glad she hadn't grabbed the cake—as tempting as it was—because her books would have been covered in frosting as well.

Once the ice melted, her ankle felt a little better. She tried to wrap the cold towel around it, but it wouldn't stay tight. Then she stashed the food she'd taken inside her fridge. Each sandwich and piece of fruit brought a new wave of tears. She hated stealing. She hated that her father had left her to this. She was beginning to hate Daniel.

"Shannon?"

Shannon shook herself and rubbed her eyes. Maggie was patting her hand, worry in every feature of her face.

"What?"

"Oh, my. I thought maybe you'd had a stroke. Are you okay?"

"Yes. Yes, I'm fine." Shannon looked around and realized she'd gained the baristas' attention as well as a few other patrons.

Krista came over. "Do you need me to call an ambulance?"

Shannon's face went hot. "No, I'm fine. Just a little tired." Krista looked at her like she didn't believe her.

"Is your blood sugar low?"

"No." Shannon held up the remaining bite of bagel. "I'm okay. Really. No worries."

As Krista walked away, Maggie leaned closer. "What was that?" She took Shannon's hand and the warmth from her skin seeped in and comforted her.

"I'm having PTSD episodes. It's not like panic attacks or anything, I just get drawn into a memory and get stuck. Like the hook of an old song rolling through your head at 2 A.M."

"Like watching a movie, but you become the actor?"

"Yes. Yes, exactly. Have you ever experienced that?"

"One time. After they took my Amber away. I couldn't sleep without her in the house, and my mind would bring her to me. It only happened for about a month." Her mouth creased. "I wished it stayed, though. I missed her so much."

Shannon squeezed Maggie's hand back. "I'm seeing someone about it."

"Good. Does Amber know?"

"Yes. And Justin. He's going to be giving me rides if I need it. I don't feel—" Shannon took a deep breath, having trouble admitting it—"safe. I don't feel safe."

"If there's anything I can do, please let me know."

"I will."

"Back to the matter at hand. Your father? I think he would like an apartment very, very much. I've been talking to a counselor at the church, and they know a drug program he could get into, too. But he claims to be clean. It doesn't explain his episodes, though."

"He's bipolar and possibly schizophrenic. He's never been willing to take his meds. He used to medicate through other means."

"They'll help him manage that. But they weren't willing to take a chance on him if he didn't have a regular place to stay. Since he'll be living with you, I think they'll go for it."

"No."

"What do you mean by no?" Maggie drew back.

"Daniel isn't going to be living with me. And I don't want to help him in any other way." Shannon's voice went cold.

"I don't understand. With you back in his life, he might have a chance."

"I've arranged an apartment, but I don't want to be in his life."

"But surely you'll tell him who you are."

"I won't. And I don't want you to, either. Promise me that, or I'll tear up the lease and he can stay right where he is." Shannon's voice was hard.

"My dear, you don't mean that."

Shannon's jaw clenched. "I do. Trust me. If you can't promise me this, then I'll walk out of here right now."

Maggie sank back in her chair, clearly upset. "You need to forgive him, my child."

"You have no idea what a hell that man made my childhood— my life. What I had to survive." Shannon choked on her words. "I don't want him to suffer, but I don't want to be part of his life ever again."

"Ah." Maggie's eyes teared. "I'm so sorry."

"Don't be sorry for me. And don't be sorry for him. He's done this to himself. He's driven everyone who ever loved him away. He could have had a wife and a family. But he was too selfish. I won't be put in that position ever again, Maggie." Shannon got to her feet. "I need you to respect my choices in this matter, or he'll stay on that corner until he's driven off by the weather." The harshness in her tone shook her. Until that moment, she didn't have any clue how angry she was. Not really. All her altruistic feelings vanished. She'd made a huge mistake taking pity on Daniel. She'd let her guilt get the better of her.

Her guilt? What did she have to be guilty of in the first place? Surviving?

Because that's all she'd done. She'd just survived until she reached adulthood. Until she'd aged out. And now?

Now she wasn't going to ever let him put her in that situation again.

"Promise me."

Maggie pursed her lips. "Very well. I don't approve, but his safety outweighs my disapproval."

"Good."

CHAPTER 20

S hannon sat at a café's outdoor table, down the street from the church where Maggie's group met and where Daniel was camped. His tarp took up a larger area now. He'd obviously been collecting items. In the three hours she'd sat here, he'd been given money, a bottle of water, clothing, and a blanket from a passionate youth group canvassing the downtown.

He stood and stretched, then nearly fell over. He was probably drunk or strung out, but for some reason that didn't keep people from feeling sorry for him. He'd been charming and handsome when she was a girl. He probably still was.

Customers came and went, the sun dipped below the rooflines of the businesses across the street, and a chill filled the air. People moved inside, and still she sat. The cool of the metal chair made her shiver. Glancing at her watch, she saw it was nearing five. Daniel moved to the church and knocked on the door. Maggie opened it and let him inside.

Thirty minutes later, Daniel emerged carrying a donut and a thermos.

Her reasons for finding him a home dissipated. He was warm enough, and fed. For someone living on the street, he had a pretty good gig. He leaned down to put his thermos on the ground and toppled over into his tarp.

Shannon gasped, jumped up, and ran down the block, across the street and came upon Daniel wrestling with the plastic. Instead of worried, though, he was laughing.

"Are you okay, Da...mister?" She pulled back the blue crinkly sheet.

"Been better." He chuckled. "It's awful getting old. Arthritis." He rolled to a sitting position and looked up at her with his startling clear eyes. The haze of the month before had cleared.

"You're the hamburger girl." His scraggily, bearded face changed from wary to warm. He put out a shaking hand.

She didn't take it. "I was passing by again."

"I'm glad you did. That hamburger? Saved my life. It was the first decent food I'd had in ages."

"Dumpster diving not meeting your nutritional needs?"

He drew back as if she'd burned him.

"No. I expect not. Thank you."

Her anger subsided. She needed to get this over with. As soon as he was settled, she'd know where he was, and maybe her memories would back off without the threat of coming across him unexpectedly. "I've been thinking about you, too."

"You have?"

"You remind me of someone." *Don't go too far, Shannon.*

"Father, grandfather, brother?"

"That doesn't matter. He's been gone a long time. But I found an apartment the other day that's looking to lease to a hardship case. Are you interested?"

Daniel rubbed his scruffy chin in thought. "You mean leave all this?" He waved a hand over his belongings with an air of sarcasm. "That's a hard one."

Shannon couldn't wrap her mind around this joking version of her father. "Is that a yes?"

"What do I have to do?"

"Stay off drugs and look for work."

"Done."

"Really?" She couldn't hide the skepticism her in voice.

"Sure. I actually have been drug-free for quite a while. Years."

That didn't sound right to Shannon. "You seemed pretty out of it the last time I was here."

"Diabetes. I'd been living on donuts. Beggars quite literally cannot be choosers—sometimes hunger gets the best of me. Can't afford medication, so it makes things very, very tricky."

"Diabetes? I didn't know you had that."

His brows furrowed. "It's hard to tell from appearances. Like I said, that burger saved my life. Not living on the street would go a long way to extending my life, too. I'll take it. Can we go now?"

Agitated by this unexpected turn of events, Shannon took a step back. "Now?"

"No time like the present."

Her mind rushed. "Um. Okay. Let me call a friend for a ride." She pulled out her phone and dialed Justin, turning away to keep the conversation private while Daniel gathered his things with deft speed.

"Daniel is ready to move now. I'm so sorry to ask this, but could you come and pick us up?"

"Absolutely. Are you at the church?"

"Yes. I'm so sorry to trouble you."

"It's okay. Does he know?"

"Know what?" Shannon looked over her shoulder and watched Daniel roll up his tarp. Everything else was already stashed in black plastic bags, near to capacity. Her eyes locked on those bags, and her mind flashed to every time she'd been moved from one place to another. She'd always had her backpack, the only thing she had left from being with Daniel. But that didn't hold all she had. She had a pillow from an outreach group and three pillowcases. She had four sets of clothes, six pairs of panties and socks, and two books. Her toothbrush, hairbrush, and school books took up her backpack. And her go-bag.

Her hands started stuffing her belongings in the bag, and she heard someone call her name.

"Shannon?" Justin yelled into her ear. She jerked the phone away and stared at her other hand—empty.

"You okay there, miss?" Daniel was standing in front of her, concern etching his weathered face.

"Yes. I'm fine. Sorry." She put the phone back up to her ear. "Sorry, Justin. Yes, we're in front of the church. We'll see you in a minute."

She tucked her phone back in her pocket.

Daniel eyed her. "You sure?"

His concerned tone was the one she remembered from his good days so long ago. It tugged at her heart, but she shoved the emotion away. "Yes. Of course. You ready to go?"

"I want to go tell Maggie where I'm going. Do I have an address?" He gave her a charming grin. She didn't return it.

Shannon pulled a slip of paper out of her pocket and wrote the address on it. "I'll go with you." Following Daniel into the church, she tried to shake herself to the present entirely. The memories seemed to reach out with a growing ferocity, pulling her into a crevasse. It was happening more and more frequently, as if no part of her life was off limits.

"Maggie?" Daniel called, and Maggie came out of her office. She'd been hired in the past few months as an organizer as well as the support group counselor. This church really walked the walk.

"Hi, there. Hi, Daniel."

"This young lady has a place for me to live. Come to think of it, I don't think I know your name." He looked at Shannon expectantly.

She didn't think to lie. "Shannon."

Daniel went still and then his eyes searched her face. Shannon could play poker with the best of them and revealed nothing. Even so, a tiny part of her heart hoped he'd recognize her. He didn't.

"This young lady, Shannon, has found a place for me to stay."

"Isn't that wonderful?" Maggie's tone sounded oddly expectant to Shannon, but Daniel didn't seem to notice.

"Are you ready to go?" Shannon didn't want to stay any longer than she had to.

"Yep. Just wanted Maggie here to know I wasn't kidnapped."

"Of course. There's no phone at this time."

Daniel read the address to Maggie.

"Oh, that's not too far."

Shannon interrupted. "I'll arrange a cell with a prepaid card for him. And I'll make sure he gets clothes for interviews. If you hear of any jobs in the area, please let me know."

"I'll be glad to." Maggie patted Daniel on the shoulder. "I'll miss your company."

"I'll be around. I can assure you." Daniel's voice was thick with intentions, and it startled Shannon. She'd not realized he might have begun to care for Maggie as more than a source of food. Maggie's smile radiated toward him. Could it be mutual? She hoped Maggie knew what she was getting involved in.

They went outside, and Justin was already loading the back of his car with Daniel's things.

Daniel put out a hand. "I'm Daniel."

Justin took it. "I'm Justin."

"Is Shannon here your girl?"

Before Shannon could interrupt, Justin answered. "Indeed. Although I can't quite convince her of that yet." He winked and kept loading. Daniel helped, and before long they were on the road, heading east.

Within ten minutes, they'd arrived. Daniel climbed out of the car and looked around. A strange, worried expression crossed his face.

"Everything okay?" Shannon questioned.

"I've been here before." His voice implied he was uneasy.

"Huh." Shannon acted as if it didn't matter and led them to the door and up the stairs. "This will be your place. The manager is number two. You can't use, drink, or party. If you do, he'll kick you out. You need to find employment fast." For his sake as well as hers.

She unlocked the door to number three and flipped the lights on inside the one-room flat. Daniel took a deep breath and smiled, apparently pleased with what he saw.

"New paint." He went over and opened the fridge and found it empty.

"We'll go shopping in a bit here and get you set up." She opened the cabinets and saw they were pretty dusty inside. The floor wasn't all that clean, either. When she'd first seen it, it had appeared clean—but maybe that was because she'd been comparing it to the streets.

She'd buy cleaning supplies, too.

Daniel rummaged through his things that Justin had just brought up and pulled out donuts and three sandwiches and stashed them in the fridge. Then he tried the tap at the kitchen sink and entered the bathroom. "Just a shower and toilet in here?"

"Yes, you'll use the sink out here to wash up."

"Fine by me." He sat on the bed. "Don't know if I'll sleep too well on this. I'm used to the ground or the brick-hard mattresses of the shelters." He bounced, and the springs under the mattress groaned.

"I'm going to head to the store, and you can unpack. What size are you?"

"It'd be more fun to go shopping together, don't you think?"

Shannon's nerves went on alert. She opened and closed her mouth trying to find the words. She needed a moment to collect herself. Justin put a hand on her arm, calming her. How he knew she needed it, she didn't know. Maybe the wide-eyed look of fear in her eyes? She swallowed down her emotions and took a shaky breath.

"I'll take you. We'll drop Shannon off at her place," said Justin.

Adrenalin shot through her. She didn't want Daniel knowing where she lived.

"That's okay. I'm going to go for a walk." She handed a prepaid debit card to Justin. "The pin is 2345. You keep the card with *you.*"

Justin looked at her questioningly but took the card. "Got it."

She put her hand out to Daniel. "I hope this works out for you."

"I'm sure it will. This is within walking distance of the church and there's the emergency grocer downstairs. I'm sure I'll be able to find work pretty fast once I'm cleaned up."

"Why don't you grab a shower before heading out?" Shannon suggested.

"I'll do that. Won't you change your mind and come with us? Please?" Daniel graced her with another charming smile. It would have been more charming if his teeth weren't stained and rotting. They looked painful. She ached inside, empathy getting the better of her.

"Yeah, it'll be fun." Justin begged. He could see her weakness like no other. It made her uneasy.

Shannon agreed and sat down helplessly at the two-seater laminate table, her legs leaden with emotional exhaustion.

Daniel grabbed one of the black bags and dumped his things out, collected a few items—including a towel and washcloth that looked newer—and headed toward the bathroom. Shannon remembered something she'd brought along.

"Just a second." She dug into her purse and pulled out a travel bag and handed it to him.

Daniel unzipped it. "Hey, there's toothpaste, toothbrush, razor, shaving cream, and soap." His voice was one of pleased surprise, like a boy on his birthday. He gave her an award-winning wink as he headed into the bathroom.

It was all she could do not to smile back.

Justin joined her at the table. They could hear Daniel singing in the shower.

"You've made him really happy." He took her hand. "You really impress me, you know that?"

Shannon's eyes teared up and she wiped them away, pretending to rub them from tiredness.

"I figure if I'd do it for a stranger, then why shouldn't I do it for him?" There was so much more than that. Layers of complicated emotions. Her doctor was going to want details and motivations. Right then, she didn't know herself why this was so important.

"I'm glad you've forgiven him."

Shannon gave him a sharp look. "I haven't. He doesn't know who I am, and I don't want him to. This isn't about what he needs. It's about what I need."

He frowned. "And what is that?"

"When I figure it out, I'll let you know." She pulled her hand from his and clasped her fingers together in her lap.

"You checked out when you were talking to me on the phone, didn't you? It's getting worse, isn't it?" He tipped his head in a way that reminded her of a puppy, and it usually melted her heart. She was tempted to lie, but if Justin was signing up for this gig, she didn't want any of it built on lies. Lies only ate away and destroyed at the base, and no matter how good the rest of the structure was, it would get too heavy for the false foundation and crumble into a mass of sharp concrete, rebar, and choking dust. There was no coming back from that.

"Yes."

"Does Amber know?"

"I haven't talked to her in a couple days. Ethan is back in town, and they are struggling." Amber had enough on her plate. At least, that's what she told herself. Part of her didn't want to admit to Amber how low things had sunk. She knew Amber would drop everything and be there for her—but Shannon was used to being the strong one. Admitting any weakness—

"I've been praying for you. My parents are praying for you."

Shannon's head shot up in panic. "What do you mean? What did you tell them?"

Justin put up his hands. "Just that you are going through a difficult time." He put a hand on her shoulder. "I would never betray your trust. Ever."

Her heart rate started to return to normal. "Okay. Thank you." She really needed to meet Justin's parents.

"They want you to come over for dinner soon."

"Soon?"

Justin's brown skin darkened on his cheeks. He was so cute when embarrassed. He ran a hand over his spiky hair.

"My mamá said Sunday would be good." His voice lilted, and his eyes widened like a hopeful little boy.

She sighed aloud, feeling backed into a corner. In truth, his parents did sound pretty amazing.

"Okay."

"Really?" He sat up straight, excitement lighting his face.

"Really."

Moments later, Daniel opened the bathroom door. Before them stood a different man. Clean shaven, except for the mustache that was now nicely groomed. He had on a blue T-shirt and a pair of stained, but clean, jeans. He brushed back his hair in a slick and tied it back with a rubber band.

"I could use a haircut, but hopefully I look presentable now?"

"I have an excellent barber. You'd look good with a prohibition cut." Justin waved his hand around his head as if he held a razor.

Daniel laughed aloud. "Perfect. In every way." Then he rubbed a finger over his teeth. "They sure are squeaky, even if they don't look so good." Behind him, he'd cleaned up his dirty clothes and hung up his towel.

"We need to make you an appointment with a dentist. First we'll get you on the Oregon Health Plan and then we'll track down a dentist."

Daniel grimaced. "I don't remember the last time I saw one. A couple got so bad this year that I pulled them out myself." He gave them a pained smile, and Shannon's mouth ached in sympathy. "I think the last time was before they took my daughter from me."

Neither of them said anything to this offered information.

"I made sure she went in a few times, but then it got to be too expensive. And I lost my job. And then they stole her from me." He looked at them, but didn't see them, his eyes were in the past. She knew the look.

"Well, it's going to take time to remake this man, but I'm well on my way. You two ready to go?"

Shannon saw the grin on Justin's face as he nodded. He was falling for her dad. It was easy to do. Daniel was kind and jovial when he was on the upswing—the manic part of his illness. It was the ensuing downswing Shannon needed to brace herself for. A little voice in her head said maybe things would be different this time.

That voice needed to shut up.

CHAPTER 21

Shannon watched Daniel and Justin choose bedding and curtains from three aisles away in the Goodwill store. They were laughing together, holding up avocado and burgundy paisley sheets, matching comforter, and curtains. A niggle of jealousy ran through her. Justin could be so easy with her dad, but he didn't know Daniel like she did. He didn't have the damage. He'd never been let down by him. Yet. The other shoe would certainly drop, and she'd have to pick up the pieces. As always. All her warnings about Daniel fell on deaf ears.

The last thing she wanted in her life was Daniel. To even be in his vicinity put her in run mode. And yet, here she was. She pushed the cart to the cooking aisle to pick out some decent pans and dinnerware. She found some casserole dishes, matching plates, and a few sets of silverware. She piled in four glasses and some mugs. Then she chose a coffee maker that had an IT WORKS sticker on it. At least something still did.

Heading to the electronics aisle, she found a couple power strips and two lamps. It reminded her of prepping for college. All the other girls in her dorm had new things, bought by parents who lavished them with trips to Ikea and Bed, Bath & Beyond—not the secondhand, stained things she brought with her. Or the hand-me-down dictionary and thesaurus with dog-eared corners she traded old novels in for at the used bookstore. All her money from working went to film and photo developing fees. She couldn't afford to play-act with her classmates. This wasn't a filler of time, an excuse to party, or a place to get her MRS degree. This was her life and her future—and the only chance she'd get at a college education. She'd earned it in scholarships and late nights studying past all the challenges she faced in her foster homes. Camped out in the library until they'd kick her out, and then moving to coffee shops until they'd closed. And then moving to 24-hour diners, eating fried zucchini and drinking copious cups of coffee. There was a Denny's and a Shari's with wait staff whom looked kindly on her and didn't mind her taking up one of their normally empty booths.

She moved down the row of secondhand microwaves, deciding against them, and onto rugs, then brooms and a mop and newly massed packs of sponges someone must have donated from an overstock store. She could still hear them laughing. It rankled her. Justin loved easily.

Wasn't that what attracted her to Justin? He used to say the same thing about her. She used to believe it. Didn't she take up the underdog's plight? But those underdogs were strangers. Shannon had no backstory with them. They were old creatures in a new light, a clean slate between them. Danie,l on the other hand...

Shannon's mind skipped off, pulling her along like a child dragging an adult to their favorite play spot. But this wasn't a safe place to play. Shannon became a spectator in this latest memory, feeling the child's shivering hand in hers, pulling away. She stopped walking and watched as though it were a movie, not her past. "Wait, come back. It's not safe."

The younger Shannon looked at her with great empathy in her brown eyes, and full knowledge of what would happen next. She walked into the fray and played her part.

"No! I don't want to go." The caseworker gathered Shannon's clothes and tossed them into a black garbage bag as the police officer stood to the side, taking notes on her pad.

"Sorry, kiddo. Your dad signed the papers in agreement. He'll go away for a while into drug therapy and counseling, and you'll go to a safer place."

Adult Shannon looked at Daniel, standing stock still, a blank expression on his face.

"Daddy, please. We'll be okay. I don't want to go. I can take care of us. Please don't make me go."

"Your father's finally done the right thing, Shannon."

Shannon's head snapped around. "What did you do? What?" A scream ripped through her.

The police officer and caseworker shot looks at each other.

"He's going to be giving up custody permanently, so you'll be safe. We met yesterday, and we're all in agreement that it's the best thing for you. The house is being repossessed, and there's no place for you to live."

"What?" Shannon looked around her room, the only place she ever felt safe. Well, sort of safe, anyway. She looked at her toys, her collection of rocks and shells, her photographs pinned on the walls, her camera, her band posters. "You lost the house? How could you? Grandma and Grandpa left it to you."

"Apparently there are at least two liens against the property," the caseworker said. Shannon hated that he knew more than she did about her own life.

Daniel looked down at the floor. "We had to eat."

"Eat? I cook when I can find food or when the nice lady from the church around the corner brings it. I don't even like mushroom casseroles or those weird Jell-O salads. But I eat them because there isn't anything else. What did you do?" Young Shannon wiped at her nose with her sleeve. "You take all the change I make doing the weeds for Mrs. Hemple, or taking down the garbage for Mr. Johansson. You take it all."

Adult Shannon felt the significance of this exchange. She'd suspected, even as a kid, that the neighbors felt pity for them and found jobs just to help how they could. She'd seen Mr. Johansson lifting some boxes in his garage one day and realized he didn't need help pulling down the cans. Shannon's cheeks went red with shame, and she'd yelled at poor Mr. Johansson that they didn't need his help.

But they did. So badly.

Daniel just shrugged. "It'll be better this way, my little wise one."

"Don't call me that." It was Daniel's way of deflecting and making her feel special. It wasn't working this time.

"If you knew how hard it was to raise you without my Mayuree." He shook his head.

How Daniel could blame her mother and also lay the responsibility at her own feet at the same time was beyond her. In the past, she would have felt the significance. She was too much to handle. She wasn't good enough. If she'd been easier, Daniel could care for her. But she wasn't, and he couldn't do it alone.

The truth rolled through the adult Shannon. He'd let her mother die. He'd provided drugs for her. He'd taken drugs himself. And somewhere in the back of his addled mind, he blamed her, and she took responsibility for it.

Young Shannon sobbed as the caseworker ignored her pleas for her camera, for her photos, for anything that made her herself.

"Why am I being punished for him? I can take care of myself. Please, let me stay. Please." She wasn't begging anyone but Daniel, and he refused to look at her. She tried to pry the caseworker's fingers from her arm. The shame of what was happening poured down like a heavy rain, clinging to her, weighing her down for being too complicated to care for—to love.

"You did this!" Shannon yelled, and all of the players in her memories looked at her. Young Shannon looked tearfully at her. "Then why do you blame yourself?"

"What?" The shock roiled through her.

"Hey, there you are." Justin popped around the corner, jolting

175

her out of the memory like someone shaking a kitten out of a pillowcase—her fingernails still clinging to the fabric. His smile quickly faded. "Are you okay? You're so pale." He took her shaking hand in his.

She felt the comfort, but her anger burned through it. "I need to go. I'm sorry. I can't do this. He doesn't deserve it." Shannon pulled her hands free and started to walk away, but Justin grabbed her arm.

"Wait, will you? What's happened?"

She clenched her eyes closed. If he saw her eyes, her story would pour out on the tears that built, streaming out all her damage, all her brokenness, and make her more vulnerable than she'd been since that day. He'd see it all, and that was a cost she couldn't pay.

"If you want to help Daniel, go ahead. But I can't."

"Shannon, remember when we started to help the homeless together? We felt like God was calling us to help the downtrodden and forgotten. It was a sacred duty. How can you love strangers but turn your back on your father?"

"If God wants to save my father, He can do it through someone else." She pulled free, pushed the debit card into Justin's hand, and left the store. She heard Daniel ask where she was going, but she didn't say a word. She needed to get out of there. As soon as Daniel could pay his own rent, she'd walk away entirely.

CHAPTER 22

H ave you gone back to see Daniel?" Amber was moving around her apartment with ease, setting the table and making them lunch. A stranger wouldn't know Amber was blind at all. She had memorized where everything was, the distances. She made it look easy—but Shannon had tried with her eyes closed one day at Amber's insistence and ended up with bruised shins.

Amber carried their sandwiches over to the dining table. "Coke or iced tea?"

"Water is good." Shannon had noticed that caffeine put her on edge, and that was the last thing she needed. Amber put a glass of ice water in front of her and sat down.

"How's Ethan?" Shannon wanted to keep the subject off Daniel for the time being.

"Better. I mean, now he's back home, he sees how his folks were coddling him." Amber took a gulp of her Coke.

"That's good. Did I tell you Brandon loaned me his camera for the time being? He's also hired me to make a marketing pamphlet for the school."

"I'm so glad you're feeling up to it. And that's amazing. I'm so happy for you." Amber sighed. "I'm sorry we missed our chance for a road trip."

"I still have a lingering dull ache if I turn my head too fast, but otherwise, good as new." Shannon ignored the other comment.

"We'll plan another soon. I got some pieces planned out on our trip to Boston. But—it's not the same. You and I are a team."

Amber's words warmed the chilly spots in Shannon's heart. Maybe everything would work out after all?

"Sisters all the way. I wish I could show you the shots I took the other day at the school." Shannon had gone and taken two-hundred candid shots of students and teachers. She got about ten solid ones she'd be printing up soon. She'd been so busy worrying about Daniel that the project had almost slipped to the side.

"I'm sure they are incredible. Did I tell you Rafe had this great idea?" Amber's tone was evasive.

"What's that?" Amber's agent, Rafe Applegate, had helped Amber find her footing in the local and now international art scene. He was a little stuck on Amber, but he didn't overstep. Shannon thought he loved her work more than he was interested in Amber as a person—he was just getting his feelings confused. He was brilliant, though, and had great connections.

"Don't say no," begged Amber.

Shannon laughed. "That's a great way to start a conversation."

"I know how you feel about this. You don't like publicity."

"Uh-oh. Okay. What's the idea?" Shannon liked anonymity—despite her flashy hair, she really was an introvert on the highest level.

"He thinks we should do a joint show. Your homeless photos and my paintings. He saw some of your work and flipped."

"Where?"

"Where what?"

"Where did he see my work?"

"Here. I have one of your old portfolios on the book case in there." Amber pointed in the direction of the living room. "He was looking through, waiting for me to gather some paintings for him, and his mind was blown. He'd like to help promote the shelters in the area and use your work to make a statement. He'd do a big push and invite some of the wealthier patrons who are interested in philanthropic programs."

Shannon chewed the last bites of her sandwich before she answered. "One wonders what kind of statement. But, okay." Shannon needed the exposure, and she needed the money.

"If you'd just give it a chance," Amber began but stopped. "Did you just say okay?"

"Yeah. I'm not in a position to be snooty about promotion right now. I need the money, and if I sold a couple prints, that would help. Of course, I don't have a hook like you do—can't beat blind girl paints." She teased in a loving tone.

"Shut up. Hey, why do you need money?" Her eyes, as though seeing, bore into Shannon's. Sometimes when that happened she would forget her friend wasn't sighted, and then it would hit her all over again. Amber's life was going in a positive direction, but Shannon had been there on the last day—the day they'd always use to mark the before and after of Amber's history. The day she'd lost her sight altogether.

"To replace my camera. I can't keep borrowing Brandon's." She took a deep breath and plunged ahead. "And I rented an apartment for Daniel." Her tone was nonchalant, but it didn't do anything to temper Amber's excitement.

"Seriously? Where? In your building? Did you get him a job? Is he going to take his meds?"

When Amber got going, Shannon could do little to stop the flow.

"In an old neighborhood we used to live in. I went to make amends for stealing from this little market way back when I was a kid." Shannon stopped talking. "Shoot, I forgot all about that."

"You stole?"

Amber had no idea how many times. "I was in dire straits. I do intend to make amends." But Amber had already moved on, apparently unaffected by her confession.

"And you rented an apartment for him? I'm so glad you're working things out and forgiving him."

"That's not exactly right. He doesn't know it's me." And forgiveness was ages away. If ever.

"You mean you haven't told him?"

"No. Justin helped us move his stuff in. They went shopping together." She left out her part of the shopping trip. "He thinks some outside source is helping him. He's been looking for work for the last couple days. He called today to tell me he'd found one but didn't say where. He left a message on my phone. I didn't call him back."

Amber coughed, and tipped her head down slightly, eyebrows gathered.

"Okay. Spill it."

"What?"

"I know that cough. And that look on your face. What?"

"I think I know where he might be working." Amber hedged.

"Where?"

Amber cleared her voice. "With my mom."

"Jennifer? How in the world did they even cross paths?"

"No, my other mom. I think the church hired him as a janitor."

Shannon sat back against the chair. "Oh boy."

"Maggie sounded really happy about this new hire. But she didn't tell me who it was, only that he used to be homeless."

"I should have been clearer with Maggie. She has no idea what she's getting herself and that church into."

"Maybe he's changed?"

Why did everyone keep saying that? They hadn't had a lifetime of regret like she did. Of hoping he'd take his meds—the legal ones. Of hoping he'd keep a job and feed them both on a regular basis. That they'd have heat and she'd have clothes that fit. That she didn't get sent off to foster care again and again. And then finally hearing if he'd just tried, if he'd just said he wanted to try to get better, they would have let her go home.

"Maggie's a grown-up. Tell her the extent of his mental illness and let her take care of herself."

Amber had no idea what she was suggesting. "And if he decides to break up the church or steal money for drugs? If he crashes and stops showing up for work?"

"Is that likely?" Amber worried.

Shannon's voice raised. "Yes. It's highly likely. This is a man who gave the state his kid. This is a man who has been in jail for theft to support his drug habit—but not the drugs he was *supposed* to take." Shannon's chest went tight as her self-control ebbed away.

"I'm sorry, Shannon." Amber's face filled with sadness, her eyes tearing in sympathy. "I know how much he's hurt you."

Only an inkling, though. How could Shannon explain it so Amber might have a clue what she'd faced? It wasn't only that her father let her down, it was that in his letting her down, she was so injured. Over the years, it wasn't the abandonment that burned inside, so much as what happened during that time.

"It's not just the hurt he did to me, Amber. It's the side effects of being abandoned. It's the neglect and fear. It's going hungry and being terrified. It's forgotten birthdays and Christmases. It's my never being enough for him to even want to try. It's the abuse at the hands of foster families." Her voice cracked. It was the being given away like she wasn't anything to him. She couldn't continue. Amber slid her chair closer and took Shannon's hand in hers.

Shannon looked at Amber's face, knowing she could hear her distress rather than see it. "Do you know who I blame for all that abuse?"

"God?"

Funny that. She'd never blamed God. The little girl she had been always felt His supply, and the adult she was could look back and see His protection, weirdly enough. She knew a lot of people did blame God. For everything. Knowing He was omnipotent, she could have drawn the conclusion that He could have orchestrated a different path for her life. But over time, she'd come to see that His power wasn't about manipulation of time and people like a puppet master, but instead of pulling them out of their situations, loving them where they were, giving them strength and peace in the midst, and guiding them along. Providing.

"No. Not God. Daniel. If he'd been even half the father he was supposed to have been, I wouldn't have been hurt." The hardness in her heart grew, and the sadness deepened. Nothing could take away what he'd done—or what he'd *not* done. For the rest of her life, she'd be marked. A gaping hole would mark her side forever.

"I know, sweetie. I wish I could take that away or make it that it never happened." Amber hugged her, emotion filling her voice. "I hate that this happened to you. I'll get through to Maggie and make sure she's being realistic and cautious."

"Thanks." Shannon sniffed and blew her nose on her napkin.

"I'm also sorry I haven't really gotten this before. I'm used to you being so strong." Amber shrugged. "That sounds stupid. And I'm sorry for that."

"No big."

"It is big though. And I think I've been living in this mental fantasy that we were just sisters living at different houses and you were the same as me. But you weren't. You've faced things I never had to. And I really am sorry I've been so dense."

Shannon leaned in to Amber, feeling the relief of being fully understood, of that mantle of holding it all together lifting. She released a long pent-up sigh.

"Knowing you understand this means everything to me." Shannon wiped at a stray tear.

"I've got your back." Amber squeezed her again.

"Vice versa."

"How have your episodes been?" Amber released her grip on Shannon, and Shannon straightened.

"Justin's been giving me rides."

"Good. I'm glad you've taken him into your confidence. He's trustworthy."

Shannon was beginning to feel that way, too, which made her even more on alert. Dropping her guard had always been dangerous in the past. She was letting Justin in a little at a time, unveiling the scars one at a time—like an actor taking off cake makeup when the play was done. Layer after layer had to be wiped away before clean, shiny skin was revealed—scars and all. Whether he could accept the sight of those scars—some faded, some pink and fresh—remained to be seen.

"I have a side question."

"Yeah?" Shannon leaned back.

"I know these terrific people who are getting married next month, and they need a photographer."

"Super. I'd love to. Is it anyone I know?"

"This is where the difficulty comes in. I know you're going to be very busy that day. But I'm kind of hoping you can wear two hats."

"What are you talking about?" Most of the time, Shannon could see Amber's thoughts playing out over her features like a picture developing on photo paper.

"It might be kind of hard being maid of honor and taking the photos at the same time." Amber's face filled with hope and uncertainty.

"You're serious? Really?" Shannon grabbed Amber by the shoulders.

"Yes. Really. Will you?"

For as much as Shannon thought she'd hate this announcement and feel like she was being displaced by Ethan, she felt joy for her friend instead. It wasn't Ethan, after all, it was the thought of Amber not being there that had threatened her security.

"Yes. I will!" She pulled her best friend in for a huge hug. "I'm so happy for you. And we're all unconventional. I'll stand by you and then I'll take pics. Everyone who comes will think it's funny, or they can just go home."

"That's what I was hoping you'd say." At that moment, Mocha leapt on the table and grabbed the last bite of Amber's sandwich before darting to the couch where he wolfed it down.

"You little thief. You can't let him get away with that, Amb."

"What? What did he do?"

"He stole the food right off your plate."

Amber broke into hysterical laughter. "Oh, thank goodness." She put her hand to her chest. "It must have been him all along. I've been reaching for where I remembered food being on my plate and it's missing and I kept thinking I was losing my memory or having a stroke." Then her face fell and she turned a little green. "I wonder how long we've been sharing bites? Okay. Gross." Amber took a shuddering breath and put a hand up to her mouth.

"He's definitely got you right where he wants you."

Mocha jumped into Shannon's lap and purred contentedly. Shannon scrubbed his head. "Scamp." Mocha purred louder, happy with his new reputation.

"So when's the wedding?"

CHAPTER 23

Justin and Shannon occupied an outside table at their favorite restaurant, Manny's Mediterranean Mecca, sharing veggie and tofu kebabs over rice. A concrete wall, the city-built barrier, shielded the sitting area that protruded into the street.

Shannon dipped her triangle of pita into the olive oil and baba ganoush. She loved this place. They made their own everything. She and Justin had become regulars, and the staff knew their names and their favorites.

A couple of homeless people ambled by on their way to the mission up the street, and the sun silhouetted their forms. Shannon pulled out her camera and took the shot, seeing the shape of them, their clothes defining who they were, their belongings burdening them, the brilliant setting sun casting orange and yellow over the darkness.

Shannon sighed contentedly. Nothing else in her life brought her such pleasure as taking photos to reveal people for who they really were. Except sculpting. She and Justin had that in common. Although, it proved hard to do in her small apartment. Photography took up little space these days with everything going digital. And there was just something about capturing the light, about reflecting it in a new way that she longed to communicate to another—the desire to share the beauty of God shining through the brokenness of others nearly overwhelmed her.

She glanced at Justin, hoping to see a familiar longing, but instead he seemed engrossed in his meal. So far, their date had been a silent one. She could feel the questions buoyed on the wind around them, hanging mid-idea, like leaves caught up in a dust devil, swirling up and down but never moving on.

Justin looked up at her and caught her staring. Her face went hot.

"Yes?"

"Nothing. Just wondering what you were thinking about."

"I know you don't want to talk about Daniel."

What a way to start a conversation. She thought he'd want to talk about *them*, not Daniel.

"And I respect that. You'll share when you're ready." His voice trailed off and she could tell he wanted her to be ready now.

That was a huge assumption. She felt a snarky answer rise, but Justin didn't need to bear the brunt of her anger toward Daniel.

"I can't even begin to hope you'd understand, Justin."

Justin's face morphed into hurt. "What's that supposed to mean?"

"I didn't mean it to sound like I don't think you're capable of being empathetic. It's just that I lived through it, and I don't expect anyone outside of myself and Daniel to really get it. Although, Daniel didn't get it the first time around, so I have little hope he'll grasp it this time."

"So, you're going it all alone in this? Can't you trust me a little?"

Shannon reached across the table. "I trust you. More than I can say." She did, too. Outside of Amber, he knew her best. She'd never let a guy get this close before, and she couldn't imagine she'd ever let another.

"Then share with me?"

"Are you sure you want this?" She waved a hand over her whole self. Deep down there was a part of her who wondered if she and Amber could ever have bounded like had if they hadn't grown up together, in between trips back to Daniel. Like, if you grew up loving someone, knowing their baggage in a natural way,

186

it was easier than having it all poured into your lap at once. She pictured her history like a cement truck backing up, up, up and the lever being pulled, dumping out gritty, slimy cement, having it harden over you like an impenetrable shell. Because after that, nothing else would ever get through. They would see you through that glaze of impervious slurry for the rest of your life and never let you break free.

She could hear the backup sounds of a garbage truck down the street and appreciated the irony.

"I want this. I want you."

His words lit a fire in her stomach, and she felt her angst turn to ash and a new amalgam of nervousness fill the void.

This was one of those moments that could break them. One of those moments where every heartbeat, every breath breathed, every brush of the wind and tingle of nerve could be counted and realized. And with a misspoken word, all of it obliterated.

Time stopped. She'd heard the term used loosely before but had never experienced its control. Their waitperson froze while taking an order next to them, the busboy came to fill their glasses with soda—the stream of sparkling liquid, frozen; a baby stopped mid-cry. Time held fast, like a fossil trapped in mud until a hammer chipped it free, exposed and examined, saved for later to be analyzed and dissected. Words that should have been said, words that still needed saying, flashing to mind at two A.M., niggling and nagging until dawn.

"There's no going back." It had to be said. She understood that he wanted to peel back her exterior and see what made her tick, see which infections lay under the surface, because on some level he thought his love was the antidote. Hardly. That was the kind of thinking that would cut deep and leave a lasting scar. There was only one Healer to do that job.

"I know." His eyes said he did.

The waiter seemed to realize he was trespassing at an inopportune time. He cleared his voice and sat the next couple far from them, leaving them in their own little circle of privacy. An oasis set in the concrete, hidden by the mirage of city life.

"Where do you want me to start?"

"Where you left off those weeks ago on the curb."

"You knew that wasn't the whole tale?"

"I know you. At least I think I do. I can tell when you need to avoid a subject for a while. Usually." Justin, humble to a fault.

"No. You know me." This sentence brought a sparkle of joy to his eyes. That sparkle cut like shards when it reached her heart. She would tell him all of it. He deserved to know if he wanted to go further with her. She was damaged goods in so many, many ways.

And if this was it? It had been a beautiful, mostly wonderful, time. A memory she'd hold onto forever. Because if this didn't work, she would never try again with anyone else. He reached over and took her hand and waited.

Tears filled her eyes and swelled in her throat, as if to cut off her words. She closed her eyes. *Lord, help me share this in a way he'll get. And if this goes poorly, please comfort us both.* When she opened her eyes, he was just opening his—he'd prayed with her. Her heart leapt in hope.

"Amen?" He coaxed, squeezing her hands, and a tear slipped free down her cheek.

She started her story, as far back as she could remember. Her father dancing with her and her mother in the middle of the living room one moment, and his ranting the next. Her memories were a jumble of ecstatic joy and indescribable fear—matching the rhythm of Daniel's manic behavior.

"The first time I was taken into custody by DHS, my mother lay dead on the couch. They tried to shield my eyes, but they didn't know I'd seen her already. I'd tried to wake her. I thought she was really, really tired. Daniel was off scoring a hit—my mother had gone through their stash I guess, and he'd gone off to get more. She'd gotten sick. I never knew from what. He was trying to bring her comfort the only way he knew how. But it was the wrong way." Another tear slid free.

"My mother was so beautiful. I can see her in my memory, her black hair, her once rosy lips and cheeks bluish and still. I knew something was wrong. I curled up next to her, covering her with all the blankets we owned, until he came back. But she stayed cold." Shannon rubbed her arm, and Justin put his hoodie around her shoulders.

"When he walked in and saw me, the look in his eyes—the only way I can describe it is horrified. Here was this little kid cozied up next to her dead mother. He pushed me off and started CPR, but it was too late. He shrieked like I'd never heard before, throwing chairs and kicking over things. I felt like he was blaming me. I know I took responsibility for it for years. He broke a window with one of them. I ran and hid under my bed. The police came, covering me with one of the blankets that had been on my mother, and then they took me."

"Oh, no." Justin moved his chair nearer, putting his arm around her as if to replace the imagined blanket with his loving arm.

"I lost all my things except what they grabbed for me. I saw them cart my mom out to the ambulance, covered with a sheet. But I knew it was her. Somewhere in my head I thought they were taking her to the hospital to wake her up. Then they wrestled Daniel, handcuffed, into the back of the other police car. He kept screaming 'Mayuree' over and over in this inhuman tone. Now I know it was his grief, but it frightened me so much that when he got out and had visitation with me, I wouldn't go to him for a few weeks. I'd just hide.

"Eventually he detoxed, got a job, went to counseling, stayed on his meds and got custody back. I lived with two families in the meantime. Daniel got me back, and we moved into my grandparents' house when I was seven. I'd never met them, and apparently my grandfather had died years before I was born, and then my grandmother died while I was in custody. I don't know if they asked her if she wanted me." Secretly Shannon suspected they'd asked, and she'd said no.

"Daniel passed all the visits, and they declared us fit and left us alone. And then Daniel went off his meds, sure he was well. Again and again he repeated the cycle. By the time I was finally taken from him, I'd been in foster care three more times. I used to do things for the neighbors to pay the bills."

"When you were ten?" Justin tried to hide his horror and failed—his eyes shifted slate gray and cold with anger.

"And before that. The neighbors seemed to know. They'd leave casseroles sometimes. He'd go off for days and leave me alone. I'd take myself to school, eat out of cans, try to wash my own clothes. It was really bad one time when I had lice. The school sent information home, and I had to figure that out. It took me a while to get clear. The school nurse kept nit-checking me before she'd let me back in class, and I felt like she talked really loud. The whole school seemed to know. I was mortified." She shivered. Getting up her nerve, she looked into Justin's eyes and saw the darkening storm brewing. She tried to smile him into a lighter mood, but it didn't work.

"Where do Amber and Jennifer fit in all this?"

"When I was home, Jennifer didn't allow Amber to come over. But when I was in care, she did. It made me feel pretty conflicted, as you can imagine."

"No doubt." He shook his head.

"Each time I was taken, I lost more and more of my things. I just quit wanting stuff. Except my little camera. That was the first thing I'd grab if it was out. I learned to keep everything in my pack that I wasn't using at the moment. Daniel was convinced more than once that the CIA was out to get him, so he made me keep a go-bag of things. I got really good at keeping everything of importance in that backpack. I still have it."

"Wait. The purple backpack in the cabinet?"

"It's still ready to go." She shrugged.

"Promise me you won't use it."

"I won't." She laughed it off.

"Promise me." His words were deadly serious, eyes nearly black now.

"I promise."

His eyes lightened some, and she continued.

"That marked a particularly dark time in my life. I won't go into all the details, but suffice to say I was abused at the hands of an older boy. And one time a foster parent got physical with me. Luckily my DHS caseworker became a stable woman who followed me closely and noticed my behavior changes. I got shifty. I started hording food, ready to run. She got me out of there."

"Like all the non-perishable food you keep in your cabinets?"

"Yeah. Like that." It was a habit she could never break.

"At least you had Amber."

"Oh." She smiled. "Meeting Amber was the only bright spot in my childhood. We met the first time I was taken into custody. In between foster families, I was in a group home, and one day there was Amber. She'd been shuffled a couple times. Her folks adopted her when I was in care, but Amber begged to see me and so they set up playdates and started following me. Amber can be pretty determined, if you haven't noticed."

Justin laughed, and it lightened the moment and his eyes shifted to gray-blue. "I've noticed."

"Jennifer made sure I had good clothes and snacks. Much of that got stolen, but she tried. She took me to doctor appointments. She mothered me."

"Can I ask why they didn't adopt you?"

This. This would be hard to admit. "Russ wanted his family to match. He didn't want questions. He'd always wanted kids they couldn't have biologically—and I didn't fit." She held up her hand, revealing her peachy-brown skin.

"Seriously?" His ire rose.

"Seriously. It was a different time. He had a very strong vision for his family."

"That's a copout."

Shannon pressed her lips together, thoughtful for a moment. "Yeah. It was. It is."

Justin leaned back in his chair, shaking his head. "I don't get that vibe from Jennifer."

"No. She really wanted me, thus all the clothes and caring for me. But he wouldn't bend. It was especially ugly when we went to him about my abuse and he called me a liar."

"He what?" Righteous anger spilled out.

"He didn't want to believe that by not adopting me he'd be condemning me to abuse for the rest of my childhood. He couldn't deal with the guilt. So he hid."

"I can't believe it."

"It's been hard to swallow." She laced her fingers together in her lap. "Hard to forgive." People had layers and damage and complications and fears and baggage. She'd tried to make excuses for Russ over the years, to sort it out in a logical way—there just wasn't one that made up for what he'd done to her.

And yet, Justin kept shaking his head.

"He could have spared you so much."

"It wasn't to be." Again, a mantra she'd told herself again and again. Because if she let her mind continue to hope as a kid or fantasize now in "if only land," she'd be crushed. She swiped a tear from her cheek with a couple shaky fingers. So far, this talk was going better than she'd expected. Shannon knew people who couldn't handle bad things, who balked and ran. She'd seen it countless times. Her admiration for Justin grew, but her stomach still held the tension and fear of being abandoned.

"Eventually I aged out of the system. I saw Daniel a couple times in passing. Once as a kid, and once as an adult. But I steered clear."

"Now that he's clean, do you think you'll take a chance on him? I can understand not wanting to." Even though Justin understood on one level, she could see him struggling to see the Daniel he'd been getting to know through her lens.

"It's not just that he did drugs and messed up. Or that he suffers from mental illness. That seems to go around in our family." She pointed at her own head. "But that he could have kept me. He chose to walk away. He chose to lose our house. He legally gave me up and never looked back."

"I don't know if that's true."

"Why's that?" Her voice unintentionally challenged him.

"The other day, when we were finishing up shopping, he mentioned missing his daughter and that he'd failed her."

"I get that he feels bad when he's sober and manic. That's the side of him I used to choose to love. But it doesn't erase what he did." She took a shaky breath. "It'll never be enough."

"What if he was Magic Stan?"

"What do you mean?"

"If he was Magic Stan—mentally ill and homeless—and his daughter showed up, you'd tell her what?"

Shannon swallowed hard. "I don't know." She pulled her hands from his.

"Yes, you do. You'd bring them together to work things out. You'd help her figure out a way to keep Stan's medication going."

"That's not fair." She sat back, arms crossed. The sun had lowered, and the streetlights came to life. The chill in the air penetrated through her clothes. Their waiter turned on the outdoor heat lamps and then came and lit the candle on their table.

"Can I get you anything else?"

Shannon heard the hopeful tone in his voice.

"Hot tea?" Justin asked.

"Coming right up." The waiter rushed away. They were probably tying up a good table for him.

Shannon checked her watch. "We've been here for quite a while. Maybe we should wrap it up."

"Hey, don't shut me down."

Shannon looked away, up into the branches overhead. The leaves curled from the cold against the rising twilight sky. She pulled out Brandon's camera again and took several shots. Then she turned the lens on Justin. He gave her a pained smile, but he let her.

There was more to say, but her emotions were frazzled and raw. She didn't know if she could continue.

"Can we shift the subject for a minute?" Justin seemed to respect her need for a break.

"Yes, please." Relief washed over her.

Justin leaned down and pulled up his backpack. He unzipped it and extracted a package, holding it out to her.

CHAPTER 24

"What is it?" Shannon hadn't ever gotten a gift from anyone outside of Jennifer or Amber. She couldn't hide her excitement. But when she opened it her heart sank.

"It's a camera. A very expensive camera." She looked up, worried. "This is *your* camera."

"True. It is. But you know I'm much more into sculpting now. It's my thing, and my job." He shrugged. "I know you need a camera of your own. It's not as fancy as the one Brandon loaned you, but it'd be yours."

Something in his tone tipped off a warning signal in Shannon's mind. "I really can't let you do this."

"Sure you can."

"Your parents gave you this camera when you entered art school."

"Yes, they did, indeed."

"What will they think?"

"They understand. I've already talked to them about it. They agree."

"Seriously?" Shannon couldn't get her mind wrapped around the idea. She'd only met his parents once. Briefly. And that was before they began dating.

"What will they think of me? I've never even gone to their house for dinner." Shannon groaned, remembering. "I was supposed to go two weeks ago, and I blew it, didn't I?"

"You were pretty upset. They understood. I made your apologies about it."

What had she ever done to deserve him? He didn't understand it at the time, but he gave her grace.

"Speaking of. Sunday. Six P.M. Be there."

She laughed. "Okay."

"Really?"

"I need to apologize to your parents. I don't want them to hate me."

"Quit worrying about my parents. Will you take good care of my camera?" Justin teased.

She laughed at his comparison. "Of course I will."

"Will you let me borrow it once in a while?"

"Don't be silly."

"Then what's stopping you?"

She turned the camera over in her hands. This was twice the camera she'd had. It wasn't quite as expensive as Brandon's, but that was because it was an older model. As she pondered how to respond, he pulled out another package filled with lenses. How had he fit all that in there? It must have weighed a ton. Despite herself, her heart beat in anticipation.

"I can't believe you did this. We've never gotten each other gifts."

He took the camera from her and laid it on the table, before taking her hands. "I'd like to remedy that starting now. Okay?"

"What if we...?" Shannon didn't complete the sentence. Suddenly the thought of breaking up with Justin, which she'd been so ready to do only a month ago, felt like the end of the world. She'd crossed a line she had promised herself she'd never cross.

"Listen to me. This is a no strings attached camera."

How did he know what she was thinking? And how did he always seem to say the right thing?

"And then you can give Brandon's camera back to him." Justin began to fiddle with his dinner fork.

Shannon squinted at his tone. There was something there. She pursed her lips at him and nodded. "That's it."

"What's it?"

"You're jealous of Brandon. Seriously? He could be my father."

"You father doesn't look at you like Brandon does." His guard slipped, and he scrambled to recover. "But I'm not jealous."

"I need to tell you something." She took both his hands in hers. "And I need you to look deeply into my eyes while I tell you."

As he did so, his eyes flashed bright blue and sparkly in the candlelight. He leaned in to kiss her, but she leaned back a little, stopping him. He gave her a mischievous smile.

"Sorry."

"Don't apologize." She leaned in and kissed his cheek, her lips brushing his scratchy five o'clock shadow. He almost caught her with his mouth, but she feinted away, laughing. His cologne was a mix of sandalwood and spice and something inherently him, and she knew she'd remember it forever.

"You have nothing to be jealous of."

"Okay." He didn't sound assured.

"Here's the part where you really listen."

That got him. "Okay."

"All this stuff I'm telling you tonight?"

"Yeah?"

"I've never told anyone."

Justin's eyes widened as the gravity of her statement settled over him.

"Amber?"

"She knows some of it. We lived much of it together. But I've never dissected it for her like I am for you. I've never told her the part about my mom. Not like that." She shivered, and Justin readjusted his hoodie, helping her put it on. She felt small inside the wide, long arms. Small, but safe. Cared for.

"This is big, then."

"Really big." She grinned at him but felt her heart walloping inside her chest, fear tempting her to run. To lie. To cover it all up again and act like nothing was happening.

But something was happening.

Something she'd promised herself would never happen. Something she found she needed more than she wanted to admit. But she still had to finish. And she had no idea how he would take it. She mustered her courage.

"Just so we're clear, I'm damaged goods." She gave him the most serious and intent look that she could muster so she wouldn't have to say the details aloud. "I was hurt *that way* by an older boy. And I have trust issues. And abandonment issues. And control issues." She released a shaky laugh. "You're getting more than you bargained for here."

Justin took her hand and flattened her fingers out against his chest, over his heart, holding her gently at the wrist. His heart beat against her hand, radiating life and warmth and love.

"Do you feel that?"

"Yes." She whispered, her own heart beating to match his rate.

"My heart has never beaten this way for anyone. And it knows you've got a past where you were hurt against your will. And it's so very sorry. It breaks for you. That shouldn't have ever happened to you. I wish I could go back in time and keep you safe from all of that. But since I can't, I can only promise you I'll do my best to keep you safe from now on."

Shannon almost gulped. "That's not your job."

"Not yet." His eyes colored to a deep green sea, sending her all his feelings and thoughts and intentions.

"Oh." Her voice softened.

"Yep." He covered her hand now with both of his, and for the first time, maybe forever, she felt protected by another human. By a man. She never thought she'd feel that way—ever.

"And you know something else?"

"What?" Her voice cracked.

"You talked pretty intently about your childhood, and you didn't check out once."

Shannon brightened. "You're right. Wow."

The waiter chose that moment to plop the teapot and a couple mugs down on the table. "Sorry about the wait. It got really crazy in there and our relief guy called in sick." He poured and then looked back and forth between them and backed away.

"I think we've made Devon feel uncomfortable."

"Who is Devon?"

"Our waiter." He laughed, and his chest vibrated under her hand. "He serves us nearly every time we're here."

"Oh." Her cheeks felt hot. She'd honestly never noticed his name.

"Poor Devon."

"We'll leave him a big tip." She checked her watch. "We've been here for four hours."

Justin's eyebrows rose. "No kidding? A really big tip, then." He still hadn't let go of her hand. "In all seriousness, you're not damaged goods. You are a child of the Most High God. When He looks at you, all He sees is your beautiful spirit and willingness to love and sacrifice for your fellow man. Well, that and Jesus. He's got you covered."

"I know He does. But you needed to know."

"Okay."

She'd done it. She'd bared her soul to Justin and came out not only unscathed, but closer to him than she ever imagined she could be.

"About your dad?"

She pulled her hand from his chest, breaking the link.

"I've gone as far as I'm going to go, Justin. You need to accept that."

He narrowed his eyes at her, but there was a sparkle there. "But you'll have dinner with my parents on Sunday and you'll accept the camera?"

She paused, narrowing her eyes back at him. "Yes."

"I'll take it." He broke into a huge grin.

She knew it wasn't the end of the discussion. But he had to accept her decision. Nothing would ever make her let her guard down with Daniel again. Nothing.

CHAPTER 25

The Romero home was an old-Portland style Victorian two-story on the corner of an older neighborhood across the Willamette River on the east side. It needed fresh paint, but otherwise the yard was impeccable, edged by a cute picket fence and tall hedges. Their front porch, like most on the block, was covered in lilac vines, with the last remains of summer buds withered brown and falling to the ground. The musky, sweet aroma filled the neighborhood. She closed the car door behind her, waiting for Justin to unload things from the backseat. He wrestled with a large bundle and kept getting it stuck against the door frame. Finally, he got the door closed and joined her.

"What is in that sack, anyway?"

Justin hefted the stuffed duffle bag over his shoulder. "My laundry."

"Seriously? How old *are* you?"

"Twenty-seven."

"You're a grown man taking laundry home to mommy?"

"Shush. Lower your voice." He hissed between his teeth. He came around to her, handing off a bottle of wine to her along with the flowers she'd chosen at the store to bring. The blooms were sunflowers and daisies of all sizes. "If my mamá hears you, her feelings will be hurt. I'm just lucky she let me move out on my own."

"What in the world?"

"It makes her happy. I just bring jeans and a couple shirts. I do the rest on my own." There was a lot more than jeans and a couple shirts in there. Shannon couldn't tell if he was in earnest or glossing over the inability to leave his childhood behind. Or maybe he couldn't work a washer. He always smelled clean, so that was an upside.

Shannon stopped cold in the middle of the walkway. "I just thought, do they know I'm Thai?"

"Why would they care?" His tone dismissed her.

"They might." She didn't like the unknown. It set off all her anxieties. She'd never let her heritage be an issue, but this felt different. What if they didn't want her like Amber's dad hadn't? She couldn't face the hurt and division that would cause for Justin. Before they could discuss it further, the screen door squeaked open and out stepped a tall man with charcoal black hair and a huge grin on his gentle face. He wore a pin-striped short-sleeved shirt tucked into his black jeans.

So far, so good.

Shannon took a big breath for courage and Justin leaned in and whispered, "Don't worry, they will love you, too."

Her heart stopped at his words.

"Wait. What?" She turned on Justin, wanting him to repeat that. She was sure he must love her, but he'd not said it in so many words.

Justin's eyes sparkled, and he looked shyly at her. How this man covered in tattoos and piercings, topped with a blue-haired mohawk, could look timid—it endeared him to her all the more. Before he could answer, Justin's father walked down the brick pathway toward them.

"Welcome! We're so glad you could come." He took the wine from Shannon and clasped her hand in a warm embrace with both of his.

"This is my papá, Matias. Papá, this is Shannon."

Matias gripped her hand closer. "I'm very glad to meet you."

"As am I, Mr. Romero." Shannon was immediately charmed.

He released her. "Please, call me Matias. Come inside. Come inside." He waved them toward the door. They climbed the steps and entered the comfortable home. The air was full of cumin and chilis and some sort of meaty delicious-roasting-something in the background. Her mouth watered in anticipation.

The furnishings included many antique pieces, craftsman coffee and side tables, a wood-framed couch, and color-rich photos. Prints with flashes of bright yellow, deep blues, and dramatic reds adorned the walls. She recognized some of Justin's older work. A couple were Amber's paintings. And one was *hers*. It was one she'd taken of the river as the moon rose two years ago. The scene had inspired her to pull out her camera and shoot frame after frame. Then she overlaid them, making a montage of the moon's flow across the night sky, arching over the great black-blue river. It felt so personal, it never occurred to her anyone else would like it. But when they did a teacher's showing at the school, it had sold fast. Now she knew where it went.

She felt the frame with her fingers, brushing the carved edge.

"That is one of our favorites." A soft, female voice came from behind her and Shannon turned to meet Justin's mother. She was on the shorter side, about Shannon's height, and was in the process of removing a bright blue apron with hand-embroidered flowers and tatting around the pockets. Her long, red hair was pulled back into an intricate braid. Her cheeks were rosy, and her blue eyes welled with kindness. Shannon couldn't remember liking someone so fast. She could see so much of Justin in his mother's face.

"Mrs. Romero. I'm so glad to finally meet you."

Mrs. Romero took Shannon's offered hand. "Please, my name is Josefina. But you may call me Josie."

"Nice to meet you, Josie." She handed her the flowers.

"And you as well." She examined the flowers, went in the other room and came back with them in a blue mason jar. "These are beautiful." She put the vase on the mantel over the fireplace in the living room—an obvious place of honor among the many photos of Justin as a boy. Then she motioned for Shannon to follow her into the kitchen. Shannon shot a worried look at Justin, but he seemed oblivious to her discomfort and chatted with his father. What did Shannon know of boyfriend's parents? This was all new territory, and she was terrified of screwing it up.

The kitchen was open to the dining room beyond. The cabinets were painted a light creamy yellow, and the framed glass doors encased plates, glasses, cookery items, and cookbooks. The counters were polished dark gray granite, framing a white farmhouse sink. A bouquet of bright yellow and orange dahlias sat on the counter as well as on the dining table beyond. The hand-carved, polished wood dining table was six feet long, adorned by a blue runner and set for four with yellow plates, and orange and blue bubble-glass goblets. Golden tapers were lit on either side of the bouquet.

"You have a beautiful home." There wasn't a speck of dust or dirt anywhere. Not that she would have cared otherwise, but she'd seen Justin's place. Impeccable it wasn't.

"Gracias. Thank you. Matias made this table and the others, and has helped restore it all, a little at a time. We are overdue for an exterior paintjob. What color would you suggest?"

The question took Shannon aback. "Oh, I don't have a clue."

"You have a wonderful aesthetic sense. Please?" She motioned to the backdoor off the kitchen and they went outside and looked at the back of the house. Here, too, there were lilacs going dormant, wisteria wrapping the trellis, rosebush pods at every corner, a rock garden and a little fountain with two cream-colored Adirondack chairs flanking it, looking onto a large brick fire pit. The yard was long and skinny and perfect in every way.

Grape vines and blueberry and raspberry bushes lined the right fence, where white and green huge-leafed Hostas framed the left, staying mostly in the shade. There was little grass, but what she could see looked more like bouncy stepables. Surrounding a gazebo was a four-by-four-foot succulent garden, with every shape, size, and color—blue, green, pink, and yellow—of plants. In great ceramic pots grew sunflowers and beach grasses. She recognized those pots. She reached out and caressed one. Justin had worked on those for months, trying to get them just right for his mom.

She smiled at Josie.

"They are beautiful, yes? My son is a man of many talents. I'm so proud of him."

"So am I." Shannon noted the twinkle in Josie's eyes at that and tallied bonus points.

Then she noticed a small herb garden, well-tended, surrounded by a tight wire fence. She motioned toward it. "Rabbits?"

"I am plagued by los conejos, the little *bunnies*. They love my roses." She scowled. "Matias thinks I don't see him out here feeding them, and the squirrels, scraps from my own kitchen. This is my only protection against them. But I love fresh herbs, and I love Matias, so I do what I can." She put up her hands in surrender.

As soon as she said it, a small gray rabbit poked its twitchy nose out from behind one of the Hostas and crept into the sunlight. "They taunt me." Josie sighed for dramatic purposes, but Shannon could see she actually did like the bunnies.

"Now, los colores?"

"Back to business. Right." Shannon grinned, liking Josie more and more each minute.

Inhaling the sweet scent of the recently watered yard, Shannon moved from one section to another, then through the gate to the front of the house and stood staring up at it, then moved back to her starting point and sat in one of the chairs, pondering.

"What do you think?"

"Well, I know what I like. But I don't know if Matias will go for it."

"Light blue with yellow trim, yes?" She clasped her hands in anticipation.

A laugh burst from Shannon. "Yes. But I was thinking lilac with yellow trim. It would match your kitchen and the fauna so well."

Josie clucked her tongue against her teeth. "Maybe. Maybe. He is not a stubborn man when it comes to letting me have my way with the colors. But lilac might push his limits. Yes?"

"What about a compromise?"

Josie looked at Shannon expectantly.

"Periwinkle leaning to blue?"

Josie clapped. "Just the thing. Perfecto!" She reached for Shannon and pulled her up by the hand, hugged her, and led her back into the house by the hand. Shannon hadn't had an adult woman hold her hand since her mother. Her memories broke in, and she remembered walking to the park, her mother's smallish hand gripping her tiny one. Her mother tying her shoes. Pushing her on the swing. Hugging her. A rag doll fashioned with a green silk dress. That doll was lost long ago to one of the foster homes. Somewhere. She frowned, trying to place it.

Her mind started to slip away, but for the first time in a long time to something positive—but also bittersweet, like the last round of an echo of laughter. This wasn't the time for it, though. She must stay present.

The oven's timer beeped in warning, just the thing to pull Shannon back to the present. Josie didn't seem to notice anything amiss and went about pulling out the pork roast, using two brightly patterned, red and orange oven mitts. The sweet aroma of crispy pork, oregano, and allspice filled the kitchen. The tempting memories faded, leaving her for now.

In the background, she could hear acoustic guitar music playing from the living room stereo, filling the kitchen with a homey sound. Everything was warm, welcoming, peaceful.

She never wanted to leave.

Justin came around the corner and gave her the thumbs up sign and questioned her with his eyes.

She nodded. Yes. Everything was good. Very good.

Josie gave orders to them all to put the food out and to take their seats. Parents at the head, kids at the center. Matias put out his hands and took hers and Justin's, and Josie took her other and Justin's other. They encircled the food, the table, the dining room—they made the center and the heart, together. Matias bowed his head, and they all followed.

"Padre Nuestro, we thank you for this wonderful meal, the beautiful blessing of guests under our roof, and the graceful hands that fashioned this food. Bless it to the use of our bodies that we might go forth in your holy name. Amen."

"Amen."

Matias carved the roast and passed the platter to Shannon first, as the guest. Then the handmade tortillas, followed by croquettes stuffed with jamon. A beautiful green salad topped by their own garden tomatoes followed it all. No one spoke at first, they were all too busy eating.

"This is amazing. I've not eaten so well in a long time."

Josie beamed at her and handed her the roast again.

Shannon knew it would be rude to turn it away, and besides, she had no intention of stopping eating just yet. She might be small, but her stomach took up most of her body. She looked up and saw Justin loading his tortilla with shreds of pork and salad greens. He was so at home with his parents. There seemed to be no stress between them. She'd never experienced such a thing.

"My Josie is quite a cook, yes?" Matias asked.

"Oh my, yes." Shannon answered past the bite in her mouth and covered it with her hand, laughing. "Sorry!"

"Then you will come back next Sunday." It was a statement more than an invitation. Josie stepped in, sensing the shift of energy in the room. Justin watched, a spectator, insecure.

"Now, Matias. Shannon might be very busy. She's a young, independent, career woman. She has much to do."

"No, I'd love to." She felt her face go hot and shot a look at Justin. "If that's okay, I mean."

Justin's eyes twinkled like his mother's. "Every Sunday as far as I'm concerned."

The weight of the sentence might have made her feel smothered, strangled, or imprisoned a month ago. But today? Free. Freer than she'd been in a long, long time.

After they ate, the men moved to the porch and Shannon helped clear the food and dishes.

"You go join them outside." Josie brushed her to the door with gentle hand movements.

"Not even. Please let me help."

They moved together, putting away food and washing dishes liked they'd done it hundreds of times before. The feeling of being home rippled over her. Even with Jennifer and Amber, it wasn't like this. She didn't know what was so different.

After the kitchen was cleared, Josie hauled Justin's duffle to the laundry room and got a load going. Shannon sat at the dining table, waiting for her. She could hear Justin and Matias talking together and laughing. Then Josie joined her.

"I know what you are thinking."

"About what?" Shannon went on alert.

"That I do my son's laundry. It's such a little thing, but it keeps me connected to him. We were never able to have more children, so now that he's gone, it can be empty. Matias doesn't like to be babied—and I certainly don't want to baby my husband." She laughed. "But until Justin settles down, I can do this for him. And make meals to send home. I love to do that. One day, though." She shrugged and looked passively at Shannon.

"I know that he will always need you. No matter who he settles down with. You mean the world to him. Both of you do."

Josie patted her hand. "May I tell you something? I don't wish to scare you."

Shannon went on alert again. Her heart raced. "Of course." She held her breath, expecting the worst.

"You are the first woman he's ever brought home."

There seemed to be a lot of firsts for them both lately.

At that moment Justin called to them. "Mamá, Shannon, come out here and be with us. You can pet the bunnies," he teased.

His mother said something in Spanish that Shannon didn't recognize but Matias sounded shocked.

"Mamá, really?"

Josie laughed. "Shall we?" Shannon watched her rise and go out the backdoor. So many firsts today. She was discovering that family ties were not bad things, that belonging could free you. Make you freer than being self-reliant. Being on her own, shutting out things and people that could hurt her, had always felt like the safe choice.

And yet somehow, belonging also liberated you.

"You coming, Shannon?" Justin called.

CHAPTER 26

The sunrise broke over the hills at Shannon's back, casting a peachy-gray glow over the shifting sky, like God's great hand was turning up the flame on a universe-sized gas stove, the flames going from clear to gold, to yellow and orange, then bright blue, burning off the previous losses and failures and clearing the path for a new day.

Beauty from ashes.

Shannon sat on a waterlogged snag, staring out over the ocean, once dark with slight highlights of foam rolling and swishing in, echoing the sky colors and the deep beneath, greening and graying, then like crystals capturing the light, refracting out, blazing brilliant.

With each shift, she captured the sight with her camera. They were still getting to know each other, their quirks, what drove them, what captured their imagination. As she touched the apertures, the lenses, adjusted the frames, clicked the shots, she thought of Justin, his hands where hers now were. Strong. Gentle. Coaxing. Patient.

She thought of her Savior. She'd known Jesus for as long as she could remember. Born with faith as a gift from God, coming to deeper acceptance of Jesus later and growing in Him. But she'd never seen His character played out so well. Not that Justin was God-like, but there were aspects of her savior there. She recognized them clearly. And as Jesus taught her to trust in Him more, she was learning to trust others.

God did that for her. And must have done that for others. He wove people into each other's lives to mirror His love and teach them to trust Him. The patient love of God, knowing what we needed and when we needed it, understanding our frailty.

It's why she gave out her packs to the homeless—how could they understand about Jesus's sacrifice for them when they didn't remember kindness, or grace, or love? They needed to experience to crave more. Then feel the weight of their sin against that love, and the gravity of the price paid for it by the only One who could.

She'd heard people misspeak that we needed to experience the dark to see the light. That was eastern philosophy sneaking in. You didn't need to sin to appreciate the sacrifice. But if you were in that dark place, the light would shine brighter if you opened your eyes to search for it.

A seagull floated on the currents as its cousin sandpipers raced at the outgoing waves, searching the uncovered sand for food, then trucking back up the shore to escape the tide. The seagull seemed to look down on them as if so say, "Why do you toil so? Come enjoy the day."

Shannon turned the camera over in her hands, looking at the controls, the buttons, the screen. Justin now used wood and wire and knives to carve large clumps of clay into something useful, making something out of nothing. And now Shannon caught the shape and shade and reflection of the light with his camera.

Shannon's lens captured the seagull and its gathering companions like floating kites on invisible strings, the sandpipers, the waves, the wisps of fog lifting from the stone outcroppings dotting the shore, like clouds burning off of miniature mountains. She focused on the revealed shapes of barnacles, anemone, starfish, every hopping and crawling thing uncovered as the tide rolled back like a blanket being pulled down over the sleeping sand, waking the creatures below.

To her far right sat Amber bundled in her hoodie, crouched

on a blanket, using her paints to recreate the sounds she heard, the things she felt. Every now and then she'd put her face up, listening, waiting, and then she'd go back to her work. She was going more abstract lately. Shannon felt the emotions Amber shared now were deeper than they were before. She couldn't put her finger on it, though.

"Heading to the water for a walk." Shannon hollered, and Amber waved, letting her know she'd heard her.

Walking down to the water's edge, staying just out of the ocean's reach, Shannon filled her lungs with the cool sea air. It was fresh today after a hard rain last night. The sun hadn't begun to heat the shore—although she mostly loved those smells, too. Sunbaked seaweed and salty sea from lands far away. The downside was when the blue sailor jellies washed ashore. That wasn't an agreeable aroma.

At the water's edge, she leaned down and picked up a worn, smooth rock and a two-foot-long piece of driftwood, turning them over and over in her hands. Then she tossed them onto the sand and photographed them at different angles.

Each had been worn in certain patterns, rubbed, polished, broken. The drift piece had probably come from a tree, turned into lumber by a logger, and floated down a river to be built into something else. Or crashed into the sea during a storm, tumbled until the limbs were stripped. Pitch was worked well out of the material, making it light, even when water logged. And although it might be overlooked, its use could be reimagined and repurposed—maybe into a piece of furniture she could buy from a weekend market.

A wave rushed up between her legs, a couple feet deep, sweeping the driftwood off and swirling the sand under her feet until she lost her footing and landed on one knee. She could taste the salty water in her mouth from the splash. She gasped from the unexpected cold. Holding her camera high above her head, she scrambled to her feet to escape.

Once she was well up into dry sand, she checked the camera. Safe. She berated herself for being so careless. To lose her own camera was bad enough, but Justin had entrusted this to her. She needed to take better care of it.

She scowled at the expanse and remembered that the ocean wasn't a thing to turn your back on. It was beautiful and equally dangerous. The ocean could turn the overconfident swimmer humble in a matter of seconds.

Her mind ticked like a flip-book, pages rapidly peeling to the day when she'd had enough of her life. She'd come here, to end her suffering and the loneliness. It was hard to remember what had driven her to it, now, though it had felt so tangible at the time. A cascade of memories of past hurts rushed over Shannon, and she nearly felt the despair again. There were so many, she couldn't choose just one inciting incident.

"Where are you, God?" she'd cried out, alone on a darkening beach in mid-winter. She'd found the perfect spot void of tourists, when all the regulars were home sipping cocoa and watching television with their lunches while the storm barreled in full force. No one in their right mind would be out there.

Thus, there she was.

Shannon had walked out to the raging waves. "Why? Why did my life have to be like this? Why did my mom have to die? Why didn't my father want me? Why wasn't I enough? What good is my life?" As she screamed her accusations at God, she sank to her knees and continued screaming at Him, but she'd really been screaming at herself. She'd come to give up, sure He'd have no answers, and condemn herself to the fate she felt lapping at her knees. Depression threatened to swallow her whole. And then the water did just that. A huge wave clobbered her, and she tumbled head over heels. She knew, right then, she didn't want to die. She didn't know how she'd go on, but she at least wanted the chance.

Then the waves rolled her up on the shore like Jonah being spit out of the whale's mouth.

"Shannon?"

Amber's call woke her from her haze and she noticed the water had found her again and was nearing her knees. Her feet spiked with cold and she stumbled back to safety.

"I'm here."

I'm here.

That's what God had told her, too. *I'm here. I didn't leave you. I didn't forsake you.* No matter what her father did, what the foster system did, Russ, all of it. Her Father God was with her, caring for her, bringing her along. He had a purpose for her.

Amber ambled toward her, tripping over the sand. "Give a girl a hand?"

Shannon caught Amber by the hand and drew her to her side. "Want to know what it looks like?" Amber often asked for Shannon to describe a scene. They'd done it hundreds of time now.

"Yes, please. There's a strange thing happening in my head I haven't shared with you yet. You know how, over time, you lose the memory of the face of a loved one who died—but the feelings and emotions associated with that person, they stay and sometimes deepen when the sting of their loss is gone?"

"I think so, yes."

"That's what is happening with color. The emotions I had about blues and greens and browns and grays—they are there more than color now. And they mean more to me now than ever." Amber's face looked peaceful with her admission. "Take me to the water?"

Shannon led her to the water and watched as Amber leaned over and let her hands caress the waves.

"Deeper?"

"Just a minute." Shannon took Amber's coat and hers, and put them up on the sand, nestling her camera deep inside. Then she came and took Amber out, one slow foot after another. The icy water rolling at their knees and then their thighs.

"Let me go?"

"I'm right here."

Amber grinned widely as Shannon let her go and she put her hands in the water, letting the waves bump into her.

Shannon described the scene. "It's clear at first, but before the waves break, they are slate gray. There's yellow and green seaweed on the rising tide. There's black oystercatchers floating in the shallows and combing the rocks." Shannon turned full circle. "There are plovers sprinting over the sand. There is a chocolate-brown sea lion basking on a rock about forty feet out. Browns, muddy and gray, sunlight glinting like fool's gold in the bottom of the river, blue sky, puffy white clouds with tinges of dark gray."

"Perfect. Thank you." Amber sighed. She took Shannon by the hand. "Are you okay? Your voice sounds funny."

"Memories."

"High school?" Amber knew everything. Shannon only needed to stick a pin in a date and she knew. But she hadn't talked about this very much.

"Yes."

"You never said why." Amber gripped Shannon's hand tighter.

"I just didn't think I could face another day in that place. And the thought of not being able to escape my situation made me want to escape everything. All the questions running in my head. All the doubts. All the hurts."

"I'm glad you didn't. I don't know how I could have, or would have, survived without you."

"Me, too." She hugged Amber sideways.

"Have you talked to your counselor about it?"

"Yes." Shannon didn't elaborate. She'd mentioned it, but they'd never analyzed it. She'd kept it light, as she did with Amber. Deep down, she knew her counselor would come back around to it one day. She shivered.

"I think we need to get out before we freeze."

Amber agreed, and they waded back to shore, stopping for their things. They went to where Amber's easel was set and took turns holding up a blanket for them both to change out of their sodden jeans into dry sweatpants. Then Shannon dug a pit and built a fire.

"It wasn't because I wanted to die." Shannon spoke at long last.

"What do you mean?"

"I just didn't want to feel the pain anymore."

"Did God take the pain away?"

"In measures. But mostly, He made it so the pain didn't hold as much weight. It's like you say about colors. The incidences are still there, but the sting has gone out of them and I can look back and see where God used those experiences to grow me. It brings me comfort, too, knowing nothing is wasted—I can really understand the hurts of others and be there for them."

Shannon stuck a stick into the fire to let more air in and the flames licked higher. Sparks emitted into the air like fiery-orange confetti. Grabbing her camera, she framed just the right angle. She shifted the stick in the embers again, lifted her camera and was about to take the shot when Amber interrupted her thoughts.

"Except for Daniel." Amber had a way at poking the right spot at the wrong moment. The sparks flickered up and the log shifted and sank, almost snuffing out the fire.

CHAPTER 27

As she paced the sidewalk, the rain started to come down. Her eyes kept darting to the church where Daniel worked under Maggie's guidance. She needed to see how he was doing. If he was really sticking to his meds, then she might be able to forgive him. A little voice whispered that it wasn't how forgiveness worked. But Shannon didn't want to be hurt again.

What did forgiveness mean anyway? Did she wish him harm? No. Did she want him to be safe and happy? Sure. To be honest, maybe not at first. Not that she didn't want him safe, she just didn't want to get involved. Why was it so hard for people to understand where she was coming from?

Deep in her spirit she knew bitterness still hung in the eaves. Her counselor said forgiving him would help her healing process. Probably. But what if she couldn't tell him? She didn't necessarily need to tell him, did she? Wouldn't that just put her at risk again?

Shannon turned to pace back up the street and ran smack into Daniel's chest.

"Hey, there. Careful. Oh, it's you." He gave her a dimpled grin. "I hoped I'd see you again."

She frowned up at him. "You did?" She could definitely...well probably...forgive him if he asked for it. If he apologized, then she'd probably forgive him. Shannon waited.

"I wanted to thank you for the great apartment. The manager and I have shared a meal here and there. The neighborhood is really quiet. Just what the doctor ordered."

"You're seeing a doctor?"

"Figure of speech."

Her shoulders sagged in disappointment.

"You should come over with Justin tonight."

That brought her up short. "Justin is coming over for dinner?"

"Yeah. He comes over a few times a week. He's a great guy." His blue eyes shone down on her. "He's invited me over to his parents' house for dinner. I thought I'd bring Maggie. We're kind of seeing each other."

At these tidbits of information, Shannon gasped so sharp that she made herself cough.

"You okay?"

"Yes. I have to go." Shannon looked both ways and tore across the street and into the church. She had to see Maggie. She needed to put a stop to this immediately.

The church was dark and cool. The distant smell of wax candles and that particular aroma all churches had of burnt coffee and carpet deodorizer met her. She headed to the room where Maggie set up for the blindness support group.

"Maggie, are you here?" She peered through the dark room, trying to discern movement. "Maggie?"

"Yes?" Maggie came up behind Shannon, making her jump.

"Oh shoot. Don't do that." Shannon's heart beat up into her throat.

"Sorry, sweetie. Is there something I can help you with?" Maggie reached over and switched the lights on and set out the box of donuts she carried. "I hope you don't mind if I keep working, I'm a little behind."

"No. That's fine." Shannon cleared her throat. She wasn't sure where to start, so she jumped in. "Are you seeing Daniel?"

"We're friends. But that's not what you meant, is it?"

"Maggie, the last thing in the world I want is for you to get hurt. You have to know Daniel is a risk. I thought I explained his history. And I know Amber did. But you hired him anyway."

"He's doing really well. He's helpful to the pastors and the church secretary. He's very thorough. They haven't had to ask him to redo any of his work. He's always on time, even though he's walking four miles to and back."

"I didn't know he was walking."

"One of the parishioners is going to donate a bicycle for him next week."

"Good." Why hadn't she thought of that?

Maggie patted one of the student desks, motioning her to sit, and then sat down next to her.

"I know you have past baggage and you are rightly concerned. But he's doing really well."

"Please don't," whispered Shannon.

"Don't what?" Maggie's eyebrows creased together.

"Don't fall for my father. He's charming. I know it. And he's got this little-boy way about him. He means to be honest. And then?"

"Bipolar is a complicated illness." Maggie reminded her.

Understatement of the year. "Yes. No one knows that better than me."

"Daniel does. We've talked about it. He's living with many regrets."

Shannon's head sagged against her chest. "I'm sure he is. But he's not under a doctor's care, and that means he's not on his meds. At any moment he's going to hit the depressive cycle and it's going to implode."

"What if it doesn't?"

Shannon put her hand on Maggie's arm. "It always does. Always. You can hope for change, but without his wanting to, it won't. He's going to be an addict for the rest of his life. He's going to avoid his meds for the rest of his life. It's who he is."

It was Maggie's turn to drop her head. "Listen, Shannon, we don't talk faith much, but with God..."

"Please don't misquote Bible verses to me. All things are possible for those who love Him and who abide in Him. I believe that. I have no proof Daniel does."

"He talks about God all the time."

There was no getting through to her. Or Amber. Or Justin. And now Justin's parents were getting sucked in. She had finally found a family for herself after all these years of waiting. Not only that, when this all exploded, she'd be blamed. She'd lose all she'd built. Even though she warned everyone, it'd come down to her. Why, oh why, had she tried to do the right thing?

She had to call Justin for one last try. She didn't want Matias or Josie hurt. Or worse, robbed. Because when Daniel went down, he'd head right for the drugs. She'd seen it a hundred times.

"I need to go."

"Can I share something with you?"

Shannon was pulling on her coat. The donuts called to her and she realized she hadn't eaten all day.

"Sure."

"Daniel told me he's been clean a number of years. I know this is hard for you. But I hope you'll at least give him a chance."

"You have no idea how many chances I *have* given him, Maggie." She whipped out of the building, not wanting to hear any more reasonable arguments from Maggie, all the while desperately hoping to catch Justin before he left for Daniel's place.

●────── • • • • ──────●

By the time she got a hold of Justin on the phone, he was pulling up outside Daniel's apartment with a lasagna.

"It's all cooked. Do you want to join us?"

Shannon realized she was four miles away and really shouldn't be driving.

"No."

"I can hear it in your voice. You know you want to. It's your favorite."

Lasagna was her favorite? "What?"

"Amber told me."

"Oh. Right." Amber made her a lasagna recently with her new cooking skills, and Shannon had wanted to be encouraging. It was coming back to bite her. "Amber didn't make that, did she?"

Justin laughed. "No. It's just a frozen one I cooked up. Smells amazing. Let me come get you."

"Fine. I'm at the church."

"Let me take this upstairs to Daniel's and I'll be right there."

Twenty minutes later, Justin pulled up. She climbed in, and they headed across the bridge to the east side.

"I told Daniel I was bringing you. He was pretty excited. I think he wants to show you gratitude for what you've done for him."

Shannon's heart raced. "But he doesn't know what I've done for him, does he? He can't know."

"He knows you got the ball rolling is all. Are you sure that's the right thing to do with all of this?"

"I wish everyone would just let me feel the way I do and quit trying to fix something that's not fixable." Her voice rose in the tiny cab of Justin's car and he pulled over, mouth agape, in front of Daniel's place.

"I'm sorry." She looked down at her fingers, intertwined, turning white from the pressure.

"No, I'm sorry. I'm only basing all this on what I've seen over the past several weeks. That's not a lifetime of disappointments like you've faced. I promise not to put any more pressure on you."

"I just don't want to lose any of this. You or your parents." Because she would. Like an atom bomb incinerating every good thing in her life.

He leaned over and hugged her, and she melted into his embrace. His scent, his arms, his warmth brought her instant comfort.

"About the other day at my folk's house?"

Shannon pulled back. "Yeah?" She had to keep Daniel from going to the Romeros'. Her mind conjured up an image of Daniel breaking things, tossing a chair out of their window because suddenly he couldn't abide something that had happened. Visions from her childhood clouded her vision and drew her away.

"Did you hear what I said?" Justin sounded hurt.

"No. I'm sorry. I drifted. I'm just so worried about the collateral damage with my dad."

Justin pulled back. "I think it goes deeper than that."

"What's that supposed to mean?"

"You're holding onto stuff you shouldn't. You're worried to the point of having anxiety attacks and PTSD events. When's the last time you talked to your counselor?"

"I don't think that's any of your business." Shannon's back stiffened.

"It should be, shouldn't it? I'm supposed to drive you." He took her hand in his. "Shannon, I just told you I loved you, and you didn't even hear it." He let go and climbed from the car, leaving her by herself. Shannon's eyes widened. She'd missed his first declaration entirely. Her eyes filled with tears. She followed him, coming around and taking his hands in hers.

"Justin, I'm so sorry. I don't know what's wrong. I don't know how to do this. I know you care about Daniel, but I don't know how to have peace with my father."

Just then the door to the stairs closed and she spun around to see a shocked Daniel, face pale, eyes tinged pink and filled with alternating happiness and grief.

"Shannon? *My* Shannon?"

"Oh, no."

CHAPTER 28

A mber's gown was one Shannon and she had planned for years. It had lace sleeves, a low-cut bodice, and a short train. They'd shortened it to make it safer for Amber to walk. The beading was intricate over the lace sleeves. If Shannon would ever marry, she'd use the same dress and detach the sleeves. At least that was the plan in the ninth grade before Amber had grown two inches taller than Shannon.

She moved to the foyer and got pictures of the flowers, then to the entry of the long hall and up through the sanctuary. Shannon had always liked Amber's church. It had an open floor plan with removable chairs for reorganizing. She moved up to the wedding party and took those photos. They didn't want to spend much time after the ceremony taking pictures. Shannon put her camera on the tripod and raced up for the bridesmaid and bride shots. Then, she took one with both the moms, Amber in the middle.

As Shannon took photos of the bride, she continued to re-imagine the dress for her wedding someday. She'd lift the hem and take off those sleeves and they'd be good to go. She shook herself. Wedding? Who was she fooling?

Two weeks ago, she'd missed Justin saying "I love you" for the first time. Not to mention Daniel knowing she was his daughter. Tensions were still high, and with all the wedding plans, they hadn't had time to clear the air and work through it all.

Shannon took the last shot, shooed them from the room and

called to the groom and best man. Ethan came in on crutches, pale and nervous. Justin followed with a big grin on his face.

"I was just teasing."

"No, man. That's just not cool."

"What's going on?" Shannon took some candid shots.

"I told him all these lilies were for a funeral, but we got a great discount."

"That's mean." Shannon giggled.

"Oh, I remember now, they're going to keep the flowers up for the funeral tomorrow." He laughed.

"Seriously, dude." Ethan shook his head at him. "So not cool. Don't let Amber hear you."

"Don't let Amber hear what?" Amber's voice shot from around the corner.

"You can't be out here." Ethan panicked. He was good at that the last few days. "We can't see each other."

"No problem," Amber snickered.

"You have an unfair advantage. But it's the groom that's not supposed to see the bride." He walked to the corner.

"Hey, Amb, do you want one of those corner-holding-hands pictures? You know, where the bride and groom hold hands but don't peek?"

Amber put her hands around the corner of the stage wall and Ethan took them. Their expressions filled Shannon's heart. They were perfect for each other. She got several shots. "Okay, you, head out." Amber followed orders and Shannon took the shots of the men. She had trouble remembering she was supposed to make Ethan the focus. Justin looked so sharp in his tuxedo. And his eyes bore into hers as she framed each shot. They really needed to talk. She followed up their set with Ethan's parents. They were a tight-lipped couple, putting on a happy act for their son. At least they could do that. Then his grandmother stepped up on the stage.

"Grammy, please, stop." She licked one of her fingers and

touched up Ethan's hair. Amber was right, they all treated him like a little boy. "Grammy, really. No."

Ethan's grandmother withdrew her fingers and sighed. "If you don't care that your cow-like is showing, then I do not care either."

"Cowlick."

"This is what I said." She shrugged. "The cow-like. It looks like the cow all spiky in different directions."

She was a feisty one. Ethan planted a kiss on her wrinkled cheek and told Justin he needed to get some photos of Amber and Shannon. He came forward to get the camera as Ethan ushered his family out of the room.

As her fingers brushed with Justin's she felt an electrical spark. "Ouch."

"I have that effect." He laughed at his own joke. She would have given him heck for it, but right then, all she could think of was:

"I love you, too." Did she say that out loud? Oh, yeah. Did she ever.

Justin's eyes widened in surprise. "Yeah?" His grin grew as he took in her face, her dress, her all.

"Yeah." She sighed.

"Finally. Let's get these shots." Amber's matter-of-fact tone startled them both. They hadn't noticed her enter.

"Is that all you can say?"

"It's my wedding." Amber pulled Shannon into a hug and whispered into her ear, "I'm so happy for you both. Really." She kissed her cheek and followed up with, "and I'll take good care of the dress for you." And she winked to her right—at no one—because Shannon was to her left.

"Dork." Shannon nudged her.

They both fell to laughing. Justin took several candid shots. And then, as he looked through the lens, Shannon felt his gaze and knew he was struggling with the same issue she'd had. She was about to joke with him when she saw Maggie entering at the back leading Daniel by the hand, and all thoughts of jokes and romantic gazes were smothered by the fear that Daniel would ruin the day for everyone.

Shannon stiffened.

"What is it?" Amber put her hand on Shannon's arm. "Are you okay?"

"Daniel is here. With Maggie. I think they're here together."

Amber understood. "Please try not to worry. This day is going to be wonderful, and nothing and no one will get in the way of it."

Shannon wished she felt so assured. She went to one of the ushers and asked him to announce that they'd begin seating. Then she led Amber off through the side door, around to the waiting room. Jennifer came in, sniffling, dabbing at her eyes and nose with a tissue.

"The church, your dress, Ethan..." She choked on a sob. "You're all so beautiful." She hugged Amber. "I always hoped you'd marry. Then it didn't seem like it would happen."

"Thanks, Mom." Amber smirked teasingly.

"You know what I mean. Boys came and went and there just wasn't anyone worthy until Ethan. And he's just so perfect for you. He doesn't let you get away with anything. And he doesn't treat you like a blind person."

"And I don't treat him like a disabled person."

The unspoken fear that Ethan's cancer would come out of re-mission hung on the air, but they acted like it didn't exist. Today wasn't a day for borrowing trouble. Shannon decided then and there not to let Daniel's presence shake her. This was about Amber and Ethan and that was that.

There was a knock on the door. "Can I come in?" Maggie called.

"Yes, please do." Amber squeezed Jennifer's hand. "If you're okay with it?"

"This is your wedding, Amber. And she's your mom, too. If you want her, she's in."

"Thank you, Jennifer. I'm grateful daily that my girl became your girl when I couldn't take care of her anymore." Maggie passed through the door. "I know I can't see you, but I know you are a beautiful bride." She made her way toward Amber, and Shannon helped her close the gap. Maggie touched Amber's face in a gentle caress. "I remember brilliant green eyes and your beautiful golden-red hair. You have carried the love of your father and I and your mom and dad with you, encased in your heart all these years. And now you'll share all your love with Ethan. And one day your children will carry it all, too. And at the core, your love of your heavenly Father, knitted through it all. What a beautiful heritage." Maggie rubbed Amber's arms, as if warming her.

"All those years ago, I never imagined I would get to attend my daughter's wedding. Praise God we found each other. That we were reunited. I will be forever grateful." She turned to Jennifer. "And thank you for allowing me to be a part of this. You did such a good job raising her. You certainly don't need to share this day with me. I feel so blessed."

Jennifer reached out and took Maggie's hand.

"We are blessed, Maggie. We have the best daughter in the whole world."

Shannon felt the sting of tears and a niggle of jealousy but pushed it away. This was Amber's day. They were sisters. That's all that mattered. That's all she needed. She didn't need a mom. Or a dad. She had Amber and Jesus. And now Justin. What more could she want?

A voice down deep told her she might not fully believe that, that she had an opportunity for more with Daniel, but she ignored the implications.

She picked up her camera and took several more candid shots of Maggie and Amber hugging, of Maggie and Jennifer hugging, and of all three of them laughing over a private joke. And then a final knock came on the door. Shannon peeked out and saw an usher.

"It's time."

"Got it." She turned around to the ladies behind her. "It's time."

Amber and Shannon held each other's hands as the moms excused themselves.

"This is it." They both said at the same time. "I wouldn't let you do this if I didn't think Ethan was the best man for the job."

"I know you wouldn't." They held each other for a minute. "And don't get mad, but I feel the same way about Justin for you."

"Today is about you, sweetie." They backed away from one another and blew their noses simultaneously. "I'm so happy for you." Shannon hugged Amber.

"Thank you. I love you."

"I love you always. Sisters forever." They linked hands, and Shannon led Amber out to both her moms and they escorted Amber to the sanctuary door. Shannon took the photo. Then she picked up her bouquet from the table, entered the wedding hall, and walked up the aisle, using the lilies, magnolias, and roses in her bouquet to cover the camera. Then she stashed the flowers and took shots of Amber, escorted by both of her mothers, up the aisle. Shannon turned and got shots of Ethan. His face glowed with peace and wonder at his bride.

And Justin was glowing at *her*. She slipped up on the stage near the pastor and waited for Amber's mothers to pass her to Ethan. Then he led her up the stairs, and Shannon took one last shot and handed the camera off to Jennifer to take some photos while she stood next to her best friend, her sister in life, as she bonded to another.

The jealousy she'd expected to feel was gone. She only felt happiness and excitement for Amber to start this new journey, even though they weren't taking it together. Love really wasn't jealous.

The rest of the verse was rattled off by the pastor, "I'll be reading from first Corinthians, chapter thirteen, verses four through eight.

"Love is patient, love is kind. It does not envy, it does not boast, it is not proud. It does not dishonor others, it is not self-seeking, it is not easily angered, it keeps no record of wrongs. Love does not delight in evil but rejoices with the truth. It always protects, always trusts, always hopes, always perseveres. Love never fails."

The pastor started his talk on love and persevering, but all Shannon could hear echoing in her ears was *love keeps no record of wrongs*. She could see Daniel sitting over to the side with Maggie. He was holding her hand. Fear threatened to seize her, but she pushed it back.

Was she keeping a record of wrongs? Was it just hurt and betrayal that kept her away from being able to forgive Daniel, or was she keeping a record of every time he let her down, every time he hurt her, forgot her, and put himself first?

Did she want to be *that* person?

And if not, how could she stop being *this* when it was all Shannon knew? It would take a miracle. It would be a huge undertaking.

"In sickness and in health, forsaking all others, until death parts us." Amber and Ethan repeated the lines back to the pastor with the utmost solemnity, looking deeply into each other's eyes. So many couples rattled off that part of the covenant as if they were just words without promises attached.

But Amber and Ethan knew already how fast life changed and what the future could hold. They weren't going in with blinders on, so to speak. Ethan's cancer could come back. No one knew how much time they'd have together, and theirs might be shorter than expected. Shannon felt tears streaming down her cheeks and wiped hastily at them. She shot a look at Justin. His eyes were pink. He knew, too.

"I now pronounce you man and wife." A few people in the audience hooted. "You may now seal the deal."

That drew a big laugh, and many "awws" as Ethan and Amber kissed for the first time as a married couple. Joy overflowed from Shannon's heart.

"Ladies and gentlemen, may I present Mr. and Mrs. Ethan and Amber Griffith."

The room exploded with claps and yells of celebration. Ethan took hold of Amber's hand and they helped each other carefully down the steps, then down the aisle to the entryway. If ever there was a portrait of marriage, that should be it. One leaning on the other.

Shannon turned to take Justin's arm and caught Daniel's eye. He still carried a stunned look in his eyes, mixed with hesitation and hurt.

Shannon didn't know what he might see in her eyes. She was trying her best to keep a blank expression when it came to him. She didn't want to let down her guard and invite discussion. But conviction rushed over her, and she tried to smile at him. He smiled back, tentative but hopeful.

The very thought of letting him closer filled her with a cold fear—the unknown and the known mixing in her imagination. Could she handle being hurt one more time?

Justin leaned over as they walked out, arm in arm. "You okay?"

"We'll see."

Okay, God. Let's go keep no record of wrongs.

CHAPTER 29

The church auditorium was decorated in pale greens and aqua, streamers cascading from the ceiling in every direction, like a tent. Wires of white and blue twinkle lights edged the walls and chased up the streamers. The DJ was playing dance music intermixed with love songs. A long buffet table ran the length of one wall, with drinks and food of every kind. There were about two-hundred guests, but food enough to feed them three times over.

Jennifer had arranged for the food and décor—and she spared no expense, even though Amber asked her to keep it low-key. Then she'd relented when Jennifer reminded her she was her only daughter and they'd never get this chance again.

In lieu of a first dance with her father, Amber danced with Ethan and invited everyone else along. Shannon took photos of the guests lingering at the buffet, dancing, sitting at tables, illuminated by candlelight.

Justin came up behind her. "Care to dance?"

She didn't look at him but teased instead. "I need to take photos."

Justin leaned over to whisper, "Don't tell Amber, but Jennifer enlisted her secretary."

"Debbie? Where?" Shannon swirled around and spied Debbie taking candid shots. She was hurt, but only for a moment. This would allow her to enjoy herself, too. She waved at Debbie, who waved back with a worried expression on her face, having been found out. Shannon gave her a thumbs up and Debbie's shoulders relaxed.

"In that case, okay." Stashing her camera in its case, she put her hand in his, and he drew her out to the dance floor, assembled for just this purpose. She had to admit, it felt very natural being in his arms.

"We've never danced together before." He pulled her closer as they swayed to "I Want to Know What Love Is."

"I guess we haven't taken time to do the traditional dating thing." Technically, she'd never done the traditional dating thing with anyone. Amber hadn't been the only one protecting herself from heartache.

"I don't even know what that means. I think the way we've done it is perfect. Natural. Nothing forced." He rested his lips against the top of her head as she leaned into him, her face resting on the chest of his tuxedo.

"You are radiating heat. Feeling okay?" She hoped he didn't have a fever.

He chuckled. "Yes. I'm just not used to holding you yet. I hope I never get used to it."

"Oh." Shannon's face went warm.

The music changed to a techno eighties song neither of them recognized, so they moved off the floor to sit down.

"Can I get you something to eat or drink?"

"Yes. I'm famished. I don't think I've eaten anything today."

"You're lucky you didn't pass out on stage." He looked worried. "I'll be right back."

Shannon massaged her neck before reaching for her camera bag. Pulling out her camera, she took several more shots of the couples dancing and then stood for closeups, snapping several of children and toddlers jumping to the rhythm.

The song changed to "You Are So Beautiful." An ache filled Shannon's throat as she watched Amber and Ethan sway to the music. Ethan was singing into Amber's ear. They really were perfect for each other, no matter how long they had. She chided herself for dark thoughts on such a light occasion.

She knew only too well how things could and did change, often for the worse. She blamed it on the song. She'd not heard it in years and avoided it when it came on the radio.

A familiar voice from behind startled her. "I used to sing that song to you and your mom."

Shannon didn't turn around. "I remember."

"Can we talk?"

She turned to look at Daniel. He was decked out in his suit. He'd been to a barber, his shoulder-length blond hair was trimmed up in a modern cut. And it appeared he'd had some dental work done. He didn't look like a homeless person anymore. He looked like her dad. But looks could be deceiving.

"Okay." She steeled her heart for what would come. Innately, she wanted to trust him. For him to be the dad he could be. But the weighed evidence came up too light.

Justin came to the table with a plate of food for her and a glass of punch. She wasn't hungry anymore.

"Do you want me to join you?"

Did she? She didn't know. She looked up at him, begging him to make the decision. "If you'd like to."

"Justin, could you give us a minute?" Daniel asked.

Justin didn't look at Daniel. He kept looking at Shannon, waiting to see what she wanted him to do.

That made her decision for her. "I would like him to stay." Justin set his food next to hers and took a seat.

Daniel looked disappointed, but Shannon felt only relief.

"Why didn't you tell me who you were?" Daniel asked.

Ah. That's how he'd take this conversation. Not how he'd missed her, how sorry he was that he'd let her down. No apologies. None of that.

"Why should I have?"

Daniel sat back, gobsmacked. "I guess I don't have a reason for you."

"Neither did I." She didn't say it to be mean. It was the truth. She'd spent her childhood raising her father. It was a job she'd grown weary of and didn't really want to take on again.

"I'm glad you found me. I've been looking for you for a long time." He tried a different tact.

Shannon shot a look at Justin and back to Daniel. "I wasn't looking for you." Again, the truth. She didn't want to tell him she'd seen him in passing years ago. She hadn't been sure then, but she was now.

"I'm glad anyway." Daniel shot her a charming and disarming smile. It didn't have the effect he wanted.

"I'm not sure what you're hoping for here, but just because I've helped you get off the streets doesn't mean I want a deeper relationship. The time for that has passed."

"We could try."

"Daniel, I've spent a lot of my life thinking about all the trying. I tried. You didn't. Those are the facts. And a grade-school-aged kid shouldn't have to try. My job was to eat and sleep and go to school and play with friends and hang out with my parents. I never got that."

Daniel frowned, his voice deepening. "I did the best I could."

Shannon looked at Daniel, her eyes dissecting every aspect. He wasn't sorry. He was still making excuses. "If that's true, then there's really nothing more to say." She moved to get up but sat back down when another thought crossed her mind. "Tell me one thing?"

"Anything."

"Maggie said you were clean, and I can see that today you are. But are you taking your meds?"

"I don't need meds. All my issues came from drug abuse. I don't have any of that anymore."

"Any of what?"

"All that crazy mental stuff." He shrugged it off like it'd been nothing more than a slight annoyance.

Shannon nodded slowly. "You might think I don't remember, Daniel. I figured it out a long time ago. You started taking illegal drugs to control your mental illness because those drugs were more to your liking than the legal ones."

Daniel stared openly at her. "That's not the order of things. You were young. You just don't remember."

Shannon leaned closer and spoke clearly. "If you don't stay clean, and you don't start taking doctor-moderated lithium, or whatever the new trial med of the day is, then you won't be able to keep the apartment and you will be right back where I found you. Do you understand?"

"I keep telling you, I'm clean."

"It's like we're on two different planes of existence. I keep talking and you aren't hearing me."

"I hear you. You just don't have the pertinent facts."

"Pertinent facts" was her father's way of deflecting. He knew better, and she was ignorant. Except she wasn't. Daniel was never a stupid man. And maybe that was the problem. He thought he could work through this on his own. And he couldn't. Anyone on the outside could see it.

Justin put a hand on her arm. "Let's dance, okay? This is Amber and Ethan's day." He stood and pulled Shannon after him, but she resisted, wanting to return for her camera and purse. "Give me a minute. I need to get my things."

Daniel stayed at the table, looking hurt until Maggie arrived. Shannon watched them from her spot on the dance floor. Maggie started patting Daniel's arm and comforting him. Daniel spoke and Maggie shook her head. Great.

"I'm sorry." Justin's voice cut into her thoughts.

Shannon looked up into Justin's face. "For what?"

Justin tipped his head toward the table. "I didn't really understand."

"You couldn't have known. I lived it. I know he thinks he means well, but I can't let myself go there again."

"I agree."

"But I do have to do something." She frowned as she watched Daniel and Maggie move to the other side of the room and take a distant table.

"What?"

"I need to warn Amber about Maggie. She's falling for Daniel, and I don't want to see her hurt."

"But not today?"

"No. Not today." Her mind slipped sideways, and Daniel was holding her up as she stood on his feet and they danced in a circle, father and daughter, laughing and enjoying a rare, lighthearted moment. She felt herself sucked into the memory like someone had turned on a vacuum and pulled her mind to a different time. The upbeat music played in the background, food cooked on the stove for the first time in months, and Daniel kept laughing and spinning her around as they danced. She laughed.

Justin's arm tightened around her, and she was yanked back to the present. She was a bead on a rubber band, stretched from one time to another.

Now she knew she had to do something else, too. She had to get over her childhood, and extricate herself from Daniel's life for good, or she'd never be able to move on. And she had to do it soon.

CHAPTER 30

The meal at the Romeros', once again, was exquisite. Shannon and Justin helped Josie clear the table as Matias moved to the back porch.

She whispered to Justin, "Does your dad ever help?"

"Not when I'm home." Justin's wry tone made Shannon laugh.

Josie clucked at them both. "Your father helps out often. He still works all week, so I want to give him a chance for respite. It's the least I can do."

"I didn't mean any disrespect, Mrs. Romero."

"None of that. You call me Josie." Then Josie's eyes narrowed. "Why did your father not join us tonight?"

Justin interrupted. "It's best for now. Daniel has a lot to work through."

"I remember what you said. Perhaps it is for the best, yes?"

Shannon nodded. "I don't know when he'll be ready, but I want to keep you both safe."

"He is not a safe man?"

"He's mentally ill and refuses help."

"Ah. I have suffered from depressions." Josie moved around her kitchen, wiping counters and putting the last of the items into the refrigerator as if she'd said nothing more than she'd gone for a walk earlier that day.

"I didn't know that, Mamá."

"It was long ago. Sometimes it still comes to me. You know we wanted other children?"

237

"But you couldn't," Justin responded in a rote manner.

"But we did."

Justin looked up surprised.

"Sadly, I had three pregnancies. You are the only one I could carry to term." Her eyes filled with tears, and Josie took Justin's outstretched hand. "It broke my heart into tiny pieces. Each baby took a piece of my heart with it when it passed." She patted Justin's face. "This is why we are so *in your life*, as you say. You are my treasure." A tear slipped down her cheek.

Justin's eyes teared. "I'm sorry, Mamá, I didn't know."

"After you, the doctor said I shouldn't try anymore. The miscarriages took such a toll mentally and physically, he and Matias worried for me. So you were our only living and last." She squeezed his arm, and he hugged her.

"But now, maybe we will have another in our family? And then another?" She hugged Shannon.

Shannon knew Josie meant it as a kindness, but right then, she couldn't imagine being a parent. She was having enough trouble taking care of herself without adding more hormones to the mix.

"Can I ask, Josie, did you take medication? Sorry if that's out of line, you don't need to answer." Shannon balked at her own forwardness.

"It's okay. I don't mind talking about it. I took medication for a while. Then the counselor and the Lord carried me through. I'm not against medication, mind you. The Lord can heal with medicine as much as miracles. Sometimes He carries us along, and sometimes He takes us out of our difficulty. Sometimes we are healed, and sometimes we have a burden to carry until the end—but through His power, we *can* carry it. Grace be to God. His choices we don't always understand, but we can trust in His goodness and mercy." She sighed as if all was right in her world. And Shannon could see it was.

It was a conversation she didn't even know she needed to have.

But Josie's words settled into her, giving her confidence in God's wisdom and power.

"I have problems." Her voice, barely audible, drew Josie and Justin's attention. "I'm seeing a counselor."

"It's PTSD," Justin explained for her.

"It's depression, too. I can't control my thoughts. They skate off on a will of their own. I don't know all the triggers and I don't know how to break their hold."

Josie took Shannon by the arm and led her into the living room. Justin followed. Josie pulled Shannon down to sit next to her on the floral-cushioned couch. Then she looked up at Justin.

"Can you tell your father we are out of ice cream?"

Justin's eyes reflected understanding. "You okay?" he asked Shannon.

"Yes."

He leaned down and kissed the top of her and his mother's heads. Then he went on out to the porch and invited Matias to the grocery store.

"I know this might make you nervous for Justin. I want you to know I'd never ever do anything to hurt him."

"Justin cares deeply for you. I assume you've shared this with him?"

"Yes. Well, not all. At my last psychologist's session, she suggested medication. I've never been against it when it was for someone else."

"But it is harder to accept when it is for you."

"Yes."

"You feel like you are admitting weakness. You are telling the world you cannot handle this alone."

"Yes." Tears welled in her throat. "How can I insist my father take meds to control his bipolar condition when I don't want to take meds for my own issue?"

"It's always easier to see what will help the other person before ourselves. I felt the same. I was frightened. What if they made me worse? What if they changed my personality? What if?"

Shannon nodded.

"I shared my fears with my doctor, and he assured me if we needed to change medications or doses, we would. That I was not on my own. I enlisted Matias to help keep an eye on me. By God's grace I got the right one the first time. But knowing they would listen to me, and watch me, made all the difference."

Shannon's hands shook, so she clasped them together in her lap. "Do you think I should take medication?"

"That's not a decision I can make for you, mija." *My daughter.* Shannon's breath caught at the loving and inclusive nickname. It conjured up additional Sunday night dinners and holiday celebrations. Of a possible history. A hope of family.

Amber was her sister, and Jennifer had been so kind and loving, but it wasn't like this. To have a mother and father who chose her when they didn't have to—the idea tempted and terrified. You couldn't be hurt if there wasn't anyone to hurt you. At least that was what her overprotective central nervous system told her.

It wasn't true, though. She'd been hurt plenty of times being shut out of family events, by being alone, or from having to grow up much faster than she should. She'd gone hungry, knowing kids in other families were fed and clothed. Loved.

"Josie, I'm afraid. I'm scared I will let you and Matias down. I'm afraid of hurting Justin. I'm afraid of what Daniel will do. I'm afraid of not being enough for anyone—and at the same time being too much to handle. I'm afraid if I take medication, it will work, and I'll have to take it forever. And I'm afraid if I don't take it, my thoughts will stay out of control and I'll lose everything and everyone important to me." Tears streamed down her cheeks and the older woman took her in her arms and held her.

"Shhh. It will be okay." Josie patted Shannon's back. "There is no fear that can control us inside of the Father's love. Perfect love casts out all fear and ushers in perfect peace."

"But I do trust God." She wiped at her cheeks. Didn't she?

"If you trust Him completely, He will give you the strength to face all of your fears." She continued to rub circles on her back. "Shall I tell you what I did many years ago?"

"Please."

"I was terrified. Justin was very young, but it was time for him to go to school. I'd never let him out of my sight before. He had always been within reach. And now I had to take him somewhere and leave him. Not only that, he'd have to ride a bus with strangers. He'd be with people I didn't know. Then I realized this was only the beginning. He would always be with someone I didn't know. He'd one day grow up and move out. He'd go away to college. And I realized I'd been trying to be God for him. To protect him from life and the hardships he might face." Josie's eyes welled with unshed tears.

"He was my blessing from God. He was my only child."

"You'd probably feel like that even if you'd had more children." Shannon tried to comfort Josie. Seeing her so distraught tore at her heart.

"Possibly. But you cannot reason with your fears. Reasoning means you're trying to talk to them and talking with them gives them life. It gives them power they do not have when they are only distant thoughts. The more you talk to them, the larger they grow. Their tendrils start to sneak into every avenue of your life. First, it's fear for your child, then it's fear for your husband, then it's fear of others, fear of failure, fear of the future. They will immobilize you. You will be, how do you say?" Josie searched her memory's English dictionary for the right word. "You will be petrified like the wood turning to stone." She put a hand over her heart. "First your heart, then the rest. Soon, all stone."

Shannon's mind wrapped around what she was saying. Fear didn't stay isolated. It grew and took over.

"How did you do it? How did you escape the fear?"

Josie clucked her tongue and laughed lightly. "You cannot escape. Fear cannot be broken free from or escaped from—it will only find you again. But it can be overcome and overpowered by the Lord. It can be crushed. You can do it on your own, people do. But it keeps coming back to life, stronger the next time. Like an infection treated with the wrong antibiotic. Like weeds you kill and don't dig up and cover. It leaves the open space for twice and three times and ten times the weeds to come back. Soon you are choking again."

Shannon pictured herself in a corn maze with no exit, but instead of corn stalks, they were wild blackberries, and every time she chopped at a section, they would double and come back, their thorns catching her clothes, entangling her hair, scratching her skin leaving long, red, bleeding welts.

"It feels hopeless."

"If you try yourself, it is. But with God all things are possible for those who love Him. God says, 'Fear not, for I am with you.' He says, 'I am the one who helps you.' He says, 'He will go before you.' He says, 'I will be with you, I will never forsake you.' He says nothing can separate us from Him. Nothing. If you put your full trust in Jesus, He will never let you down. You might face hard things, but never, ever alone."

When Shannon was little, she knew this to be true. Now she needed to realize it again.

"Will he help me forgive Daniel? I know I need to, if not for him then for me. I can't carry around this heart of stone for him and still love others fully."

Josie nodded. "I know that is true. If you have a hardness, you cannot be wholly free. It's like the hard ground, when you water it, only the weak spots can accept the water of life, but the rest resists and nothing can take root in such hard ground. It might take a while. But if you go prayerfully, He will help you. And I will pray for you."

"You said you'd tell me how you did it. How God overcame your fear?"

"Much prayer. Much study on the Word of God. And then? I wrote those fears down on slips of paper. I took them out to the fire pit in the back and I lit each one on fire. The paper turned bright yellow, then golden, then to ash. When I am tempted to fear, I take it to the Lord, then I write it down and I burn it up as an offering to the Lord. That I trust Him more than I trust myself. Fear has never overcome me again." Josie sighed. "Not that I am perfect, I have fears. But I don't let them stay. I take care of them as soon as I recognize them."

Shannon imagined her fears on paper, burning them up. What a bonfire that would make.

"When I'm ready, can I use your fire pit?"

Josie's smile creased every wrinkle on her face. "Yes, mija. Yes." And she hugged Shannon like she'd not been hugged ever before. There was love and acceptance in that hug. There was healing and kindness. There was peace.

At that moment, Justin opened the front door and announced they had ice cream. He must have seen the tears streaking down Shannon's face.

"Are you okay?"

"I will be."

"I got the no-problems vanilla, the double-problems mint chip, or the quad-fix-extravaganza of chocolate-fudge-brownie-mocha."

"I think we'll need the quad-fix-extravaganza today."

"Gotcha covered." He headed to the kitchen to start scooping.

By the time she was done, she might need an IV more than the bowl.

CHAPTER 31

S taring down at the kitchen table and the photos arranged on the top, Shannon moved the prints around deftly, gathering like ones together, highlighting others. She needed to take the proposal over that afternoon. Unfortunately, the entire project had slipped to the side during the wedding and all the resulting stress with Daniel.

He was still seeing Maggie, which was upsetting on many levels. She'd hoped that Maggie would listen to her warnings, but Daniel was being so charming, Maggie couldn't believe he'd ever be anything else.

It'd been three months since Shannon had found him. Three weeks since the wedding. He still appeared to be on the straight path. For Maggie's and Amber's sake, she hoped he would stay there. Maggie didn't deserve that kind of pain after what she'd endured in her life. Maybe if she could see Daniel with her own eyes, she'd feel different.

It was a foolish thought.

Meanwhile, she taught at the school, and on long walks, she had gotten in great shots and needed to get them printed off for the mock presentation with Brandon. Tomorrow was the real deal. As much as she told herself it was just some extra cash, she realized that somewhere in the middle of if all, she'd fallen in love with the project.

The phone rang. Rafe Applegate. She answered.

"Shannon, darling, how are you, my dear?"

"Good. I'm good."

"Have you given any thought to the showing I suggested to Amber?"

"I really haven't had time. There's just a lot going on in my life right now."

"I would love to set it up for late November. The rains are here, it's gray and dismal. It will enhance the mood of your photos and pull on the heartstrings of those who love to invest in projects right before Christmas."

"That sounds really callous." She hadn't meant to say it aloud. "I mean..." she stuttered.

"I'm a pragmatist, my dear. It's darkest before the dawn. And the dawn brings in money from the well-intentioned. They are going to give it away somewhere. Why not give it to a place you're invested in and also take some of that money for yourself?"

"What are the margins?"

"Fifty, thirty-five, fifteen."

"The fifteen percent is for you?"

"Yes. I'm a businessman. I wish I could be entirely philanthropic, but there are bills to pay, and I need to eat."

She knew from watching Rafe work his magic at these parties, he ate very well. Still...

"Fifty percent for the shelter sounds amazing. Especially right now with Thanksgiving around the corner."

"You and I are on the exact same page."

She doubted that. Though Rafe was, at his core, a nice guy. She knew at least that much. Had a stranger come to her with such a proposal, she would have balked.

"What's the sell-line?"

"I happen to know many people who are on the cusp of the homeless issue, doing studies and research. And they know people who want to invest and be part of the solution. Their reasons are their own, but the money will go to places you trust and have a relationship with. It's all well and good to donate food and clothing. But the shelters, too, have bills to pay. Electricity, water, upkeep and infrastructure takes up a larger chunk than people want to admit."

"I know that's true. You can't pay the city with sleeping bags or shelf-stable foods." The shelters were often hard-pressed for cash. It was easier for people to grasp the idea of keeping someone warm and fed with tangible objects, so that's what most gravitated to. But they really did need to keep the power on and the toilets and showers working.

"I'm glad you're seeing my side. Can you come over this evening?"

"I've got to turn in a project presentation at the school. It'll be late. Is that okay?"

"The coffee bar is open until ten."

"It won't be that late."

"Dinner is on me. We've got fresh salmon salad with smoky gouda and hand-crafted croutons and crusty bread."

"Oh, shoot. I want to come by now. I haven't eaten today."

"You could certainly come by now."

Shannon looked down at the messy arrangement and knew she had at least two hours ahead of her.

"Thanks, but seriously can't. I will be there tonight for sure."

They said their good-byes, and Shannon grabbed a banana and went back to the task at hand. She put the special needs classes front and center, then the youth classes to the sides. She showcased some of their best students as well as some of the beginners. When she was satisfied, she opened her computer, repositioned the photos and added the text and their school's logo.

Two hours fell away fast. She printed the final and slipped it into the protective sleeve and into her portfolio. She grabbed her water bottle and filled it. She double checked to make sure she had everything she needed and opened the door.

Daniel stood on the other side. His face showed she'd taken him by surprise.

"I didn't know if you'd be home."

"I don't have time right now." She started to close the door behind her, but he put up a hand.

"Please. I really handled things badly last time."

"How did you get my address?"

"Maggie gave it to me."

Shannon flustered with anger but didn't know how to react to that. Instead she pressed him to leave.

"I've got to be at my school to drop off a presentation. I really can't do this." She waved a hand back and forth between them.

"Can I have just fifteen minutes?"

Shannon's shoulders sagged in defeat. "Fine. But just fifteen. I really need to go."

She invited him in and pointed him to the dining table where he pulled out a chair and she joined him. She didn't offer him a drink. She didn't want to extend their meeting.

"At the wedding, I just wanted to say—I really messed up."

Shannon could hear the regret in his voice and could see it clearly in his eyes.

"I should have let you know how grateful I was that you have helped me when you owe me nothing but animosity. I let you down. I'm very sorry."

The words hung in the air, waiting to be accepted—but she didn't know how to do that. She immediately wished Josie were there to counsel her. She didn't want to continue to hold a grudge against her father, it would just fester in her spirit. But this felt like an ambush. She was about to ask him to leave when she caught him staring at her neck.

"What?" She put a hand up protectively.

"That's your mom's necklace," said Daniel in awe.

Shannon fingered it and then tucked it inside her shirt.

"It's all I have left of her."

Daniel's head hung low. "I wish I could make things up to you."

"I feel like we need to talk about a lot of things, none of which I have time to do today."

"Please." His tone shifted. He was begging. And something else was off. Shannon scrutinized his features. He was perspiring at the temples, his leg was bouncing, his hands were shaking.

"You have the DTs?"

"No. I'm clean. I have been for months. I'm just really nervous. I missed breakfast because I want to make things right with you."

Anger bubbled to the surface faster than blinking. Her heart raced, and words rushed from her lips before she could stop them. Part of her relished laying him out, but most of her was horrified.

"Make things right? And how do you propose to do that? Rewind the clock and remove all the abuse I suffered in foster homes? Remove the neglect from you and Mom? And later when you were strung out? Make up for all the nights I went to bed hungry? Go back and stop Mom from killing herself on drugs *you* brought home?" She laughed, horrified and on the edge of hysterical. She'd never felt like this before. Hot rage zinged through her like bolts of lightning, striking whatever was in her path.

Daniel sat back, away from her, eyes full of pain. Shannon watched as each accusation hit home, like an unpredictable storm rolling in off the ocean, taking out trees and homes indiscriminately.

"Can you make up for all the nights I slept in the house afraid? Or the times I went out to find you and bring you home? Did you remember I'd go into those drug-infested, needle-strewn dumps to find you? Do you even know how old I was? How is that right for a six or seven or even nine-year-old child to do?"

Her voice rose to a pitch so high she didn't recognize it. Her throat burned from emotion and strain. She covered her mouth with both hands and stopped. Her breaths came in gasps through her fingers.

"I don't know." He exhaled, grasping at words that seemed to be too hard to find. "I'm sorry. I wish..." He stopped, looking at her with red-tinged eyes full of amazement and awe and horror. "There's just..." His voice cracked with emotion. "I'm sorry."

There was nothing he could say to her to take away the burning anger, the bone-deep hurt, the broken spirit, the betrayal. Nothing. *Sorry* simply wouldn't do it.

"Your fifteen minutes are up." Her voice was raspy. She grabbed her things and opened the door, pointing him out with a shaking finger. Then she locked the door behind them and raced down the stairwell, skipping steps and stumbling. She had to get out of there. She had to get away from Daniel. And somehow, she had to get away from herself.

CHAPTER 32

Shannon was out of her car, stumbling up to the school, her portfolio slipping out of her grasp as she fumbled her keys before she realized where she was. She looked back at her car, realizing with a start that she'd driven. Once she saw there wasn't a mark on it, she breathed again. Somehow, she'd made it there safely, but she didn't recall any of the streets. She didn't even remember getting in the car.

She just remembered wanting to run, and the sinking realization that Daniel would see her go-bag if she'd grabbed it. A niggling voice in her head said she'd need to find a new apartment. She couldn't have him knowing where she lived.

Her heart raced, and her hands shook so hard she dropped everything on the front step of the school. The sky opened, and rain poured down. The streets emptied of pedestrians. As Shannon stood under the overhang, the musky aroma of tar rose from the rain-soaked asphalt and filled her senses. The rain came down in sheets and the wind whipped up, blowing like ocean waves at her. Her hair stuck to the side of her face, and the wet started soaking through her light coat to her T-shirt beneath. A chill raced over her, but it was like it was happening to someone else.

The door opened behind her.

"Hey. You better get in here." Brandon helped her gather her things, and she followed him inside, down the hall and to his office.

He was talking but none of his words made sense to her ears. What was she doing here?

"So, what do you think?" Brandon was sitting at his desk, looking up to her.

What *did* she think?

"You're really dripping. Let me get you a towel and then we'll look at your proposal."

The proposal. Right. Dripping?

Shannon's brain was full of rattling, loose lines set at cross purposes, like someone had ripped a component out of a computer and left bare ends of wires exposed. Brandon brought in a towel and she took it as if on auto pilot, drying her hair, wiping her face—of tears or rain she wasn't sure and didn't know if it mattered.

Once she was dried to his satisfaction, she wiped her hands and then the portfolio. She tossed the towel over a chair back, and opened the folder, revealing the plan inside. Brandon looked it over with great scrutiny. He unfolded and refolded the brochure several times, looking at it from the back to the front and over again. A wide smile crossed his face.

"I love it. I think we'll have it reproduced onto heavier cardstock, but otherwise? The colors are stupendous, the layout professional, and I like the reboot of the logo. It's incredible." He grinned at her.

"I'm very glad you like it." Was she? Shannon felt split down the middle, one side reasonable, the other in a numbed stupor watching from the outside in.

"I think if you ever wanted to, you could start a commercial art business. This is as good if not better than what those other bids offered."

"And at an affordable price."

"You can't beat free."

Shannon stared at him. "Funny."

"Can't blame a guy for trying."

Shannon's mind wandered and found purchase. "Oh, here."

She pulled out Brandon's camera bag, lenses and extra paraphilia from her bag. "I was given another camera. Thanks very much for letting me borrow this."

Brandon's eyebrows creased. "Of course. I kind of thought you'd want to use it for a while."

"Justin gave me his old camera. It took an hour or so, but we're getting along very well."

"This one is superior."

Shannon's head cocked to one side, as if to see if his offense would make more sense from that direction.

"I am very grateful to you, Brandon. I certainly wouldn't be so far ahead without it. You're right, it's superior, but my new camera fits me well, and it's mine. It's not the latest greatest, but as you can see from the photos, it's hard to tell which camera I used for which shots."

Brandon studied the pamphlet as if the photos would scream out which camera had been used for each of them.

"I guess you're right." He backed down.

"I hope you know how much I appreciated your trusting me with such a magnificent piece of equipment." The numb side of her couldn't believe the other side was being so overt and gushy. It worked, though. Brandon dropped the argument. He pulled out his checkbook and wrote out a check for the project.

"If you would drop those by the printers, it'd be great."

"I can't. I'm on my way to another meeting." Was she? The awake portion of her brain looked around, taking in the rough texture of the tweed guest chairs in Brandon's office, comparing them to the slick and smooth vegan leather desk chair that had probably cost more than three months' rent.

"Oh, of course. I'll be able to do that in a bit. Will you be there for the main presentation?"

"When will you give it?"

"Tomorrow."

"Yes. I'll definitely be there. What time again?"

Brandon said but she didn't listen. She was packing up her things, pulling on her drenched coat, and readying to leave. She shook his hand and closed his office door behind her. When she got to the hall, she couldn't remember which way the parking lot was. Her legs moved her west, and she found herself outside. She went to her car and started to tug on the door handle. Her fingers kept slipping off from the rain. It was locked.

She pushed her hair back from her face and dug into her pocket, extracting the keys. Something in the back of her head warned her not to try the lock. It told her to walk away. Instead she went to the trunk of her car and popped it. Inside was a warmer coat and gloves. She emptied her current coat pocket of change and her phone and put them to the side where they'd be safe from being dropped. She tossed her keys on top of the tiny pile before taking off the wet coat and tossed it to the opposite side. She tugged on the dry, winter jacket, zipping it up to her neck and pulling on the hood lined with fake fur. Then she pulled on the gloves.

Shannon stretched her fingers inside the gloves, the blood warming them, the tingling cold leaving. She kept her bottle of water, hooking it to her jeans with a carabiner under her coat, but dumped the portfolio. She stuck her wallet in her pocket and left the purse. Then she slammed the trunk closed.

With the keys. And her phone. Inside.

Her head dropped in exasperation. She went back to the school, intending to use the phone to call Amber. Shannon kept an extra set of her keys at her place for just such an emergency. And Amber did vice-versa at her place. Except Amber was on her honeymoon and there was no way to get in without her *keys*.

"I'm an idiot." She spoke to the sky.

She'd go inside and call Justin and stay at his place until she could figure out a game plan.

She got to the school's glass door and tugged, but it was locked. She leaned in, cupping her face to the glass in order to see inside the darkened school building, but only spied the emergency exit lights. Brandon's office was dark. He must have gone out the other side. She ran around to the other parking lot but found that door locked and his parking space empty.

Now what? The numbness in her brain was waking up. She'd never shut down quite like that before, but as it was waking up, the pain she'd felt from her confrontation with Daniel seeped in, and she wished it would go numb all over again.

She checked her watch. She was supposed to be at the gallery soon. She could make it on foot. She was in good shape. It was only three miles. The walk would warm her up and give her time to think. The wind chose that moment to pick up, and the rain slushed out the building runoff chutes, creating rivers over the sidewalks and then down street gutters. Shannon pulled the strings on the hood of her coat tight to protect her from the onslaught, and she headed down the street.

There were quite a number of businesses who relied on the nine-to-five crowd to keep them afloat. They were closed or in process. Coffee shops and luncheonettes, food carts, all shuttering for the night.

They used to stay open later, but this part of town had become inundated with the homeless. Most of whom just wanted to survive, but there were bad elements here just as in every other part of society. And those bad elements defined how the world judged the rest of their community.

She'd been walking for about thirty minutes when she came across the golden-statue at Pettygrove Park where she'd lost her camera those many months ago. Shannon hadn't realized she'd been avoiding this area since the incident. It had historically been one of her favorite spots during fall. She'd come and take pictures of the trees changing color, the pedestrians bundling up, and the birds and squirrels racing like mad to gather food and supplies for winter. Now the leaves had fallen, and it looked like a skeleton forest.

As a youngster, she'd imagined the golden fountain to be magical and come to life at night when all the people were home in bed. Then the little animals would dance and sing with the statue. She pulled her hood forward as if to hide her identity in case that thug was there, lying in wait. But all she saw was a couple of homeless people taking shelter against one of the office buildings and a few other people hitting the stairs nearby on their way to the parking garage. She sighted Magic Stan on the far side of the fountain, splashing around, frantic, in the shin-deep water.

Shannon rounded it and heard Stan muttering to himself.

"Need the money. They took the money. Need the money. Need the money."

"Stan? Are you okay?" Shannon lowered her hood in hopes he'd recognize her from their many encounters.

"If I were okay, young lady, do you think I'd be pilfering and scrounging change in this insipid, bacteria-infested fountain?"

Shannon was taken aback. "No. I guess you sure wouldn't be."

"Indeed." He leaned down and scooped up a Styrofoam cup of change and sludge. He dumped in on the fountain's edge and extracted the coins. Then he put them into another cup, sluicing them free of grime before he pocketed them.

"You seem upset." Shannon approached him with caution. She wasn't afraid for her safety as much as she didn't want to spook him.

"My queen is quite ill. She needs medicine, and we're broke. These horrid criminals stole what little we had, and that included her cold medicine."

"Oh, no. Where is Susie?" Shannon looked around but didn't see Susie Q anywhere in the park.

"She resides at home, convalescing."

"Where is that?"

Stan narrowed his eyes accusingly at her. "Who wants to know?"

"I'm Shannon. I give out books and care packages."

"Yes. The young lady with purple hair. And the boyfriend with all the tattoos and piercings." Stan shivered.

"That's right." Shannon grinned at Stan. Homelessness had done nothing to his tongue.

"Sorry, my dear girl. It grows harder to tell friend from foe on these means streets."

"I totally get that." She looked around to make sure the pimp from before wasn't there. She couldn't fight the sensation she was being watched. She knew she'd do better to stay on alert with Stan, too. She didn't know him any better than anyone else on the street. She didn't know his story. And if she'd learned anything, the most charming could also be the most devastating.

"Where is Susie, Stan?"

Stan stopped his panning for change long enough to answer. "She's four blocks over in one of the better alleys. Only the best for her, you know." He said it proudly, and Shannon once again admired the care he gave Susie.

"Will you take me to her? I can get her a doctor if she needs one. Or buy medicine if I know what it is she needs. And there's a sick room at some of the shelters."

"I cannot let them separate us."

An occupational hazard for homeless families—men and women were kept apart to keep them safe from abuse. But that also kept dedicated couples away from one another—and they often made the choice to stay on the street together than apart in the shelter.

Stan sized her up once again and must not have found her lacking, because he packed away his cups and rinsed his fingers in the fountain, dried them, and stepped from the water. He tugged on wet socks over wet feet and tucked his shoes into his sopping loafers.

"I can get you some dry socks, too. Maybe a blanket?"

"We have everything we need except medicine. On that front I would be eternally grateful."

Shannon followed Stan out of the park. The feeling of being followed didn't leave her though. They continued up considerably more than a few blocks. She was going further and further away from Rafe's café. He had said he'd wait until ten. She didn't really want to be out on the streets until that time of night, though.

Stan stopped and looked around him. Then he ducked into a long walkway snugly fitted between two tall brick buildings. There were a couple of windows higher up that faced the walkway, but for the most part, it was two blank walls and several residential style garbage bins. The rooflines over-hung the walkway just so and kept most of the rain at bay.

Shannon followed, knowing all too well she was officially off grid. If anything happened, no one would know about it for a long time. And no one knew where she was. Her steps faltered, but when she heard moaning, she picked up the pace and caught up to Stan. He turned down a tight sidewalk that dead-ended. There Shannon found a tarp and cardboard tiny house. The green and blue tarps were staked into the walls, tightly secured with ropes, and tipped to allow rain water to run off into buckets on the sides. They were reinforced with heavy cardboard, creating a warmth barrier.

Shannon ducked under the doorway, following Stan inside. The brick walls were also covered with plastic and cardboard, creating the best insulation they could find on the streets. There was a heater running off an extension cord trailing from a basement window and a mini fridge and cooler. Did the landlord know they were literally heating the outside world?

Milk crates stacked three high and three wide up the right wall were filled with plates and pots and mugs. Some clothing was stashed there, as well. There was a larger barrel filled with water and a dishpan. The exterior drain had an additional hole cracked into it and finished with a funnel with a screen over it and duct tape to affix the whole contraption. This was where they must have been dumping dish water and bath water, for those special occasions that required cleanliness.

A hot plate sat over on the right, stabilized on a tray table. Near that was another tray table, and flanking it were two more milk crates. Aged and stained decorative pillows tied to the crates provided the back to a makeshift chair, and a pillow under each for the cushion. Down the left side were four more milk crates, stacked, and full of books. *Her* books she'd given away. Her eyes scanned the shelves and saw familiar titles. Shakespeare, Hemingway, Austin, Montgomery, Bradbury, Pilcher, Tyler, Alcott, and so many more. All were misaligned, a bit tattered, and much loved.

The moaning sound drew Shannon's attention to the back of the tarp-house. She pushed a sheet back and found a bedroom-like area with two sleeping mats and all-weather sleeping bags. Inside one of the bags, Susie Q lay writhing in pain. Near her head was a battery powered camping lamp, lighting the small space.

Shannon ducked inside and went to her knees by Susie's bed.

"Queen Susie? I'm here to help. Can you tell me what you need?"

"She needs acetaminophen for fever and ibuprofen for pain." Stan spoke, as always, like one in great authority.

Shannon felt Susie's fevered brow and saw her eyes were glassy.

He wasn't wrong. Susie definitely needed medication. But for what, Shannon didn't have a clue.

"Where does it hurt?"

"My stomach. My side."

"Can you stretch out so I can press around? I have some minor first aid training." Not to mention she'd been taking care of herself forever. Survival of the fittest was a thing in many group homes. There were some tremendously great foster families, Shannon knew that. She'd seen it. But she'd never been on the receiving end of such things.

Susie took a shuddering breath and stretched out. Shannon pulled back the sleeping bag and held her breath from the odor. She and Stan were doing amazingly well for living on the street, but bathing was a challenge for all of them. She pulled her top taut and pressed lightly where Susie's gallbladder resided. Susie groaned. Then Shannon pushed where her appendix was. As she released the pressure Susie screamed.

"I'm sorry."

Stan came rushing in past the sheet doorway. "What have you done?"

"It's her appendix, Stan. We need to get her to the hospital." She felt Susie's forehead again. Hotter than it was even moments ago. "And we need to get her there immediately. This is an emergency."

All the color drained from Stan's face. "We have no money to pay. We can't take the risk of going to any place of medicine. They will separate us. We'll be indentured and incarcerated into workhouses."

"Let's worry about that after we save her life, okay?"

"But..." Stan balked.

"Stan, if ever Susie needed a hero, it's today." Shannon's words worked like a spell. Stan's countenance changed to one of determination.

"As you say, dear girl. A hero is needed, and a hero has arrived." He bowed low, then he moved in and scooped Susie's frail form into his arms.

Not for the first time did Shannon wish she had her cell phone. Just as Stan exited with Susie in his arms, Shannon heard a struggle in the path outside.

"There's no time for such shenanigans. This is an emergency, don't you see?"

Cruel laughter met Shannon's ears, expletives and threats. In the midst of them all was a familiar, frightening voice.

"We like your place, old man. It's ours now."

CHAPTER 33

Shannon heard scuffling feet and Stan cry out. She ducked back and hid behind some plastic sheeting, all the while searching with her hands for a weapon of some kind. The sun had set outside, and it was impossible to make out anything except large shapes in the little space. The light illuminated Susie, but little else. Shannon's heart raced, thudding in her chest as she slipped from one side to the other, only finding clothes and blankets and ratty old pillows.

Suddenly the sheeting was yanked back, and a flashlight flooded the space, washing out her sight.

"Hey, he's got a girl back here," a man with a croaking voice called to his companions. The flashlight darted over Stan and Susie and came to rest on Shannon's face, blinding her.

"I know you."

The man who broke her camera.

Then she heard a thud, and Stan cried out before he stumbled back inside the tented area, carrying Susie with him. He had a bloody nose and was breathing heavily.

Shannon felt her mind slipping to that dark place of memories when another dangerous man had tried to force her to do something she refused. She'd escaped *him*. But he'd been alone.

Another man came around, wielding a thick tree branch. "Nice set up you have here, man. Room for three or four, I'd say. Water and electricity? Who ever heard of such a thing." The man pulled his dirty blond hair back into a messy ponytail. Shannon saw he sported a scar that ran down the side of his face.

Stan glowered at him. "You may have all of our belongings if you will only let us leave in peace. My queen is quite sick. This is her nurse. We must be on our way."

Shannon felt the weight of his words. Their little house must have taken months to scout out and supply, and Stan was about to lose all of it to these thugs.

"I'll tell you when you can go. You've been living here off the grid for how long?"

Stan showed his reluctance, so the man shoved the sharper end of the stick into his stomach. "You'll answer me."

"For near on two years."

The greasy man with blond hair shot a look at the shorter, heavier man—the man who had attacked her. "Sounds like the perfect place."

Shannon wasn't sure what they were up to. They had to have other safe houses for their victims. Why did they need Stan's place? There wasn't any use trying to reason with them. She'd somehow help Stan and Susie to find another hiding place. But for now, she needed to get them out of there.

"Will you let us go? She's very sick, and I'm afraid her appendix might burst." Shannon showed them respect rather than deference. She knew if she showed fear, this type would milk it for all it's worth. They were school bullies that never grew up, they just changed locales.

"The old man can take that head case to the hospital. But you'll stay here. You owe me." His dark eyebrows drew together, and he scowled at her.

"I wouldn't allow such a thing. Besides, she is much needed." Stan stood in their way. Shannon didn't want Stan hurt, but she also didn't want to stay there any longer than necessary.

"Sit down, old man." The short one pushed Stan. Stan surprised them both, though. He pulled a pole from the side and the roof caved in. Then he pulled another string and a second pole dropped. The two thugs were immediately encased in water and plastic, rolling around and cursing. Shannon felt what must have been Stan's hand pull her up and out. She saw Susie on the ground and went to her. She was burning up with fever, delirious.

Stan threw the hot plate, the heater, and a couple of partially loaded milk crates onto the tarps. With each thud a yelp of pain followed. He stood as one passing judgement on the filth of the earth, backlit by streetlights, towering over them. The men underneath cursed in anger as each item landed. Then Stan grabbed a hand-sized bag from its hiding spot inside one of the brick gaps and lifted Susie in one fluid motion.

"Come, my child, we must depart."

Shannon, still in shock, followed after Stan. He moved at a clipped pace, limping but without his cane.

"Stan, how did you do all of that?" She'd never seen anything like that outside of movies.

"My brain, more busy than the laboring spider, weaves tedious snares to trap mine enemies," came his gasping reply.

Shannon, despite her fear and exhaustion, laughed aloud in great surprise. Stan, for all his eccentricities, could quote Shakespeare at the most poignant times. His eloquence and speed energized her pace.

Susie gave a sharp cry and then her moaning—that had been accompanying them this whole time—vanished. Stan stopped short and moved the blanket back from her face. Shannon leaned in and felt her neck. Her pulse was rapid, her skin dry, and her breath labored.

Her mind, stress induced, shifted. She couldn't let that happen, or Susie could die.

"Stan, I'm not feeling well. But you need to get Susie to the hospital. Here, take my wallet." She handed it to him. "Let them know I've been helping you." Did she just give a homeless man her wallet? It was her only hope of help. *Please God, help Stan to get it to the right people.*

"Where are you going, child?"

"I don't know. I'm just not feeling myself and I don't think I can...keep...up." Shannon leaned against a building as the memories reached out and grabbed her like weedy black claws rising from the pavement. She saw Stan lugging Susie up the street, and then she was in another place. Her mind was filled with vivid images running from the man in her past, and that mixed with one of Daniel ranting at the bills piling up and then leaving the house, running up the street, yelling at the night sky, at the streetlights, at the cars in passing. He demanded answers. Shannon chased him, screaming for him to come back. Her little feet ached from sharp chunks of loose gravel and pebbles.

"Daddy. Please come back."

But Daniel raced off into the night, leaving her freezing and alone in the rain.

And then she was a teen, on the streets. Fighting to stay alive and out of the clutches of sex traffickers. The latter was far more difficult than the former. It happened so fast. A man approached teen Shannon.

"Hey, you look really cold and hungry. I've got a place not too far. Good food."

"No." Shannon pushed by, knowing if she stopped it would be dangerous.

"Your folks must be worried about you."

Shannon said nothing. If he knew no one was worried about her whereabouts she'd be in worse danger than she already was.

"You're way too pretty to be out here alone. There are some unsavory folks on the street. I'm a police officer, I should know."

He flashed a badge quickly. Shannon didn't know if it was fake or not. Most police were kind and helpful. Maybe he'd be nice?

264

"Seriously, my apartment is just up the block. You don't even have to come in. I'll get you some clothes and food. You can wait outside."

Shannon's guard dropped. Her fingers ached from the cold, and her feet were numb. She nodded.

"Great." He started walking off and she followed. "What's your name?"

"May." She gave her mother's nickname instead of her own.

"Nice. Suits you." He stopped in front of a rather beat up door that opened into a stairway. "You wait here, I'll be right back." He motioned to a chair under the awning, and she sat down. It was nice to sit and be out of the rain.

The downpour continued, and the night sky darkened. The business lights across the street turned off. Pedestrians drifted away like wraiths into the shadows.

Adult Shannon raced down the street, then up an alley, then down another street. Daniel. Where was he? Was he coming back? Would he hurt everyone she knew before he disappeared for good?

Because he would leave. He would disappear and leave her in pieces and her life shattered—hurting everyone around her and destroying what she'd built. How could she ever hope to forgive that?

Questions without answers pushed and shoved into her consciousness. Was she a child or an adult? Was this night or day? She slipped down and sat against a brick wall. Maybe the thing she'd run from all her life was really inside her? Whatever gene Daniel carried—had he passed it on to her? How could she ever hope for a whole life with Justin when such darkness loomed on the edges of her mind? And children? She'd never wanted children before. But now? The thought that something working inside her would keep her from even making the choice filled her with a desolate helplessness, a pit so black it absorbed every bit of light.

Her mouth was so dry, her tongue stuck to the roof of it. She found her water bottle and tipped it up to drink, but somewhere along the way, it'd been cracked and was all but empty. She tossed it aside and stared up at the dark sky.

Justin wanted to spend his future with her—and she was barely able to stay in her present reality. Exhaustion, fear, and the frigid night overtook Shannon, and she slipped into a kind of dreamless sleep.

The sun rose over the city skyline, and she felt the filthy puddles lining the alley soak into her jeans. She watched the black brick wall turn rust, then red, then pink as the sun lifted the cover of night and revealed her surroundings. She was hemmed in by two dark blue, sour-smelling commercial garbage bins. Their looming shadows hiding her away from whomever passed by.

The cold settled deep within, and her hands stung. She examined them, finding them raw and scratched. Her legs were weak. She couldn't move.

Shannon patted her pocket. She had no identification. She had no phone. She was anonymous on the street.

She'd been there before. Years ago. Between high school and college. She hadn't earned enough to live on her own, but she'd aged out of the group home. There was a halfway house for kids in her situation, but they were rough and edgy. She didn't want any of it. She wanted to take her chances. More than once, she'd snuck into Amber's bedroom and slept on her floor.

Only years later did Jennifer admit she knew.

Then why didn't Jennifer invite her to stay rather than sneak in? The love from that family, save Amber, was sideways and confused.

The scattered, shattered memories and broken shards of hopes and dreams rambled around in her memory. A homeless woman shuffled by, checking the garbage cans, but saying nothing to Shannon. Shannon looked like one of them, but not. Her clothes and hair were too clean.

She wiped her scathed hands on her jeans and tried to stand, but her legs went out from under her. The thought came again that no one knew where she was. Nor would they. And if she died here on the street? Who would find her and who would report it?

Stan was unstable, and it was unlikely anyone would listen. Besides, she wasn't sure if she was anywhere near where she and Stan and Susie had parted. As for anyone else, Justin wouldn't know where to begin looking. Amber didn't return for another week. Shannon's father certainly didn't care.

"God. Help."

CHAPTER 34

Several other homeless people shuffled by Shannon. She lost track of time and had no idea how long she'd been in the ally. It could have been overnight, or days. Her psychologist had wanted her to try medication, and she'd been reluctant. She'd wanted to handle this on her own. She and God. But what if God wanted her to get outside help and heal her through medication?

But if she took medication, she'd have to admit she couldn't handle life.

Like father, like daughter?

The thought chilled her even more. She'd run her whole life from being like Daniel, and here she was, exactly like him.

Sitting in a stinking alley. Freezing cold and starving.

She frowned. Had she ever found Daniel in an alley? Her mind reached this time for any familiar inkling. Not that she could recollect. Shannon stared up at the sky, a single strip of blue brushed with white mists framed by two city buildings. Rainbow-tinged gray pigeons cooed to one another as they clumsily waddled up the alley, pecking at odd items and perching on the fire escape above her. She felt like the buildings were closing in on her, surrounding and crushing. Wind whipped past her, and dark rain clouds rushed overhead. It started to sprinkle. Birds took to higher, dryer ground. But all she had was this spot.

She could feel her chest congest, her nose plug up, and knew she'd be full-on sick soon. How had she managed as a teen to stay safe from the natural elements or the streetwise ones?

No. She never looked for Daniel in an alley. But she'd found him in flophouses and in bars. And sometimes she never found him. That was scarier than this.

Sounds of a fight down the alley met her ears—she recognized the voices. She shrank back, not sure where to hide. It was the men from last night. The ones who had taken Stan and Susie's belongings and run them off when all they'd begged for was mercy.

There were four main types of people living on the street. One group, the mentally ill. Another set had fallen on hard times and were trying to get back on their feet. Another, larger group were the drug abusers. The fourth, completely interconnected with the drug abusers, were a heinous type of person. They sold humans for drugs and money. They stole from the poor and harassed the weak. They were treacherous, living as if they had nothing to lose.

Laughter trailed up the alley as they joked with one another, hitting the cans and knocking over containers with an object of some kind as they made their way along. She clenched her teeth, held her breath, and pushed as far into the slimy corner near the garbage can as she could. Her feet slid and made a grinding sound as she slipped in the muck.

"I can't believe we lost that nut last night. He was fast." Voices agreed.

They passed by.

She let her breath go, immediately sorry that she had. The rancid smell surrounded her and rushed into her nostrils. As she stood on shaking legs, she moved cautiously out from between the cans and the men were suddenly there, heckling her, pulling on her hair, tugging her clothes. They'd been waiting for her, toying with her.

"Leave me alone."

"Oh, sure. We'll leave you alone." The man who'd broken her camera pulled her from her hiding spot. "You reek. You know what, we happen to have a nice little camp just a few blocks away.

You can clean up, and then I'll warm you up, and we'll see how the day goes." They sneered and chuckled. Shannon didn't think she could get any colder, but her shivering became more violent.

"Consider it pay back for those four girls you took from me." He trailed a finger down her face and chest while the other two held her fast.

Shannon never felt so small and helpless. Weakness stole over her. She'd never be able to escape—or fight them off. She thought of offering her wallet and remembered faintly that she'd given it to Stan.

What was she thinking?

She wasn't. None of this was about thinking—it was desperate instinct. And right then, instinct told her to scream loud.

"Help!" She screamed and kept on hollering. The men dragged her down the alley. She kicked their shins, she scratched at their faces. They struck her, the sting burned into her eye socket, shutting her up.

No one was coming. The only people out on the street at that time were the street people. Everyone else was in their warm houses, eating cereal and drinking coffee, talking over the day with their loved ones. They'd watch the news or read the paper. They weren't interested in what happened as the sun rose and set on this town.

Her feet slid against the pavement, the sound of tennis shoes grating on rough pavement echoed all around them. She found herself focusing on the puddles filled with oily rainbow swirls. God's promise was in a rainbow. He'd never leave her or forsake her. She prayed under her breath, "God, help. Send someone. Help, please." Her shoulders burned from the strain of the men's fingers digging deep and yanking her along against her will.

"Listen to her." They mocked.

"I don't like it." One of the men stopped. He was much younger than Shannon had realized. Maybe sixteen. She glanced at the two that held her, both scruffy-faced, teeth rotting out, drug abusers. But not the boy. Not yet. She hoped.

"Help me, please." She begged him. His eyes were full of fear— but the fear amplified when he looked at her captors. Then his gaze dropped, and he moved to the side.

Too late, he'd been broken by them. He'd never go against them now.

"He ain' gonna help you. He's ours. And now you are, too."

A certain reason settled into Shannon's mind. She would be sold. Then moved to a new city against her will. They would try to break her with violent acts and make her believe she wasn't worth any more than what she got from dirty men who convinced themselves that prostitutes wanted to do what they were doing.

Even if they didn't, she'd never be the same. They'd never leave her alone. She'd never escape. And no one would ever know what happened to her.

Was this her fate? As much as she wanted to say no, she knew how weak she was. Shannon didn't see an exit, and she nearly always did.

And the last person to see her would never remember he'd seen her at all.

As they made it to the end of the alley, she screamed as loud as she could. The sound tore from her body, burning her vocal cords, leaving a hollow shell behind.

Rapid footsteps slapped the pavement, something akin to the sound of a linebacker raced toward them, and struck the man on her right so hard that she was thrown free. She pried herself out of the grasp of the other and sprawled out of the way. Shannon gasped sharp breaths, trying to fill her lungs.

She saw her hero, aglow in the sun's light. She never imagined him like this. Protective rage flashing in his eyes. Teeth grinding in righteous anger. Fists pummeling and striking them. Grunts and yells filling the air. Then the men ran off, and she was caught up in his protective arms as if she didn't weigh any more than a blanket. He shushed her and patted her as he raced up the block, away from the danger, to safety.

"I've got you, baby. Don't worry, Daddy's got you."

CHAPTER 35

S hannon stirred under some blankets. The aroma of chicken noodle soup filled her senses. She opened her eyes and found herself in Daniel's apartment. She glanced down and discovered she was covered in three quilts. The register under the window hissed, filling the room with the most delicious heat. She would never take being warm for granted ever again.

She turned her head and spied Daniel's back at the stove, stirring a pot. There was a knock on the door. Daniel opened it and Bill, the landlord, entered carrying a pair of woolen socks, a T-shirt with PORTLAND printed across the front, and a pair of felt pajama pants. He laid the items on the table.

"This is all I could come up with in my shop. Sorry."

"This is great. Thanks, Bill."

Daniel pulled out his wallet, but Bill waved him off. "None of that. You just keep doing what you do for me around here, and we'll call it even."

Bill left, and Daniel locked the door. When he turned around, she saw the relief in his eyes.

"Hey, you." He came over to the bed and crouched down next to her. "You warming up? You were pretty close to blue when I got you here."

Shannon's teeth chattered. "I am better. Thank you."

"You had us all pretty scared."

"How did you find me?" Shannon's teeth chattered together.

"It wasn't easy. We didn't really know what was going on. Some guy named Rafe called Amber, looking for you about the same time that a nurse at the hospital called her and said a homeless man showed up with your wallet, claiming you were in danger."

It was all so fuzzy in her mind. "I remember giving it to Stan, so someone would help Susie." Although her reasoning didn't make any sense right then, it had seemed like the best plan at the time.

"Amber called Justin, and he called me, and we hit the streets, not sure what was happening. Stan was pretty out of it and got violent when the police questioned him. They took him in."

"Oh, no! He saved me. You need to let them know."

"We'll work it all out. I called Justin to let him know I found you. He'd filed a missing person's report—I'm sure he straightened it all out with the police."

Shannon sank down against the pillows, her mind spinning. She'd really messed up this time. "I'm so sorry I worried everyone." She shivered under the blankets.

Daniel felt her cheeks. "I think you have a fever. I'm finishing up the soup, do you want to try and shower? Bill found some clothes you can change into. I hated to leave you in those filthy wet ones, but I didn't have a lady around to help you out. I figured you'd been through enough without any more uncomfortable situations." His eyes crinkled at the corners when he smiled, but she saw the worry and pain in them, too.

"Yes, please. I want to get all that off of me."

"You got it." He helped pull the covers back and lifted her to standing. He walked her jittery form to the bathroom, carrying in the clothes, and pointed to a fresh towel.

"Takes a while for the water to heat up. If you get in any trouble, just yell and I'll come in with my eyes closed."

"Thanks."

He shut the door behind her, and she moved to the little glass door-encased shower. The bathroom was miniscule, but Daniel had made it homey with a couple framed postcards on the wall of a sunset over the Pacific and a panorama shot of the Columbia River and its bridges.

She peeled the clothes from her body like she was sluffing off an outer skin and tossed them in a smelly heap. Then she stepped in and washed the grime from her skin. Her hands stung from the soap.

For someone who had it all together, she sure was a mess. To top it off, she'd been attacked by sex traffickers twice in the past few months. Maybe she needed to rethink her life. She'd survived so much, she considered herself resilient and untouchable. Not. Her thoughts turned to Daniel and his heroics, and she felt her heart melt a little.

She looked down at her feet and watched the sudsy water circle them before pouring down the drain.

She heard a knock at the bathroom door. "You okay in there?"

"Yes. Thawing out," she called back.

"Soup's ready when you are."

Shannon let the water run until it began to chill, and she quickly wrenched the handle off. She'd had enough of cold to last her the rest of her life. She stepped out, dried off, and dressed in the clothes. They were a little scratchy and baggy and the best thing she'd felt in ages. She came out, pulling her hair back into a ponytail.

Daniel's face softened. "You look so much like your mom sometimes. I mean, you look like you, but at angles, and coming out doing your hair like that. It took me back." He shook his head.

"I don't have any photos of her, and I don't remember." Shannon shakily took a seat at the table.

"I do." Daniel pulled his duffel from underneath the bed. He unzipped it and pushed some clothes to the side. Then he tugged out a lacquer box. It was orange and black with a cherry tree painted on the top. It was about the size of a shoebox, with latched top. He pulled out his keys and flipped to one and put it in the keyhole, and it opened with a tiny click.

He put it on the table and lifted the lid. Inside were handfuls of loose, faded photos. Shannon couldn't take her eyes from the box. She hadn't seen it for so long, she'd forgotten it existed until just then.

"That was Mom's box."

"Yes. And her mother gave it to her. She'd come over from Thailand when she was young." His face fell. "She thought she was coming to a safe country, getting away from the drugs in her town. She ended up falling in love with the wrong guy." Guilt and sadness laced his voice. "I wish sometimes that I'd never said hello to her. That I'd let her alone in that park and just watched from a distance. It would have been better for all of us." His fingers flipped through each photo until he found the one he wanted.

"I wouldn't be here."

He looked intently into her eyes. "Did you ever wish you'd never been born?"

Shannon considered his question. "No. Even though I had to live through all that, I'm glad I'm alive. And I'm a survivor. And I help people." She gave him a level look. "I wish you'd never done drugs though."

Daniel nodded. "Me too. Every day. Every single day, little one." Tears filled his eyes, and he handed her a photo of her mother.

Mayuree held baby Shannon on her lap, nuzzling the side of her fuzzy black head. She had a huge smile on her face, and Shannon was laughing.

An intense ache built in her chest. She didn't remember her mother smiling. Or laughing with her.

"She would sing to you. Oh, how she loved you." Tears flowed freely. "I'm sorry, you know. So sorry. I'll never be able to atone for what I did. Never."

"She made choices, too." Shannon didn't lay all the blame at his feet. Her mother could have turned down the drugs.

"I just felt so..."

"Numb."

He frowned. "What?"

"The drugs numbed you from your illness."

"No. That's not it. They took away the pain. All the pain. The disappointment. The not being enough for you and your mom. The fear my mental illness brought. They made me feel light. They made me feel able. It was a lie. But I believed the lie. I wanted to believe it. But it was never about being numb from everything—just the pain."

"My doctor wants me to take medication." This admission depleted her energy even more, and her head felt like a weighted bobble-head doll.

Daniel's face fell. "Do you have bipolar or schizophrenia?" He stated it as if she had to have one or the other.

Shannon sat at attention. "No. Who had schizophrenia?"

He pursed his lips. "Your mom. It came on after you were born. Like a switch in her brain flipped. She'd be so happy one moment and then delusional. The only thing that kept her from the delusions was drugs. And not the ones they wanted to give her. Those shut her down and stole the light from her eyes." He sighed. "I'm sorry. I thought you knew. Some gene pool you were born into, huh, kiddo?"

Gene pool. Her kids *could* inherit this.

"But meds are better now. I bet if—" Shannon stopped. If she wasn't willing, how would she ever think her mother would have be willing? The idea scared her to death. Suddenly all the judgement she'd carried toward her father and mother lightened. She saw the situation from their point of view. She didn't like it, didn't agree with it, but there was a glimmer of understanding.

"Who took the drugs first?"

Daniel chewed the inside of cheek. "It doesn't matter, really, does it?"

Shannon shrugged, but deep down, she knew. Her father didn't want to cast shade on her mother's memory.

"Are you still clean?" Shannon felt a wave of dizziness pass over her, and she listed to the side and caught herself on the table before she toppled out of the chair. She hadn't eaten in over two days.

Instead of answering, Daniel got up and served them a couple bowls of soup and brought it to the table with a loaf of bread and cube of butter. He handed her the knife, and she slathered a piece of bread in butter and ate it. Then she took several spoonfuls of soup.

"Did you make this?"

"You remember my chicken noodle soup?"

Shannon loaded her spoon with noodles. "I always thought that was from a can."

"Nope. It was your mom's recipe. The only thing she ever made successfully. I'll show you how one of these days." He took a bite of bread. "Yes, I'm still clean. I won't go back to that life. Ever."

"Are you getting treatment?" Because he'd made that promise before.

He sighed and nodded. "I haven't had an episode for a couple years. Until the other day at the wedding."

Shannon's shoulders sank.

Daniel put up a hand. "No guilt. I needed you to give it to me straight, little wise one. And you did with both barrels. It sent me spiraling. Maggie helped me get in with a doctor." He pulled a bottle out of his pocket and put it on the table. "It took a week, but they seem to be making a difference. It's not like it used to be where I felt all disconnected. And maybe that was due to the drinking and drugs mixing wrong."

"You think?" She gave him a bitter look but tried to cover it. He still hadn't mentioned getting help with drug and alcohol abuse—but she didn't want to condemn the steps he was taking.

"Yeah. I think." He scrutinized her face. "What does your psychologist want you to take medication for?"

"Depression, anxiety, and PTSD is all." She tried to put a light spin on that. It didn't work so much.

"Oh, that's all." His mouth drew down. "I sure didn't give you much of a life."

Even yesterday she would have agreed with him, but today something was different. His serious tone, his regretful eyes, or his recusing her—risking life and limb—mixed together with her emotions. She didn't respond, but instead focused on her food. He brought her seconds, and then thirds.

"You sure can eat. Your mom could eat." He nodded. "Boy, oh boy, could she. This one time we went to a Chinese buffet and she kept going back for more. The manager came out and asked us to leave. Said we were stealing food. But I had him check her purse. It all went into her, that tiny frame. We used to joke that we'd hit the country fair circuit and she'd become this famous food contest eater—pie being her best event."

Shannon laughed. It was so good to laugh.

"Now that you're fed and warm, I need to call Justin." He pulled out his phone, but it rang before he could dial. Daniel held it up as if to say, "see?"

"Yeah, I've still got her. She's safe here at my place. Sure." Daniel handed Shannon the phone.

"Hey," she croaked.

"You okay?" Justin's voice sounded demanding and terrified.

"Yes. I am now."

She watched Daniel go still at the sink for a moment, listening, and then he hummed a nonsensical tune, pretending not to listen.

"Thank God. Thank God. I was so afraid."

"I'm sorry. That whole thing with Stan."

"Not just Stan. I found your car. And there was no sign of you. I called your phone and it was ringing in your trunk." He trailed off.

"What?"

"I kinda broke into your trunk. I was worried someone stuffed you in there. But when I found your phone and your purse and your keys, I freaked."

"I'm so sorry. My head was in a bad spot and I made some pretty hasty decisions. And locked myself out of everything. And then I found Stan, and Susie was sick."

"I called the police to update them, and they let Stan go."

"Poor Stan."

"Don't sound so accusing. You have no idea what this looked like. He was ranting and spouting Shakespeare, waving your wallet around with one hand and holding Susie up with the other."

"Is Susie okay?"

"Yeah, they did surgery on her appendix. She's going to make it. You going to be there for a while?"

"Yes. I'll be here for a while. And when I need a ride, I'll call you."

"And not drive unsafely across town." He reprimanded her, but she didn't mind. He wanted her safe. That was a good thing.

"Yeah, and not do that."

"Good. I love you."

"I love you, too." Their endearments still felt fresh and new, like the spring buds of a garden breaking the soil, tender and unprotected. Anything could happen.

"I'll call Amber," Justin said in a leading manner.

"Oh, no. Her honeymoon." Shannon leaned her head against her hand.

"It couldn't be helped."

"Of course not." They said their good-byes, and she hit end and handed the phone back to Daniel. Minutes later, the phone rang. Shannon knew who it was without looking. She put her hand out and Daniel plopped the phone into it.

"Hi, Amb."

280

"What in the world? I cannot believe you."

"It's not like I did it on purpose." Shannon stirred the noodles in her chicken soup from one side of the bowl to the other, watching them rise and sink and flop around at her whim.

"No. *That* would be ridiculous. Can I not leave home anymore without you trying to get yourself killed by some criminal?"

Shannon sighed dramatically. "I guess not. No."

"Seriously."

"Wait, you're not coming home, are you?"

"Of course, we were. My best friend was missing on the streets of Portland. You think I can enjoy my honeymoon when you're lost and I'm not sure if you're alive or dead?"

"Sorry. Is it too late to turn around?"

"No. In fact, I'm telling Ethan to do that right now." Shannon could hear a muffled conversation and then laughing. "We will be gone another week. Do you think you can stay away from the dregs of society until we get back?"

"The criminal part, yes."

"Just...for a week?" Amber's voice begged. "For my sanity if not for yours?"

"I need to make sure Stan and Susie are okay. They saved my life."

"So did Daniel."

"Yes. He really did."

"Are you sure you're okay?"

"I am. I promise." She felt more okay than she had in a long time, even in her physically beaten state. "Oh, no!"

"What?"

"I missed my meeting with Rafe. I was supposed to come to the gallery the other night...was it only last night? I've lost track of time."

"It was the night before last. And don't worry. He's the one that alerted me long before Justin. He said he couldn't find you and he didn't think it was like you not to show up. I'll call him and update him. I'm sure it'll be okay."

"Thank you, Amb. You're the best."

"What do we do to commemorate this? Or is this too close to last time? I'm very confused."

"You and me both. Love you."

"Love you."

Shannon heard the silence of the ended call and handed the phone back to Daniel.

"Sorry."

"It's not a problem. You have good friends who really care about you. That's pretty special."

Shannon thought about that for a moment. "Yeah. They're my family." Shannon took a drink of water. "Thanks for saving my life." She said it more off-handedly than she meant to, so she tried again. "I mean it. Thank you."

"It's the job I should have been doing all these years. It's the job I'd like to have back, if you'll let me." His eyes begged her to say yes.

Shannon didn't know what to say to that. Part of her felt uneasy, the part that knew this could all change in the blink of an eye. But the rest of her wondered if Daniel really had changed. Saving her life went a long way to proving that. But was it enough?

CHAPTER 36

S hannon carried a large bouquet of mixed flowers through the hospital halls, heading toward Susie's room. She didn't know what Susie would like, but she got some bright and cheery Gerbera daisies of all colors (did daisies really come in teal and magenta?) and some carnations for a sweet aroma. She passed by the nurses' station. They were in busy conversation, so she continued on until she found the room. The halls were crowded with orderlies and aids handing out medications and lunches.

Pushing open the door, Shannon found Stan sitting in a lounge chair near the window, staring out on the rainy day, and Susie resting peacefully. The noisy sounds cut off as she closed the door. Stan alerted to her presence and rose to meet her, taking her hand in both of his.

"Dear girl. I was so worried for your safety with those hooligans on the loose. I have gone since to our home, and it's destroyed. Vindictive and evil are the men of these days."

"I wish they'd leave forever." Shannon hadn't meant to reveal her anger.

Stan seemed to pick up on it and spoke with clarity and conviction. "But I say to you who hear, love your enemies, do good to those who hate you, bless those who curse you, and pray for those who spitefully use you." Stan took his seat and grew distant again, leaving Shannon with the distinct feeling she'd failed to be compassionate to her enemies.

If only the man who had broken her camera—or those other

men—had been caught. They walked free, able to hurt others. But forgiveness and compassion weren't suggestions—they were commands.

It was those morsels of wisdom, those points of intense sincerity that drew Shannon to Stan. He spoke from an inner place of peace and truth that was still hooked to reality, and he always had the right words to illuminate a trying situation.

"He's so dramatic, my son." Susie's frail voice interrupted the scene. Shannon gave her a huge smile.

"Well, he's not wrong." She moved to Susie's bedside. "I'm so relieved you're okay, Queen Susie."

Susie patted the bed and whispered behind her hand. "You know dear, I'm not really a queen." She winked at Shannon. "It makes my Stan happy to say it, though, so I humor him." She brushed back her hair with a regal hand as if to say, "Just kidding."

"Is he really your son?"

"He's very much like my son. He *could* be my son. My boy died when he was a teen. He also loved drama and would quote movies. We thought he'd go on the stage. But he was killed by a drunk driver." Tears streamed down her cheeks. Shannon handed her a tissue and waited for Susie to compose herself.

"Then, ten years ago, I lost my husband and the bank took our house and I found myself alone. Destitute. Dying in solitude. Until Stan found me. He needed a mother, don't you know? And I definitely needed a son. We've been taking care of one another ever since." She waved her hand toward the table in the corner where Stan's hat resided. "I bought him his top hat." She punctuated the last sentence with gravity as if it were the most significant part of the conversation.

"It's a brilliant hat."

"I found it at the thrift store. In another town—another time. It used to be part of a magic act. It has a hidden spot inside for a fake dove." She leaned conspiratorially closer, using her cupped hand to whisper to Shannon. "That's where we keep the bulk of our savings." Then she leaned back, exhausted by her admission. "But I can't remember where we were then. He lost the dove a long time ago. And now..." She sniffled. "I guess we'll have to leave again. Our home has once again been stolen from us."

"I wanted to talk to you about that. I'm working on an art show, and I'd like to include your story in the hopes someone might be able to help you both."

"Why would anyone want to help us?"

"Because you're special to me."

"Oh, my." Susie's one good eye reddened, and she sobbed, pressing the tissue against her mouth. "It's been so long since anyone..." She was unable to finish her sentence.

Shannon offered the flowers that, until then, she'd forgotten she'd brought.

"Daisies. They are my favorite. How very lovely." Susie's aged, translucent hands reached for the bouquet. Her fingers wrapped around them, and she cradled them like a baby. "Have you ever seen anything so beautiful, Stan?"

Stan startled as if being shaken from a dream. He focused on the bouquet. "Flowers cannot grow without the love of the sun, nor can we grow within save by the love of the Son."

Shannon was taken aback. "That was beautiful. Who said that?"

He twisted his mouth to the side and looked at her as if she were being dull. "Why, I did, my dear." He shook his head at her. "Perhaps you need more rest."

Shannon laughed aloud. "I think you're absolutely right." Once she composed herself, she broached the subject again.

"I don't want you two leaving town. Please let me know when they discharge you. I've arranged a small apartment for you for a month. We'll see what comes of my photography showing, and we'll have a direction."

Stan stood, bowing deeply to her. "You do us a great kindness, lady. We will certainly not forget your favor."

She handed Stan her business card with her phone number on it. Then she left them on their own and headed to the nurses' station. Two were now sitting quietly doing paperwork.

"Excuse me. Can you please let me know when you discharge Susie? I've arranged housing for them and want to come pick them up."

The closest nurse shot a suspicious look at Shannon, but the farther one crossed over to her. Shannon remembered her from one of the homeless missions volunteer days.

"They want to get her stable, hydrated, and make sure there's no infection. They're trying to arrange an ocular prosthesis for her as well—although she's resisting. Probably two days." She took Shannon's offered card.

"I really do appreciate it. Stan saved my life, and I want to be sure they are taken care of."

"You bet, sweetie."

With this off her mind, she headed out for home. She needed to rest, and then she needed to get ahold of Rafe and hopefully pull off a miracle.

CHAPTER 37

Rafe motioned for Shannon to sit at the closest table while Justin wandered around the gallery portion of the coffee shop sipping his latte. It was upscale, in the Pearl, but people in jeans were just as comfortable as people in suits.

"I'm so relieved you're safe." Rafe took Shannon's hand and squeezed it. "You had us all very worried." His icy blue eyes warmed toward her. Rafe remained an enigma to her. He was kind to everyone she'd ever seen in his company, but he kept to himself. There had to be a deeper story, but he hadn't shared it with her or with Amber.

"It was pretty scary. But it also opened up an opportunity to help a couple of very special people. Have you ever seen an older woman and a man in his fifties, very tall, bearded, with a top hat? He often quotes the Bible or Shakespeare or other poets. And apparently he's writing his own material lately." Shannon smiled wryly.

"I do believe I've seen them. They haven't been in these parts for quite a long time, though. I thought they'd moved on." She couldn't read his tone.

"No. They'd built themselves a pretty ingenious shelter between two buildings over off Couch, but it was destroyed by those thugs that attacked me. Stan saved my life at one point. I feel I owe them any help I can offer."

"Incredible. I wouldn't have thought they'd have the clarity to do such a thing."

Shannon frowned at him. "Do you have issues with the home-less, Rafe?"

Rafe looked down at his espresso. "They've caused damage to my business more times than I can count."

"Then why do you want to help them?"

He turned his cup, straightening it on the saucer. "Personal reasons."

"Sorry, I don't mean to pry."

"It's a long story." He shook his head, and Shannon waited for him to change the subject.

But he didn't.

"When I was very small, my mother and I lived in our car on the streets of England. My father was a wretch and abandoned us. We did our best, but it wasn't enough. She died from pneumonia and exposure. Something in her kept us from asking for help."

"I'm so sorry." Shannon felt the weight of his admission.

"I've never understood that. Was it pride or fear? Whatever it was, it left me an orphan up for adoption. A very nice couple adopted me, and we moved to the US. I guess I should feel lucky. But I often reminisce about what would have become of us if she'd just asked for help when we most needed it."

She had more in common with Rafe than she'd imagined.

"Life is so full of unknowns. She might have sought help without you knowing. There were few services then. Even now, while there's more, it's hard to get people connected to the right places. And there are so many out there abusing the system—it feels impossible to overcome. But since they can't try themselves, I'd like to try on behalf of Stan and Susie."

"And that sounds very interesting to me." He gave her a soft smile. "Here are some of the layout ideas I had based on the prints you shared with me via e-mail." Rafe laid out the photos in mock frames. "What if you did a focused study on your friends and then write up a piece for the paper? I know a few people that might help them get off the streets permanently. If that's what they want. I know it's hard to change people, especially those with mental illness."

"That's true. They can be very stubborn." She chided herself. "But they seemed relieved at the idea of having a safe place. I've worked it out with Bill, my father's landlord, to let them stay in one of his apartments for a while. But there are stairs, so that's not a good long-term solution for Susie."

"I'm sure we can come up with something."

"I was hoping we could." She grinned at him.

Justin returned to the table and looked at the layouts. After some redirection on layout, they came up with a solution that pleased both Shannon and Rafe.

As they prepared to go, Shannon turned to Rafe and hugged him. "Thanks for sharing your story and for helping me with this."

"Certainly." Rafe didn't seem to know what to do with her attention, so he excused himself as she and Justin exited the café.

"What was that about?" Justin looked sideways at her.

"A story for another day."

Justin seemed to take her response well. She didn't want to share confidences that weren't meant to be shared.

"How are things with your dad?" They made their way up the block, heading toward her apartment.

"Better."

"Good."

She turned to Justin. "I'm never going to have a relationship with my dad like you've had with your parents."

"I get that."

"I don't know that you do." She scrutinized him.

"I'm actually struggling right now."

"With what?" Alarmed, she took his hand.

"I really liked Daniel. And I know forgiveness isn't a suggestion—it's a command. But down deep?"

"Yeah?"

"Ever since you disappeared, I've been feeling pretty bitter and angry at what you had to survive. This week, but also your whole life."

What he was saying didn't make what she needed to share with him any easier. "There's another thing we need to talk about."

"I don't know that I like the sound of that." He furrowed his eyebrows at her.

Shannon looked around for a quiet place they could sit. She spied a bench up the street, but foot traffic ran past it like a river. She frowned, frozen, unable to decide where to go.

"Hey?" He tugged on her hand. "You're kind of freaking me out here."

"I'm sorry. I want to talk, but somewhere private."

Even though his eyes showed worry, he smiled. "I know just the spot."

They walked up several blocks and turned to the right, and he pointed to his car. She climbed in and they drove up over the hill, taking several curvy and obscure backroads to Washington Park. They pulled into the parking lot, and he came around to the passenger side door and opened it for her. He reached for her, and she took his hand. They walked down the brick walkways to the center of the Rose Garden, where the Memorial Fountain stood, crafted from great stainless-steel pillars. One post rose and crossed the gateway's center, dividing it.

The water of the two fountainheads at the edge of the arch trickled and splashed off the metal, creating a gentle tinkling sound. Justin led her to a matching stainless slab to sit. The crispness of the oncoming winter hung in the air. Occasionally, an independent walker passed them, but for the most part, they were alone in the center of the hibernating garden.

The coldness of the bench worked through her jeans, chilling her.

"I love this place. It's like they used stainless steel to mimic cement forms found in brutalism and mimicked the Japanese gate. It's fascinating."

She loved that they had an appreciation of art and aesthetics in common at their core. And their faith. They spoke the same language in so many ways. She hoped what she was about to tell him wouldn't change everything.

"Now, what's up?" He took her cold hands in his, warming them.

"It's about Daniel. And Mayuree."

"Okay."

"Daniel shared a bunch of photos with me the other day while I was recovering. Baby photos, photos from before I was born. Their whole history. It was pretty incredible."

"I bet. I can't imagine not having that until now. My mom catalogued my every breath."

"I love your mom. She's the kind of mom I hope to be someday." She knocked her shoulder into his.

This brought a flash of joy to Justin's eyes, and she immediately regretted saying it—because what she was about to say might steal that smile.

"That would make her very happy. She's going to love being a grandma. She'll be crazy. Quilting and photographing and monograming towels." He laughed at Shannon's gaping expression. "I'm serious." He shook his head. "Take whatever you imagine a dedicated grandmother is like—jack that up about ten notches."

She hoped Josie would offer the same love to an adopted grandchild.

"We talked a lot about his drug abuse. And hers." She didn't know how to say this, because it might break them. And what would she do then?

"That must have been really hard." He pulled her close and wrapped his arm around her, caressing her shoulder through her coat to comfort her. She wished he wouldn't—it made it too hard to concentrate and keep her distance in case this went poorly.

"We talked about his bipolar. And how the illegal drugs hid his condition. He admitted that he'd actually started buying drugs off the street for—" She took a deep breath—"my mom."

Justin's hand squeezed her shoulder. "I'm so sorry." He'd known her mother had died of an overdose.

"But when it started, neither of them had ever had a drug problem. My mom was taking medication for another condition, and they didn't work like she'd hoped. They made her disconnect from everything. She was sad all the time. So, they thought they'd found a better solution. It wasn't."

"A solution to what?"

"My mom was schizophrenic."

"Whoa. That's a lot to take in." His arm pulled her closer until she was fully leaning on him.

"That's not all."

"This sounds pretty serious."

She nodded into his shoulder. "It is." She took a moment to collect her thoughts. Justin's warmth seeped in and gave her the confidence she needed.

"My dad is bipolar, and my mom is schizophrenic. And I have generalized anxiety disorder and PTSD."

"Well, the PTSD is from trauma."

"Probably so. The flashbacks are pretty dramatic sometimes. Although since my experience on the street, and my dad rescuing me, I haven't had one." She'd been working on forgiving Daniel. It was a daily event still, but it was having an effect. Sometimes forgiveness was a process.

"That's great news, right?"

"I have gone into remission before." Shannon felt the immediate release of his hand on her shoulder as he turned her to face him.

"What are you trying to say? You can tell me."

"It might be genetic. Sometimes the father or mother can pass on a gene. In my case, it's doubly likely and hard to test for."

A shift in Justin's eyes told her he was following the discussion.

"It could be that any children I have would have mental illness issues."

"But we can't know."

"No, I can't know for sure. The data isn't there."

"What does your psychologist say?"

Shannon chewed on her lip. "I called her after my incident and got in to see her." She put up a hand when Justin balked. "Don't worry, I didn't drive. I took the bus."

"What did she say?"

"She said it's not definitive."

"So, we're good. We can just leave it up to God. We'll be fine."

Shannon's head sagged against her chest. "You know how much I trust God."

He nodded.

"I trust Him so much that I know if I ever got pregnant, I would rely upon Him for every aspect. I'd never once be tempted to end the pregnancy out of fear. I know He would provide and aid and help me and the child adjust should they have any of my issues."

A frigid breeze blew through the garden, and Shannon shivered. Storm clouds gathered overhead, darkening and growing heavier. It wouldn't be long before they'd be caught in a downpour.

"*If* you ever got pregnant. You mean you'd try not to become pregnant. On purpose."

"Yes."

"That's how you feel now. You might change your mind." He pulled away, leveling his gaze intently at her.

The sprinkles started.

"I can't."

She wouldn't change her mind. She loved her life, but the

struggles and heritage it came with was too much for her to purposefully give it to another.

"It breaks my heart to say it. Please know that."

"You're making that choice for both of us." Justin's hurt flamed into anger.

"Yes." She knew it sounded selfish, but having thought it out, it was the most selfless thing she could do.

"No kids."

"No, I'm not saying that." She put a hand on his arm, but he moved away. *Oh, no.*

"Then what are you saying? Because it sounds an awful lot like if we got married you'd never want us to have a baby."

"Not a baby from us. I'd like to adopt."

Justin stood and paced over the concrete bricks. A grinding sound of tennis shoe meeting gravel sounded every time he turned back to her.

"Adopt? Sure. Along with our own kids."

"They would be *our* own kids." Her voice was soft against the atmosphere of his growing frustration.

"You know what I mean."

"I do."

"I suppose Amber agrees with you? That your father backs you up? I'm the only one left to be unreasonable."

The accusation hurt. "I haven't spoken to them about this. This is between us."

Justin's eyes turned red from unshed tears and angst. "But it's not between us, is it? You've made this choice on your own."

"You can't understand." This was going categorically, catastrophically, bad.

"I can't? You're the woman—" He stopped. "You're the only one." He choked on his words.

"You're the only one for me, too."

"Then how could you decide this without me?" Hurt laced every word.

"This isn't up to you."

Justin turned away from her, mumbling something to himself she couldn't hear.

"What?" She rose and went to him, trying to hold him by the arm, tethering him to her the only way she knew how.

He looked down at her. "I was just praying. I don't know how to get through to you. Haven't I been here for you? Didn't I stand by you when Amber lost her sight and you were inconsolable? She doesn't know, till this day, how afraid you were for her, how you took that upon yourself. But I was there for you."

"Yes," she whispered.

"And when you decided you didn't want to be married, that nothing could make you want me. Wasn't I patient?"

"Yes."

"And when your dad—" His voice tore in his throat—"showed up and you started to tune out and disappear into a world I didn't understand, wasn't I supportive and standing with you?"

All Shannon could do was nod.

"And when you told me about your abuse, about your damage, did I condemn you?"

"No. Never." Her voice was barely a whisper.

"Then why, when I have done nothing but be here for you, pray for you, encourage you, take care of you, would you go and make this choice without me?"

Tears streamed down her cheeks unchecked. "I just can't. I can't wish this—" She moved her hand up and down her body—"on a child."

"Is what you live with so horrible? Is it so unlivable? Unmanageable?"

Shannon couldn't speak for the longest time. She'd not wanted to hurt him. She'd hoped he'd accept this decision and be reasonable. But with every word Justin spoke, she felt a sinking in her spirit.

"It's my body." She knew that was a dim argument. Any child they made would be theirs together. He had every right to the baby as much as she did.

"Please, don't use that on me. I don't deserve that." His hands shook, and she watched him shove them deep in his pockets. She'd never seen him so angry. At her.

"You've gotta tell me something here so I can understand, Shannon. Because if you make this decision without me, then we can't move ahead. I can do a lot. But I can't do that."

"But..." She bit her lip, trying to control her emotions.

"But what? Please. Shannon." His voice begged her for reasonableness—but there was nothing reasonable about what she was feeling.

"I'm afraid." She crossed her arms over her chest as a barrier between them, as a way to keep herself in check. As a way to stay present. As a way to keep herself from running away. Because that's what she wanted to do more than anything. Run. *Grab your go-bag and run.*

The sprinkles gathered, welding together into huge drops, pummeling the earth. As they hit the sculpture, a racket of hundreds of little hammers, of a thousand starting pistols, a race about to begin or end in abject failure, sounded and echoed around them. A cacophony of sound that she'd never heard took them over, so loud she barely heard his response through the deluge.

"Who isn't?"

CHAPTER 38

"Wat?" Shannon's teeth chattered as they stood in the downpour, soaked to the skin, in the dimming light. "Who isn't afraid?" he asked again.

"You're afraid?"

"A lot. But I trust God to know better. Mostly. Sometimes I goof that up. Do you know the thing I'm most afraid of, right now?"

She shook her head, feeling her hair sway, leaden with water, and slap and stick against her cheek.

"That I won't get you to understand that we can face anything as long as we've got Jesus. And He's in the middle of all of this. We're not alone making these choices, we can trust Him. With ourselves, with each other, and with the kids we have. All of it. There's nothing we have to keep away from Him. There's nothing we can't trust Him with. Nothing."

She stared into Justin's eyes, rain and tears mixing on his face. He was dead serious. And as soon as he said it she knew he was right. She'd trusted God with so many aspects of her life but was holding back this one thing. One thing.

"And do you know what else is really messed up about all of this?"

"What?"

He stepped closer to her, taking her freezing hands into his.

"We're talking about kids and I haven't even asked you to marry me yet."

Her mouth worked to the side, and she tried to laugh, but it came out as a strangled sob instead. She tried to cover her embarrassment with her hand, but he wouldn't let go of it.

"Are you willing to trust God, Shannon?"

God. I believe. Please help me believe. Forgive my unbelief.

Shannon nodded, unable to give him more than that.

"Is that a yes?"

"Tentatively." She smiled through the rain, through all the emotions she was feeling.

"I can wait." He reached up and brushed her soaking hair back from her cheeks and rubbed a thumb under one eye, then under the other. "Your mascara is running."

"Oh!" She wiped her face with a rain-soaked tissue she pulled from her back pocket. "Sorry."

"I didn't mind so much. But I want to see your face." He kept a grip on one of her hands and knelt down in front of her. "Because I want to see clearly into your eyes when I ask you a question."

Shannon stared down into his upturned face. The rain splatted against his nose and cheeks and into his eyes, where he blinked it away, revealing only joy.

"Will you be my wife?"

A certainty she'd not felt that whole afternoon filled her spirit. The fear dissipated. Not because of what Justin was asking her, but because the King of all kings was healing her, a little at a time, and for the first time in the longest time, she wasn't afraid of what would come.

"Yes."

Justin pulled her into a deep kiss and held her to him. They were both shivering from cold, but she didn't feel any of it, only the sweet warmth from his lips, the security of his arms around her, and the vibration under her hand of his heart that beat for her.

CHAPTER 39

The café was full to the very edges with people interested in Stan and Susie's story. Originals and prints were selling. Coffee flowed. Rafe was in his element. Amber leaned on Ethan's arm and laughed at a patron's joke. Daniel and Maggie perched on stools at the bar across the room as Daniel described different prints to her. Stan and Susie sat at a table, an island all their own. Reporters had just finished taking photos and doing their interviews with them. Everything was still in motion but slowing to a more thoughtful pace.

And in the middle of it all stood Shannon gripping Justin's hand, nervous that she would awake from this dream.

From behind her came a familiar, soon to be family, voice.

"This is beautiful. This is my favorite," Josie stated firmly.

"You said that very thing a moment ago with that one over there." Matias laughed at her.

"Oh, stop. You know I can't pick just one. First Shannon's photos, then Amber's painting, and then our boy's sculpture, how could I choose one over the other?" She hit Matias on the arm.

Justin grinned at Shannon and turned to his parents to watch them argue in the sweet way they had.

"Mamá, you are the best of all critics. Should we buy one of each?" asked Matias.

"Oh, that we could." Josie gave a huge sigh of disappointment.

"You guys know you can have whatever there is of mine for free, right?" Justin nodded with a wry expression on his face.

"And mine for that matter," Shannon added.

"Oh, we couldn't take yours, Shannon."

"But you'll take mine?" Justin spoke in mock surprise.

"You we helped put through art school. Consider it a repayment."

"So, four or five pieces and we'll call it services rendered and we're even?"

"Such disrespect." Josie clucked her tongue at Justin.

Daniel and Maggie walked over by them.

"Mamá and Papá, this is Daniel Jameson. Daniel, these are my parents."

They shook hands with one another.

"Very good to meet you, Mr. and Mrs. Romero."

"And we're pleased to meet you."

A large group of people entered and passed by them, jostling Maggie and nearly knocking her over. Daniel caught her and reddened with anger at their carelessness.

Somehow Maggie sensed his anger. "It's fine. They didn't see me."

"People can be very inconsiderate. Are you all right?" Matias moved to take Maggie's other arm.

"Honestly, I'm fine."

Justin leaned over and nudged Shannon. "Is now a good time?"

All of the parents turned at the same time.

"A good time for what?" Asked Daniel.

Justin cleared his voice, and Shannon gave his arm a squeeze of encouragement. "Um."

"Justin wanted to talk to you, Dad. But could I see you first?"

Both Daniel and Justin looked confused.

"Sure." Daniel guided Maggie to one of the tall tables, and the Romeros joined her. Then he returned, putting his arm out to Shannon.

Shannon looked up at Justin. "Don't worry. I'll be right back."

And she moved off with Daniel to a quiet, darker corner table that a group had recently vacated, leaving their empty cups and plates strewn over the table.

Daniel cleaned it away. "Some people, right?"

"Right." Shannon waited patiently for her dad to clear it all away. Then he came and sat down across from her.

"Okay. What's up?"

Shannon tucked a strand of black-blue hair back behind her ear with a shaky hand.

"This sounds serious. Are you okay?"

"Yes. It's just hard. What I have to say, I mean." She really was the worst at bringing up difficult conversations.

"Uh-oh."

"No." She put a hand up, quieting him. "It's okay. It's nothing bad. I don't think." *Oh, please shut up, Shannon.*

"All right. I'm ready. Lay it on me."

"I don't think people say that anymore."

He laughed. "I'm playing catch up. Hey, did I tell you, my doctor said I'm doing really good. I'm staying present. I'm also using some mindfulness techniques, and I'm making all of my AA and counseling sessions. I think it's going to stick this time."

Shannon felt her heart swell. She didn't know Daniel had been attending AA meetings. She knew this burden he carried could be lightened even more. And it wasn't because he'd cleaned up his act. It wasn't because he'd done anything to earn it. It was because God had given her the strength to do it. And even though this was one of the scariest moments she'd ever experienced—because this could go very bad if he didn't take it the right way, if he didn't think he needed what she was about to offer—it was because God had commanded it.

And she knew where God commanded, and she followed, then healing would come. And it was time for them both to have that healing. It wasn't for her. It wasn't for him. It was for her heavenly Father.

"I need to tell you something that's been weighing on me my whole life. I've lugged it around. I've lived with it every day. I've woken up facing it and fallen asleep with it bearing down on me, crushing me. And I know it's time to give that up."

Daniel's blue eyes grew watery before her own.

"I need you to know that I forgive you."

How could such a simple sentence bring such a huge release in her spirit? On paper it wouldn't have looked like anything. But said between two hurting people, it meant everything.

"You forgive me?" His voice shook with emotion.

"Yes. I forgive you. For all the times you forgot me, all the times you left me alone, all the times you didn't take care of me, all the times you let me down. All the times I got hurt—all the things you could have stopped but didn't. I forgive you for all of it. All of it remembered and forgotten. All of it."

"Oh, my God. Thank you, God. Thank you, Shannon. You don't know what this means to me. I'm so sorry. I didn't mean it to harm you. I never meant to harm you. I've loved you all your life. I was broken, but that's no excuse. I don't deserve it. I don't." Daniel sobbed. Shannon moved quickly to the other side of the table and held him. "I don't deserve it." His muffled voice cried into her shoulder.

"None of us do."

"I love you, you know?"

"I know." She wasn't ready to speak of her love so easily yet. That would come with time.

They held each other and cried for a while. When they looked up, no one had seemed to notice, but Shannon saw Josie wiping her cheeks.

"Now, if you're up to it, Justin wants to talk to you."

"Oh, boy." His voice shook as if he couldn't take another thing.

"It's okay. I promise." She patted his shoulder and motioned for Justin to come. Then she went over and took a tissue from Josie. Amber came up alongside her and kissed her cheek and pulled her into a hard hug that said it all.

"I'm so proud of you, you know?"

"Thanks." They let each other go, and Shannon turned to watch Justin. He had his hands tucked into his pockets. Then he pulled them out of his pockets. Then he sat down. Then he put his hands on the table and clasped his fingers. Then he started gesturing with shaking hands.

"Please, Father God, help him," Shannon whispered.

Amber, Ethan on her other arm, leaned over and whispered. "Is it that bad?"

Both Ethan and Shannon answered at the same time. "Yes."

"Then amen."

"What is going on? Is there anything wrong?" Josie's concern was echoed in Matias's face.

Then Daniel laughed and they all looked over at the table where they sat. Daniel jumped to his feet and rushed at Justin, who leapt up and took a step back before the tall older man embraced him and started slapping him on the back.

"Is that a yes?" Justin asked.

"Yes. Of course it is!" There were more slaps on backs and then Daniel led Justin back over to them. Shannon took Justin's hand, and they turned to their little group. Jennifer chose that moment to arrive.

"I'm so sorry I'm late. Did I miss anything?"

Josie smiled at Shannon and Justin, her eyes beginning to well with tears.

"You got here at just the right time, I'm thinking." She took Jennifer's hand, seeming to understand the position Jennifer held in Shannon's life.

Shannon looked back at them all. Her two adopted moms. Her

father, back in her life—for good, God willing. Her best friend and sister by faith and promise with her new brother-in-law. And her family to be—a mom and dad to love her, and whatever children they had—however they had them—forever. And her almost husband—promising all she'd ever wanted, leaning on God with her, bonding them together.

She looked up into Justin's eyes and saw the love she felt for them all reflected back to her. He pulled her close, gently kissing her lips.

Warmth. Sweetness. A promise. A vow. Their future.

It was a rag-tag group. It wasn't the family she ever dreamed of having. It was imperfect and misshapen, silly and broken, quirky and loving. All of their crooked parts puzzled-pieced together, making a whole.

But it was the family God designed for her to have. And that made it perfect.

ACKNOWLEDGEMENTS

This was, by far, the most challenging novel for me to write. Not only are the subjects of PTSD and mental illness serious, these are things I'm familiar with in my family and in myself. Writing Shannon's experiences caused me to draw on my own and the memories connected to them. Add to that, many physical challenges I had—well, this is a work of serious prayer and relying on the Father to carry me along. He always does.

Thank you to Roseanna and David at WhiteFire Publishing for all your support, prayers, and words of kindness. Thanks for believing in me!

Thank you to Jesus, my caretaker, my energy-endower, my peace and joy-giver—my all in all. I couldn't have finished...or started...this without you on every level.

Thank you to my family who are a never-ceasing source of encouragement as I face personal battles as well as physical and writing battles! I couldn't do this without you, either!

Thanks to Janet, my friend-sister-personal-assistant extraordinaire who is always eager and willing to help in any way needed. I'm grateful you have my back.

To Danika and Melody, my career-long critique partners, who routinely listen to my ramblings and insecurities and act as if I'm simply talking about the weather. You guys are incredible, and I'm so glad we're doing this together. A huge thank you to Bonnie Leon for reading, critiquing, and powering through. I value you and your encouragement so much!

And special thanks to Julie, who gave her professional and

personal comments, as well as Trina Brown who shared her experiences with me—you are both incredible warriors.

To my Encourager's Critique group—Sandra Bensman, Danika Cooley, Louise Dunlap, Kelly Fritz, Linda Hulse, Jac Nelson, Nora Peacock, Kendy Pearson, Melody Roberts, Rachel Russell, and Julie Streit—you are a team of blessings and wonders. THANK YOU all so much.

To my praying team friends—Billie Jo, Danika, Debbie, Janet, LeeAnn, Lynn, Melody, and Valerie—thank you for your faithful prayers.

And especially to my readers: you bless me. By reading my books, leaving reviews, sending notes, recommending them to others, and a thousand other kindnesses, you make all this hard work totally worth it.

NOTES ON PTSD AND MENTAL ILLNESS

Both mental illness and PTSD are very personal experiences. This book is meant to take a snapshot of fictional characters' facing fictional trials, but to stay as true to a sufferer's experiences as possible. My hope is this book can help lessen the stigma and discrimination against mental health sufferers. They could be in your school, work, or home life. It could be you.

The World Health Organization (WHO) estimates that one in four people in the world will be affected by mental or neurological disorders at some point in their lives. Mental health disorders are a leading cause of ill-health and disability.

Nearly two-thirds of people with mental illness never seek help. That's frightening. Two-thirds of the world is suffering in silence because of their inability to understand the seriousness of their condition, or (and more commonly) because they feel shamed and judged for reaching out for help.

Mental illness is just that, an illness, and no one should have to try to navigate that very painful and confusing world alone.

If you or a loved one suspects they are dealing with mental illness, please seek help through your medical provider. Don't stay silent. You don't have to face this alone.

If you feel suicidal, please call the suicide hotline at 1-800-273-8255.

DISCUSSION QUESTIONS

If you're reading on your own, consider journaling the answers to these questions. If you are in a group, remember to keep confidences with others and not to share details that aren't yours to share.

1. Shannon and Amber are epic friends who always have each other's backs. Is there anyone in your life you can count on like that? How has that impacted you (the gain or loss of it)?

2. Have you ever dealt with a difficult family member? What sort of things helped you to handle that situation?

3. Post Traumatic Stress Syndrome (PTSD) can occur for many reasons. Trauma from an accident, abuse, attack, or injury. Sometimes PTSD passes with counseling and time. Sometimes it becomes a life-long struggle. Do you know anyone who suffers from PTSD? What might be a good way to show them you are there for them?

4. Mental Illness is devastating on many fronts. It changes the person, but it also changes their jobs, personal lives, and family members. It touches all aspects of relationships. Have you ever known someone to battle with mental illness? How has their struggle affected those around them?

5. Forgiveness is hard. When we're wounded, our instinct is to react, fight back, yell, or sulk. Have you ever struggled with

forgiveness? If you were able to forgive, how did that come about?

6. Do fiction stories ever change your opinion on a matter you were pretty certain of before you started to read? Can you give an example?

7. Sometimes the biggest thing you can do for another is just sit and listen to them. Has anyone ever just sat and listened to you, or the other way around? Was it a powerful experience? What do you remember about it?

8. Have you ever made yourself available to a hurting friend? Is your friendship deeper than before? Changed? How?

ALSO BY APRIL MCGOWAN

Hold the Light

To an artist, the light is everything.
So what is Amber supposed to do when facing blindness?

Amber spent her life adapting—first to being abandoned by her birth mother as a toddler, and then to the death of her adoptive father in her teen years. Now she's moved past all that, loving life as an independent woman: she has a job as an art instructor and the perfect apartment.

But when a routine eye appointment reveals she's losing her sight, life comes to a halt. Pressures come at her from all sides. Her mother, her boss, her boyfriend and her closest friend, Shannon, all have ideas about what's best for her.

Even after her blindness counselor, Ethan, befriends her and opens her eyes to new opportunities and the possibility of a deeper relationship, one haunting question remains: How could the God she loved all her life turn everything upside down—again?

MACY

Independent...or Alone?

Macy longed for independence her whole life. Maybe marrying Arthur to escape her home hadn t been the best plan, but it seemed good enough at the time. Now, pregnant and abandoned in a diner far from anyone she knows, Macy must start life all over again. Relying on the mercy of the diner's owners, she begins to put things back together. Macy must make her own decisions for the first time in her adult life but it isn't all it's cracked up to be. And with the too-alluring Toby at her side instead of her husband, she s discovering those decisions harder to make than ever.

JASMINE

She survived her past but how can she face it?

Jasmine is a survivor. She's lived through the abuse of her father, running away at age fourteen, living on the streets, and now she counsels at risk young women giving them a second chance at life.

But when her mother dies, can she go home again and face the past she's forced herself to forget for the last twenty years? Or will the past she's now forgotten take over her present once again?

CPSIA information can be obtained
at www.ICGtesting.com
Printed in the USA
FSHW020919110620
70798FS